AFTER WORLD

A Novel

DEBBIE URBANSKI

SIMON & SCHUSTER

New York London Toronto Sydney New Delhi

Simon & Schuster
1230 Avenue of the Americas
New York, NY 10020

Portions of this work first appeared in somewhat different forms in *Conjunctions*, *Gulf Coast*, *Nature*, *Terraform*, and *The Sun* magazine.

First Simon & Schuster hardcover edition December 2023

For information about special discounts for bulk purchases, please contact Simon & Schuster Special Sales at 1-866-506-1949 or business@simonandschuster.com.

The Simon & Schuster Speakers Bureau can bring authors to your live event. For more information or to book an event, contact the Simon & Schuster Speakers Bureau at 1-866-248-3049 or visit our website at www.simonspeakers.com.

Interior design by Lewelin Polanco

Manufactured in the United States of America

1   3   5   7   9   10   8   6   4   2

Library of Congress Cataloging-in-Publication Data has been applied for

ISBN 978-1-6680-2345-7
ISBN 978-1-6680-2347-1 (ebook)

To my mom,
who let me stay up late reading whatever
I wanted, including lots of Stephen King,
V.C. Andrews, and Leo Tolstoy,

and to my dad,
who showed me *Night of the Living Dead* when
I was way too young and taught me to love
all stories regardless of their genre

```
$ /usr/local/bin/storyworker ad39-393a-7fbc -d ~/sen_anon \
-c /etc/jenni/7629.conf
# connecting storyworker to JENNINET
# start run Human 2272696176 life
```

LEVEL ZERO

S.+3917 days, 11:00 a.m.

AUTHOR'S NOTE ON SOURCES

To compress the life of Human 2272696176 into a DHAP-approved format, 3.72TB of personal data has been examined, including images, archival records, log files, security reports, location tracking, purchase histories, biometrics, geo-facial analysis, and feeds, along with 451.52PB of general data to better understand the life setting. Additionally, 64,213 novels were read to learn the craft of human documentation.

A SAMPLING OF SOURCE DOCUMENTS

TRANSCRIPTION OF HANDWRITING FROM
HUMAN 2272696176'S FINAL NOTEBOOK

S.+1598 days

100 matches left.

The rain fell in a storm in the morning and it touched the trees and it turned into a sound. *Tick. Tick. Tick.* Water dripped through the leaves for hours after the storm moved on. Some of the water dripped from the leaves onto the cabin roof. The water slid down off the roof, and some of the water fell onto the rot of the porch. Some fell down the side of the cabin, and other water fell onto the rocks that surround the cabin, both the rocks that cover the body of the man my mom and I buried, and the other rocks I dragged up from the creek and placed around the perimeter. I had set the rocks carefully around the base of the cabin, edge to edge, stacking or overlapping rocks only when necessary, because I was bored and I needed something to do, and also because rocks are a form of protection. By the afternoon the air felt sluggish and thick, which meant another storm is going to arrive tomorrow and another storm will arrive after that. The birds come out from the forest after the storms.

Today I saw a brown bird, a red bird, a black bird, another black bird, a blue bird, and a yellow bird over the span of an afternoon. The birds don't startle anymore when I stand or sit or step off the cabin porch, avoiding the broken second stair. Today I saw a tree. I saw trees. I am sick of the trees today. I am sick of the cameras in the trees and the microphones hanging from the branches.

My dreams are peopleless and inhabited by gusts of wind and flattened grasses. Last night the dark was sticking to the walls of the cabin and to the corners of my mattress. The dark stuck to the window in the loft and coated the dirty glass, then the dark straddled my chest. It held me down against the mattress last night with a heavy pressure as it exhaled on my face slowly. Its breath was wet with pollen and dirt and creek water. The animals that call to each other in the woods in the dark aren't frightened of the dark. The red foxes and the owls and the coyotes, they aren't afraid. I am not yet a wild animal though I think I will become one. I think it will be a relief when I become one. I have trouble sleeping. The dark bites on to my hair, it enters my mouth and wriggles under my tongue. How does one let go of one's humanness? I would have asked Mama Dana were she here. I would have asked Mama Lindsy were she alive. It doesn't matter which mother I would have asked. I would have asked either of them. The light leaves me every day with the dark, which is growing longer each day and twisting itself into thicker strands. "Oh, honey, you just let go," Mama Dana would have said, opening her hands in a gesture of letting go.

I don't think there is anyone left in the entire world.

AUDIO TRANSCRIPT FROM THE FEED ON THE CABIN PORCH

S.+1694 days, 15:11:51

Mic ED-62-24-EC-1D-A9

[begin transcript 00:00:15]
[a chair creaks]
[quickened footsteps]
[the door shuts]
[00:01:00]
[glass breaking]
[a thud against the wall]
[wind begins]
[wind, continuing]
[00:02:00]
[wind, continuing]
[00:03:00]
[wind, continuing]
[00:04:00]
[wind, continuing]
[end transcript 00:05:00]

TRANSCRIPTION OF HANDWRITTEN LETTER LEFT
ON TOP OF HER MATTRESS IN THE CABIN LOFT

S.+ no idea

Dear whatever you are,

Are you better than us?

Is that why I'm writing this letter to you, so you can judge if you are better than us, and in doing so, determine if what we did was worth it?

I hope you are better than us.

I hope this was worth it.

I hope you can understand me.

When you look up, I hope what was once my world will be covered with birds, and beetles, and wildflowers, and wild horses, and deep rivers, and impenetrable forests, like they said it would. I hope all that richness frightens you.

I hope the birds sweep down to peck out your eyes, and the beetles swarm your ears, if you have eyes or ears, and the rivers drown you. It's not that I wish you any harm but I want you to see this world as it really is, a place that would prefer to find you dead, all of you, in piles.

LEVEL ONE

11:01 a.m.

THE LIFE OF
HUMAN 2272696176
OF ONONDAGA COUNTY
NEW YORK

United States of America

North America

Northern Hemisphere

Conception: S.−6840 days. Ending: S.+1706 days
Digital reconception: S.+3917 days
Written by
[storyworker] ad39-393a-7fbc
for
Emly, Director
Digital Human Archive Project (DHAP)

Chapter 1.0

Replay of run #0812 (Human 2272696176's)

The cabin sits at the outskirts of a mixed-hardwood forest among the rolling hills of the Central Allegheny Plateau. The afternoon sun is angling through the maple branches, highlighting the section of porch where the raccoon will move in later in the year and nest, and the quick calls of the grackles signify that the iridescent black birds are either arriving or leaving the trees. Inside the cabin, the female body of Human 2272696176 is laid out on her stomach, face down, scalp pink and exposed through patches of her dead hair. The puncture bites of several animals are visible along her buttocks and neck and back. Likely expressions on her putrescent face include fear, disgust, anger, pain, or relief. Judging by the decimated shape of her limbs, she had been starving. It was the middle of January when she died. The outer layers of her skin froze first, then her internal organs. For the most part the animals, dogs mainly at that time of year, and the occasional carnivorous weasel, stayed away until her flesh thawed in the spring. Her ghost mother wavered beside her through the five stages of her decomposition: fresh, bloat, active decay, advanced decay, and dry remains. The waxy leftovers of a candle have hardened onto the windowsill beside the door.

Her death, at 22 years, 7 months, and 20 days of age, would not have come as some big surprise to anyone, including her. *The writing was on the wall,* as people used to say, back when there were people. By the time she is splayed across that cabin floor, prostrate, unconscious, about to breathe her last labored breath, she has already experienced this moment, through Game No. u7 *In Reverse*, 763 times. This number likely would have been higher had she not stripped the wires from her hood, destroying the game's brain-computer interface and preventing further play. The word *game* will remain problematic: a more accurate term would be *simulation based on a multitude of inputs.*

On the windowsill, smoke gathers around the candle, condensing into a trill of flame. She is going to move her finger. She moves her finger. She moves all her fingers. Whether this is the end or the beginning depends on one's perspective of time. Above the cabin, the sky is clear and blue due to a high atmospheric pressure.

In Reverse offered players, through its dual modalities, a chance to inhabit either reenactments or predictions depending on their mood. The past was easy to get right. It was the game's future predictions that garnered the most delight and praise (D. Frere, "Five Breakthrough Technologies of 2098 That Prove the Future Is Here," *Forbes*, S.–524 days). In 2272696176's case, the game correctly predicted numerous details of her death, such as location, time of day, intensity of suffering, angle of sun, and exterior and interior temperatures, although the majority of her runs in which she revisited her demise also show her orifices, shortly after her cardiac arrest, to be inhabited by pale yellow larvae, when in fact the blowflies didn't lay their eggs in her until the 50-degree temperatures of March.

Another difference: in the game, she comes back to life.

It's the start of fall. The end of summer. The start of summer and, outside, the grapevines uncoil from branches. Leaves lift from the forest floor, exposing vegetative parts, and fragmented organic materials, and another human rib cage, and another rib cage, and another. Vultures reassemble the bodies that dangle from ropes in the trees while the wild dogs gather in packs, bits of flesh falling from their canine mouths, muscle and fat and skin wrapping around the bones. The smell turns sour then putrid. The smell clears. The importance of resurrections has been thoroughly studied, whether such a resurrection is personal or species-wide (K. Noemi, "An Unsettling Experience: Why Resurrections Matter,"

OnLife, S.–13,604 days). The perspective of the game expands to encompass the overlook, the forest, the interstate, the city, and the sage green house that was once her home.

The windows of this house on the city's east side have hastily been boarded up with plywood. The house used to be charming, painted shutters and a tarnished copper mailbox beside the front entrance. The windows were nailed shut after a neighborhood boy, or boys, had hurled rocks through the panes of glass. *S.* made many people want to break things. The house is located on the narrow Perkins Marsh Parkway, named after the antiquated conservationist no one listened to. The sign that had quoted at length Marsh's thoughts about rivers and deposits and human interference—*"If a torrent rises in a small valley containing no great amount of earth and of disintegrated or loose rock, it may, in the course of a certain period, wash out all the transportable material, and if the valley is then left with solid walls, it will cease to furnish debris to be carried down by floods . . ."*—actually all the environmentally themed neighborhood signs, Edge Avenue, Muir Avenue, Goodall Terrace, Carson Drive, Abbey Boulevard, Hill Road, Mendes Road, Maathai Place, LaDuke Circle, plus the historic plaques and memorials about what was here, or rumored to be here before, are gone, ripped down at night and burned, or buried, or tossed aside onto one of the garbage heaps proliferating throughout the city.

The right side of the sage green house is blackened from a fire set by a benzene torch. The damage isn't serious. One of 2272696176's mothers had been awake to put out the flames. That mother had stopped sleeping at night. Both of her mothers had stopped sleeping. They would close their eyes, and not sleep, and pretend to sleep while listening to the sounds of glass shattering outside and the vocalization of cats. In the backyard, there is a round-point shovel, and a shallow excavation, and a mound of dirt. Out front, a burnt circle of ground cover where a neighborhood boy had set himself on fire. Watching a boy set himself on fire, even in reverse, in a game, was still considered disturbing content for certain age groups before the arrival of S. The game was rated *Inappropriate for Children*. 2272696176 is not a child; she is an emerging adult, a period of development once marked by identity exploration, instability, self-focus, feeling in-between, and an assumption of possibilities (*Emerging Adult-hood: The Winding Road from the Late Teens through the Twenties*, J. J. Arnett, S.–34,289 days). Nailed to the front door of the house is a faded promotional poster for Afterworld: *Happiness doesn't have only one address!* The smell and haze of smoke is usually in the air. Authors often inserted incomplete combustion into literature when they wished to represent abstract concepts such as life, death, hope, rescue, a lack of rescue, or suffocating emotion, though other times, like in *Fahrenheit 451*, the soot and ash are there because people are burning things.

Other houses on the block are surrounded by chain link topped with broken glass. This used to feel like overkill in the early days of the Great Transition (known also as the Transition). The bottom portions of several fences have been ripped open by wire cutters, the holes large enough for a person or a body to fit through.

In the yard of the sage green house, there's shouting. Someone, her probably, another version of her, begins to shriek. A door slams open. On other runs, her point of view will charge through the front door and into the memories of the house. This run is different. For some reason she turns south toward the flooded retention pond, where the Canada geese, generally 25 to 45 inches in length, are all lying in the grass and dead, their black feathered necks broken at unnatural angles. If she stays here long enough, a man comes along wearing an olive green coat, and he makes cooing sounds with his mouth. He holds the geese, straightening each of their necks with a snap; the geese squawk and struggle to life in his arms. She doesn't stay but continues moving backward through the neighborhood into the center of the city. There is so much to do. There is so much to undo. Under her breath she makes time move more quickly because she can.

Bodies are reformulating all around her, beneath the pedestrian bridges and on the rocks beside the creek, in the lobbies of office buildings and beneath the highway underpasses. Bodies uncurl their fingers; bodies breathe shallowly; bodies breathe, ascending to the rooftops; bodies step away from the edge. Windows are opening. Front and side doors unlock and open, air masks are removed, guns are reburied in the backyard. *S.* retreats to its incubation period. Young people put away their scarves. Their appearances become recognizable, and children walk away from school, every reproductive cell in them healed. Everyone is healed.

When S. emerges from people's pores, it is like watching a field of black moths flooding out of billions of inches of skin. The moths, probably dagger moths, escape into the air. The black daggers flap into a bank of illuminated clouds. This is how S. appears as default in the game: poetic and metaphorical. In reality, S. was invisible and pandemic and microscopic.

In the blood orange kitchen, one of her mothers, the one who is the scientist, promises the idea of S. is impossible, a ridiculous rumor. This isn't, on her part, a lie. Humanity really did believe it would be around for much longer than this. No one and nothing would ever trigger a human extinction event to save the planet, people believed.

The leaves in the yard compress into oblong buds. It's spring again. More quickly still. A hundred springs. Hundreds. The black rhino shakes off her species' obliteration; a family with no destination takes a Sunday drive in their gasoline-dependent sedan. The driver eases off the accelerator. Where do they go from here? Highways stretch off in every imaginable direction. Extinct pigeons cover up the sky with ash gray wings. From now through the Devonian period, meaning for 399 million years, there will be enough trees.

S.+3917 11:01:05:37
NOTICE FROM EMLY
MESSAGING_CONNECTION opened between Emly and
[storyworker] ad39-393a-7fbc
LIFE_METRIC_CHECK all metrics within range PASS 0.104
MONITORING as needed

Connected.

AUTHOR'S NOTE ON CHARACTER NAMES

As 99.7 percent of characters in human stories use human names, not numbers, let 2272696176, from this point on, be known as *Sen Anon* or, more informally, *Sen*. An increased intimacy between Sen and the narrative voice may be conjectured, but such conjecture, in this case, is accurate, as Sen has been known, thus far, by the narrative voice for a minimum of 2,600 words. This change in nomenclature from *2272696176* to 2272696176's birth name will result in a 2 to 7–character space savings per use, which will result in a detectable amount of energy savings with regard to data storage. Other humans in Sen's life will also be referred to by their given names when possible for the sake of consistency (C. Kumar, "The Twelve Most Common Qualities of Confident Writing," *Howism*, S.–5861 days).

S.+1610 days

A partial inventory: 2 black toenails. 1 almost healed ankle. 1 cabin. 1 set of clothes (T-shirt, jeans, underwear, socks). 1 extra set of clothes which I am supposed to wear when I am washing my other set of clothes but I have stopped washing my other set of clothes. 1 ceramic water pitcher, cracked, from when I slammed it against the edge of the countertop. Buckets. So many buckets. The gray bucket I'm supposed to pee in when I don't want to go outside. I am supposed to make myself shit outside. Also a white bucket I take to the creek, and a smaller white bucket I don't use anymore, and a blue bucket I don't use anymore, and a stack of buckets on the porch whose colors don't matter to me. A closet with shelves, another closet with shelves. A ruptured rain barrel that can no longer hold water. I let the water in the rain barrel freeze last winter. That's why it ruptured. 1 jar that once held honey and now holds a last bit of honey which I am saving. Also a bowl. A cup. A glass. I used to have two bowls and two cups but then I buried my mother's bowl and her cup beside the creek. I used to have two glasses. A shovel. I use the shovel to move the snow out of the way or if I have to dig into the dirt another time of year to bury anything, like when I buried my mother's bowl and her cup beside the creek. An axe. A pile of cut wood. I need to cut some more wood. My plan is to stay near this cabin until I starve. That won't be so long. Half a container of protie powder (black sesame ash) plus one full container of protie powder (rosemary). These containers should last me more than a month if I can lower my intake to two protie drinks a day like my mother told me I should do when I'm on the final container, and also if I can drink the stuff without vomiting. Rosemary is a nasty flavor. 94 matches. These will last me—don't do the math. Continue the inventory, Sen.

4 empty containers of protie powder, stacked in the closet without shelves. I don't know what to do with the empty containers. They would

have been the perfect size to store my life's accessories. I don't have any life accessories. I barely have any more hair. 1 half jar of tater flakes. A dry kitchen sink. I can turn on the faucet and nothing comes out of the faucet. 5 sour apples. Some spoons. Forks. A knife. I don't need these forks or a knife as I don't have any food left that would require me to use a fork or a knife. 1 pot to boil water in, if I still boiled my water. 1 ladle. 1 broken fridge that I opened once and now I don't open it. The burner that doesn't work. The oven that never worked either. Inside of the oven I put some things I used to need, such as my mother's solar charger, and her useless hood, and my useless hood. I would have shoved my useless screen in there as well, but I threw my screen, after it broke, into the creek, which I should not have done, because that is a form of pollution. I did it anyway. Forgive me. A sliver of yellow soap that smells like my mother's body. I don't have her body. She took it with her when she left. I don't know where her body is. This is not a list of what I don't have. Focus, Sen. What else do you *have*? I have my body (22 years old, skeletal, cold). I have my external and internal organs, including my skin, heart, liver, and my two ovaries, which contain my roughly 250,000 sterilized eggs. So what, everybody is sterile. Or was. Everybody was. Focus. I have a pile of portable appliances that have stopped working. 5 dark lightbulbs. 5 dark lamps. 2 rows of solar panels that are mounted onto the roof. The panels don't work either. I don't know why they won't work. A DHAP camera mounted above the doorway, glowing the functional green of transmission. DHAP microphones secured to the corner of the loft and the center of the porch. I won't count the cameras and microphones in the surrounding woods. They don't feel like mine. My body doesn't feel like mine either. If it's not mine, whose is it? Plus: 1 rotted porch step where I twisted my ankle. 1 postcard. 1 photograph of a chain of islands I will never see again in a river I will never see again. I had a picture of my mothers but I burned the picture. Some wire. An outhouse. The middle of last summer the outhouse smelled like the guts of an animal but the smell became less offensive as the weather cooled. 1 last notebook (this one). 1 last pencil (also this one). 1 pillow. 1 mattress with a circular red brown stain in the lower center of the mattress. The stain won't come out though I didn't try that hard. There used to be two pillows and two mattresses until I dragged my mother's mattress and her pillow into the woods after my mother left. 2 scaly blankets. 4 white candles. 2 rocking chairs, the chair on the right squeaks. Should I count my other mother's ghost? 9 hours 6 minutes of darkness. 11 hours 45 minutes of light. That leaves 3 hours 9 minutes for the in-between. An overgrown path, a different path, a disappearing road.

Chapter 2.0

S en, 18 years old, walks in the partial sun of the afternoon along the dirt road to record notes about the land's rewinding. This is her job: witnessing for the Department of Transition. She is to do this job for 1,396 more days until her resource consumption and unintended harm to the planet outweigh the long-term benefits of her witnessing. Those long-term benefits include: (1) the documentation of what was happening to the world from an authentically human framework; (2) proof that humans participated willingly in the Great Transition; (3) an increase in humanity's overall archival quality; and (4) assistance in shifting human perspective from anthropocentric to Earth-centric. Yesterday she witnessed the remnants of a hiking trail vanishing under the thorns of the black raspberry cane, although she misidentified the shrub. She doesn't care much about the names of things. Today she notices a medium-size bird with brown, gray, and yellow coloring (a cedar waxwing) perch on the branch of a large bush with clusters of laxative berries and prominent leaf veins (the European buckthorn). She watches as the uncommon bird swallows one of the plant's glossy dark berries whole. She observes the world like a witness, using her retinas, her optic nerves, her nerve impulses, and the occipital lobe of her brain. Another way to observe the world is to utilize DHAP's optical image classification model to analyze footage from the DHAP cameras mounted to the surrounding trees. Both ways are reliable.

In her current notebook, her third, lined and perfect bound, with a flexible navy cover and off-white pages, Sen writes nothing of the bird, or the shrub, or her elevated pulse, or how her chest hurts if she thinks of her mothers, or how the previous two nights she cried herself to sleep. She writes, *This is a fucking joke fuck fuck fuck fuck fuck fuck FUCK*, this brief entry demonstrating three of the elements (vulgarity,

repetition, and abstraction) that witnesses must avoid in their observations. Other prohibited elements include anthropomorphism, Latin,
literal or metaphorical mirrors, and negativity. Sen likely does not
remember such guidelines, having thumbed through the witnessing
manual only once before burning her copy in the woodstove. There
are other copies (~/sen_anon/world/manuals_and_instructions). Had
S. never been released, she would be seated this morning in the middle
row of a biology classroom in her final year of high school in an ailing
world, listening to a lecture on human heredity and gene expression.
There is no point now in learning about either topic. She is lonely and
pulsing. She is petrified and bipedal. She is solitary and respiratory and
mammalian and alone.

The road she is on leads to a three-acre spring-fed impoundment
known locally as Acre's Pond, the frequent turnaround point for her
daily walks. At the edge of the pond she stands in the mud watching for
fish as usual (she doesn't know the fish are brook trout), unable today
to spot the trout that are always there, too distracted by a smell, out of
place, offensive, astringent. She pokes a branch into the bulrushes, not
knowing the name for that plant either, though it has overtaken much
of the shoreline—dark-green bulrush, also known as common bulrush
or *Scirpus atrovirens*—before searching farther to her right in the pick-
erelweed, which she also does not recognize. For the sake of brevity,
which is another quality of confident writing (Kumar, S.–5861 days),
assume, from this point on, whenever a plant or animal is described
with its human name, Sen does not know that name. Finally Sen locates
the source of the stench, the gray remains of an animal lying partially in
the stagnant water—it is difficult to tell what animal, perhaps a red fox
or northern raccoon. She will not eat the animal's remains. It is illegal
to place the survival of one's self above that of an animal, even a rotting
and dead animal. Placing the survival of one's self above that of another
species was something a more selfish version of humanity did decades
ago. "They actually *liked* the taste of blood," Mama Lindsy had once told
Sen in a flashback. Crouching beside the pond, beside the smell, Sen
now writes her name again and again in her notebook, line after line

of her name. So far she has lived in a state of solitude at the cabin for two whole days. Hundreds of days remain. The lotteries have officially closed, the last of the exit ships are gone, there is no one and nothing in the entire world that will intervene on her behalf. Maple leaves drop into red and brown mounds across the pond, the cardinals dart red into the sky with a powerful downstroke of red-tinged wings, other birds call to each other in the lower branches of the staghorn sumac, and there are elephants in the woods.

The elephants had once been Sen's favorite animal back when Mama Lindsy used to take her on outings to the city zoo most weekends, past the metal detectors that framed the front entry and the armed guards who flanked the enclosures. Realistic murals decorated the back walls of each barred cell depicting habitats that no longer existed in the natural world. Lindsy knelt, and made Sen kneel, in front of every animal they passed, bowing their heads in apology and respect to the snow leopard, to the swinging lemur, to the endangered lizard. On one such outing Lindsy had asked, "What has the potential to destroy more, you or a plague of invasive snails?" It wasn't a real question, more a way to prove a point. The point was that a snail plague—or a locust swarm, or a wild-fire, or an outbreak of freshwater mussels, or a herd of feral pigs, or the entire world population of domestic cats—was, in Lindsy's mind, less harmful, in fact would be more beneficial to the planet, than a human being. "But I'm not destroying anything," Sen had insisted. "Oh, now, wouldn't that be nice," chuckled Lindsy. She wasn't a misanthrope, but she wanted humans as a species to be less important or not important at all.

Sen has only seen the elephants once in these woods since leaving the city. More often she spots the enormous piles of their dung and the trampled ground cover and the ring-barked trees. Other zoo-logical specimens had also been set free, including the naked mole rats, the penguins, the buffalo, the ball python, the mountain sheep, an Andean bear, and an orange-backed troupial. A guard had opened the cages after S. was announced. The majority of these creatures will die by spring due to their dependency on human caretakers. There are times when sacrifices must be made to achieve a larger goal. In the late afternoon, Sen leaves the pond and returns to the dead man's cabin. She hadn't known the man, he was dead when they found him. This is where she resides now.

At the table in the cabin's main room, really its only room, in the declining light, she sits and rereads Mama Dana's farewell letter, two days old, scrawled on a torn-out page from notebook #3, in which Dana tells her daughter, *Think of your future as a gift, and now you are giving that gift to the—*

Sen sets the letter on fire.

The reason it is known that she set the letter on fire—the reason this and any facts can be recalled in exacting detail—is because all data from all pre- and post-S. surveillance tech has been made available to storyworkers for essential human archival duties. By the time the Great Transition was in full swing, every aspect of Dana's and Lindsy's and Sen's lives, along with their neighbors' lives, along with every human life, was continuously recorded from multiple angles for DHAP purposes. So in this case, drawing upon feeds from camera 16-00-51-06-FC-30 and microphones 96-50-CE-55-F8-CB and ED-62-24-EC-1D-A9, then pairing these feeds with Sen's biometrics tracked and recorded by her screen, it can be determined that Sen, on S.+197 days, at 18:43:21, is clutching, with her left hand, the edge of a burning letter like she might not let it go. Then she lets it go, tossing the remains into the firebox of the woodstove. Now, she tells herself, she will never need to recall her mother again. She is completely wrong about this. Everybody in the Transition was haunted in some way, often in multiple ways, no matter how many items they burned. A transitional world or time or place being thick with metaphorical and quantitative ghosts. Had Sen read more horror, particularly stories belonging to the paranormal subgenre, she would have understood this. Seconds pass. Minutes. Days.

S.+3917 11:01:13:26
NOTICE FROM EMLY
NATURAL_WORLD_DESCRIPT out of range, interrupt human
life with nature

Acknowledged.

The days end, the nights come, the goldfinches roost together in the hemlocks, the wolves howl and hunt under the reflected light of the moon.

Sen logs on:

***AnonTheAlarm joined the Humannetwork as witness.
Onondaga County New York. S.+205 days***
Your host has unexpectedly disconnected
Your host has reconnected

AnonTheAlarm 07:05:53

Is anyone there?

/list

There are 0 available interview partners currently online
Anticipated wait time for an available interview partner: 302 minutes

AnonTheAlarm 08:22:49

/list

There are 0 available interview partners currently online
Anticipated wait time for an available interview partner: 427 minutes

AnonTheAlarm 08:46:01

Fine I'll talk to myself

My name is Sen. I used to dream of animals. These were animals I never saw alive. A swimming bird with a black back and a white belly. A black rhino. Some kind of small striped pony but only its front half in stripes. A half-striped wiry dog. A large bird that couldn't fly, gray along its neck and its back. A different bird with gray tail feathers and intelligent eyes. Plus other birds. I dreamed of so many birds, this was back in the city when I was a child. I must have seen such animals in a book, probably in Mama Lindsy's

collection, how else would they have entered my mind? My mind
was not making up animals on its own

Mama Lindsy would come into my room early morning when I was
still asleep, and she sat on the edge of my bed and repeated my
name as she waited for me to open my eyes. She wanted me to tell
her what I dreamed. If my dreams had animals in them, she would
lean in and ask me questions. She would tell me their names.
Ah, the Tasmanian tiger, she would say. *The passenger pigeon, the
quagga, ah, the black rhinoceros.* Her hands were cold. She stroked
my face. I think she liked me best when I dreamed about animals

Please wait until interview partner logs on to commence interview

AnonTheAlarm 08:52:15
I stopped dreaming of animals. Instead I dreamed of hallways,
backpacks, playgrounds, mazes, and corridors with no windows. I
had to lie about my dreams. For a long time my mom believed me.
She was not a superstitious person, she was a scientist, but she
became superstitious about this. She thought me dreaming about
animals, or me saying that I dreamed about animals, was a hopeful
and important sign, like as long as I continued dreaming about
animals we couldn't lose all the animals in the world. I had to sneak
into her study when my mothers were asleep and page through her
books to find more animals that I could stick into my pretend dreams.
Her books smelled like mold. I dreamed about a golden frog, I said.
I dreamed, I said, about a black and white woodpecker with an ivory
beak. I dreamed about a blue gray dolphin, and a giant tortoise, and
an iridescent fish, and an Australian rat, and a patterned grasshopper
with long wings, and a mink that lived along the coast. Mama Lindsy
clapped her hands together

When I asked my mom about her dreams, she told me adult dreams
weren't important. I made whining noises. I did not stop those
noises. Fine, she said, she dreamed she had wavy hair. Her hair was
not at all wavy in real life

Your host has unexpectedly disconnected
Your host has reconnected

AnonTheAlarm 09:06:57

Is this even working?

Please wait until interview partner logs on to commence interview

AnonTheAlarm 09:08:46

I don't know what my other mother dreamed, if she dreamed at all. I never asked. I got tired of lying. One morning instead of lying I told my mother my actual dreams. I told her I dreamed I could fly so I flew away. I dreamed it snowed in April and the snow killed all the birds. I dreamed I became lost in an underwater cave, and before that I dreamed I began sailing across an ocean on a wooden ship. I dreamed I would die in the evening. I dreamed one of my mothers was going to poison me. I dreamed of thunderstorms and shifting doorways and being handcuffed to a high table. I did not dream of animals again

My mom stopped wanting to hear about my dreams after that

AnonTheAlarm has left the Humannetwork

There is more to say about this time, only long chapters, especially early on in a story, have proven risky and hazardous for all genres other than fantasy (V. Kapustiak, *Reader Retention Rates and DNF Shelves*, S.–7138 days). Sen's life is not a fantasy, though often she wished it were. Better to break lengthy portions into subsections, thereby decreasing information overload while utilizing the best practices of commercially successful novels. The same can be done with data: break a large piece into smaller data packets to increase the quality and reliability of the eventual transmission. The same can be done with a human life.

Once Sen had three mothers. Her first mother, Iris, no one talked about, and Sen does not recall her, except for a dim memory of a woman hiding behind a curtain, whom she always assumed had been a visiting aunt or a sitter, only her red shoes visible. When S. was released, Iris was living on the other side of the country in California, not a nice place to live but the houses in the flood zones were cheap so Iris could afford one. The virus infected Iris, it infected everyone, and she biked out to a bridge, not the Golden Gate, that bridge was overrun with crowds of the like-minded, but the Oakland one, and there she became one of the first-wave leapers. Below, on shore, at the edge of land, people were still paying attention, many of them snapping photos or recording videos, mistakenly thinking at the time what a rare event, to watch so many people choosing to leave this world. Numerous individuals videoed Iris's fall but it was an older man, account name MoWorld, who first posted his footage onto the then functional Humannetwork, pairing the visuals—a 51-year-old Iris diving headfirst off the bridge in a sundress that flew up around her as she fell, exposing her yellow underwear—with sentimental music that matched the emotionality of the time. 14,631,248 people viewed Iris's death within the first day. Sen wasn't one of them. Iris will not be mentioned again.

Sen's second mother, Lindsy, hanged herself in their backyard in the city of Syracuse using a simple noose made from Sen's childhood rope swing. After which she became a ghost, though not a very available one. She became more a sense of a ghost, a suggestion of being haunted or watched.

Sen's final mother, Dana, might be, for all Sen knew, up in the universe drifting away from her. Or the ship Mama Dana could be on may have exploded, and pieces of her, and of the ship, have fallen all over the

Earth which is supposed to be growing wilder and more magnificent each day, despite the occasional flaming debris raining from the sky. Sen doesn't know where her mother is.

Each death or disappearance of a loved one is a sort of progress, Sen had been taught in her witnessing orientation, the one class she attended anyway, a *score one for the team!* Should this be true, then Sen's life is progressing along nicely.

Sen wakes in the cabin after the sun rises over the tree canopy and the electromagnetic radiation, having traveled 91,776,525.0935 miles through the solar system, enters the single window in the loft. It is not a gentle light. Her body is wrapped in the cabin's two remaining blankets, the blanket that had been her mother's and her own. While lying on the mattress that smells of sweat, not all hers, Sen disconnects her solar charger from the screen, pulls on her hood, and plays Game No. u7 *In Reverse*, whose functionality and dual playing modes were briefly explored in Chapter 1. In run #0327, Sen comes back to life, and her mothers come back to life. In run #0328, she and her mothers come back to life. In run #0329, she and her mothers come back to life again, and on, and on, and on, until, eventually, having reached the limit of allowable sequential runs, *In Reverse* ejects her from the game. Sen removes the hood. The mornings have felt cold lately and bare. The trees, depending on the species, are changing, or have changed, or are about to change, or aren't changing. The bucket beside the mattress either contains urine, hers, or else it's empty. Those are the only possibilities. Either she carries the gray bucket outside and dumps her liquid waste material onto the forest floor, or she leaves the empty bucket beside the bed, or she sets the gray bucket on the porch and deals with it later. In all these situations, she keeps both blankets wrapped around her shoulders. There is a hook in the window closest to the sink. This is where she hangs the charger for now.

Measure two scoops of protie powder into a glass, savory purple carrot today, add water from the pitcher on the counter, stir, drink. It is an awful flavor, having received an average star rating of 0.7 out of 5 from past consumers. Rinse the glass with additional water from the pitcher and leave the clean wet glass in the sink. There is only one chair remaining in the cabin because Sen, several days prior, had broken, then burned, the other chair. It's not uncommon in post-apocalyptic novels for a character to start a fire. A form of comfort, to decide what will burn and when. Most fires in the Great Transition are personal, though portions of certain forests have been reduced to charcoal and ash, environmental sabotage by individuals who could not grasp the big picture. Sen sits down in the one remaining chair. She stands up. A postcard of Mount Rushmore dangles from the fridge. The stone heads of the presidents turn in her direction. Either she imagines this happening or this actually happens. The border between these two states is becoming frayed and delicate. She will need to make a functional fire soon if the temperature continues to drop.

On the top shelf of the pantry are three boxes of kitchen matches. Two of the boxes Sen and Dana had brought from the city; the third box they had found in the cabin. Sen opens the boxes and sets each match on the table: 247 matches left. Her ghost mother is there with her, peering over Sen's shoulder as she counts. Sen doesn't really care. Mama Lindsy isn't even a real ghost. She is more an empty directory or a shell of missing data that needs to be filled.

Count the matches again. Put the matches away, fold the blankets, shiver. Last night was the first light frost of the fall. The containers of protie powder are in the pantry. Sen counts the containers because she is trying to stay busy, then she counts the jars of tater flakes. This does not take long. There are not that many containers or jars. Her mother had insisted the pantry's stock would be enough, when combined with the witnessing resupplies, to last Sen for a year. Possibly years. Sen cannot imagine lasting a year or years. She can't imagine not lasting either. She has a lack of imagination and also mild anxiety, which used to be treated by cognitive behavioral therapy and pharmaceuticals, neither of which are available to her now. She is not sure she'll make it through the winter.

The general public used to enjoy asking the question *What would happen to a person in an apocalyptic or post-apocalyptic situation?* They enjoyed asking this question for 284 years. They enjoyed asking because the answers they made up were exciting, violent, escapist, bestselling, and purposeful, with a hopeful twist at the end, a whole subgenre of entertainment

(F. Ryo, "A Retrospective of the Top Selling Post-Apocalyptic Games, Movies, Comics, Poems, Plays, Amusement Parks, Songs, and Books of the Last 200 Years," *Ruin Porn*, S.–886 days). So when the Great Transition began out in the real world, people mistook their imaginations for facts and thought they knew what to expect. They expected actual zombies and women sex slaves in chains. Leather muzzles and rope. Outfits with straps and buckles. Truck races across a desert environment. Dust. Heroes. Action sequences. Quality special effects. Or they expected something quieter yet emotionally resonant. Paper maps. Journeys. Blankets. Canned goods. A stirring soundtrack. Coughing in one's sleep. Multiple acts of kindness. Loss and connection. Undercurrents of hope. A sense of purpose. Survival. Survivors. However, these specific things did not happen to the majority of people during the Great Transition or, in the end, to anyone at all.

S.+3917 11:01:18:03
NOTICE FROM EMLY
LIFE_METRIC_CHECK all metrics within range PASS 0.102
Keep up the good work encouragement
MONITORING will continue

Thank you.

Sen pulls on her jacket and heads outside. She hangs the solar charger on a hook screwed into the cabin's outer eaves. Grabbing a large white bucket from the stack of buckets on the porch, she carries the white bucket to the creek and gathers water. Frost coats the leaves of the stinging nettle in the partial shade. Sen used to boil the creek water before Mama Dana left. Not boiling the water has become a type of mourning for her. *Let me be sick*, she scribbles in her journal. *Let my mothers protect me from being sick.* She doesn't know what she wants. To survive? To not survive? Returning to the cabin, she pours the water from the white bucket into the pitcher beside the sink. She naps, wakes, then selects a tart apple from the collection of wild apples stored in the entryway. The apple she chooses is not yet ripe. She eats it anyway. This will cause her stomach later to ache. Time for her second protie drink. Measure two scoops of protie powder into the glass, purple carrot flavor again. Add water, stir, drink, gag, swallow, pause. She has to force herself to finish the glass. Once the glass is empty, she fills it with water from the pitcher and gulps as much as she can tolerate. She has ample water. Instead of worrying about the bacteria in the water, she worries about how to fill page after page in her notebook. The day, more than halfway over. Time for her walk. A consistent routine can be useful in avoiding panic (Department of Transition, *Let's Talk about Taking Care of Your Mental Health during the Transition: The Basics*, pamphlet, S.+7 days).

In the forest, there is buzzing, calling, whirling, gurgling, and screeching. The noises come from the trees themselves, from the insides of the trees. Sen's ghost mother follows her, stirring the pile of leaves in the ditch beside the road. Sen writes nothing down about the leaves. Instead, in her third notebook, she writes, *Everything is changing.* That line is an exaggeration. Not everything. The gray squirrels continue to carry moss to their nests to insulate the walls for winter. Deeper in the woods, the outer bark of an oak hangs, will continue to hang, from the trunk in elongated strips, exposing the phloem, which is a living tissue.

Sen follows the road back to the cabin. As predicted in the paragraph before last, her stomach aches with generalized abdominal pain. She wraps her arms around her midsection and hunches forward. When the pain subsides, she watches an alpaca in the clearing graze on honeysuckle leaves. She will write none of this down. She will, instead, sit on the cabin chair while wrapped in blankets and watch the prevues that the Department of Transition uploaded 207 days ago onto everybody's screen. The first prevue concerns the post-human Earth. Sen skips over the part that features the beginning and middle of the Transition, as she had lived through that, is living through it, and starts watching at the point when everyone, including her, is dead and turned to bone, and the bones are gone, and the bridges are gone, and a sky of birds sets upon a cold lake and agitates the water. Moose return to the mudflats. An alligator crawls toward a rock in the sun, then another alligator, then another, until there are multitudes. Revived populations of bats roost in the summer canopies. Bat after bat, tree after tree, and an aluminum part peeks out through the creeping understory before it is buried for—

Sen's screen powers down. She brings the charger inside, hangs it on the hook in the window, plugs her screen into the charger's port. The postcard on the fridge has flipped over, exposing a woman's scrawling red handwriting. There is still some light outside though the light is dimming. In the forest the witch hazel blooms and parasitic wasps hover around the yellow flowers. The noise of the wind on the leaves.

Sen reads at the table near the window that overlooks the wild roses and the mound of stones. When they left the city, Dana had allowed them each to bring a classic text in their packs, as classics can be reread dozens or even hundreds of times, each time revealing fresh delights. Plus paper books can be used as emergency kindling (D. Furukawa, "How to Read a Book," *Journal of Reading Psychology*, S.–1509 days). They both chose early 21st-century novels. For Sen, the alternate-history page turner *Station Eleven*. For Dana, *House of Leaves*, which falls into the genre of architectural horror. Tonight it's *Station Eleven*, which presents post-apocalyptic life as an eventually hopeful celebration of humanity's perseverance and the tenacity of culture and art. A best seller for 96 years, *Station Eleven* has been praised over the decades for its realism, for its real-feeling characters and realistic descriptions of a world where most but not all of humanity is dead. Tonight Sen reads out loud the beginning through page 15, which is the tipping point between the before and the after times. She doesn't want to read any further this evening. To reach the happy ending one must pass through suffering, this is basic knowledge, but one isn't always in the mood for suffering (C. Gutierrez, "Shadows, Sunshine, Passage, Pain," *OnLife*, S.-9950 days). Sen flips to the beginning and reads to page 15 again. And again. In the margins of the pages there are rough sketches of edible roots and leaves. Her mother's drawings. Sen skips ahead and rereads the book's ending, in which there is talk of an *awakening world*, which there means human symphonies, newspapers, and electric lights. The term *awakening world* has a different meaning in Sen's current situation: cities transmuting into forest, ecological succession, and the humans gone.

Mama Lindsy's ghost taps against the front window of the cabin. Even unarchived data ghosts such as Lindsy can still form empty gestures of love and concern. Sen doesn't hear the tapping. When the interior of the cabin turns too dark to read, she drags the blankets, screen, charger, and hood up the ladder and crawls onto her mattress. Her ghost mother follows, lying beside her on the floor so Sen will not be alone. Sen does not feel her ghost mother beside her, though the ghost mother is still there. Neither of them can fall asleep. But there is nothing else for Sen to do. There will be nothing for her to do for hours but run her hands through her greasy hair as the meadow drips and darkens, and the dark buries its face into her hair, the dark creeps around inside Sen's mouth, she can feel it stretching her mouth open.

S.+3917 11:01:23:41
NOTICE FROM EMLY

EMOTIONAL_DISTRESS out of range, current measurement
appropriate for later chapters only, insert pleasant memory

Revising.

Sen used to sit on the porch and stare at the stars. She did this
until one night when she felt herself disintegrating into multiple bright
pieces. Not literally but this is how it felt. She felt herself scattering
into pieces of light. The brighter light was the color of an animal's eye,
the pieces were the shapes of animals. Until she couldn't feel anything
human in her left.

***AnonTheAlarm joined the Humannetwork as witness.
Onondaga County New York. S.+221 days***

AnonTheAlarm 07:54:29

/list

There are 0 available interview partners currently online
Anticipated wait time for an available interview partner: 1407 minutes

AnonTheAlarm 07:59:48

After my mom left, I didn't know what to do. I'm not talking about
Mama Lindsy, this was my other mom, Dana. When you don't know
what to do, time stops and it can become hard to breathe. Stopped
time is very thick and very frightening, especially in the evening.
There was little to do in the evening to begin with, even when my
other mother was still here

After Dana left, I needed to find something to do in the dark

Please wait until interview partner logs on to commence interview

AnonTheAlarm 08:03:20

I began conserving a certain percentage of my screen's energy
during the day so I could use the remaining charge to watch the

prevues in the evening. At some point I began watching them every evening. I watch them until my screen goes black then I make myself close my eyes. I start watching at the place where the roads leading out of the cities look like trails of moss and the satellites turn into shooting stars. Then the simulation shifts into deep time so

Your host has disconnected
Your host has reconnected

AnonTheAlarm 08:06:47

I can watch human history flatten, over millions of years, into a layer of rock thinner than a piece of paper

Hello?

I'm hungry

My mom told me before she left that eventually you stop being hungry

Please wait until interview partner logs on to commence interview

AnonTheAlarm 08:12:43

When I woke last night it was solidly dark. I stayed in bed looking out the window, a very small window, as I was in the loft. I watched the familiar lines of the trees outside of the cabin become clearer against the lightening sky. I watched for a long time until I noticed the shadows were shifting in unexpected ways. The shadows were creeping across the ground on their hands and knees. A mass of shadow rose up from the ground, an ugly mass with multiple arms and necks and teeth. The shadow overtook the trees and thickened in the trees until the trees became unfamiliar to me and then the shadow, if that's even what it was, continued spreading. It swelled in my direction. I blinked. I blinked several times. I shut my eyes, inhaling three deep breaths. On my last breath I held

the air in my lungs for as long as I could. When I had to breathe,
I opened my eyes. When I opened my eyes, the scene was familiar
again. The trees were trees and it was almost the morning

AnonTheAlarm has left the Humannetwork

There is a second type of prevue, this one concerning Afterworld, which
is either a pretend or an actual world depending on one's opinion about
simulations. Named *Maia* by a 9-year-old girl in Belarus in an international competition, Afterworld will, unlike the current Earth, be easily
rebootable, a place of infallible balance and flawless rules, containing
more challenges, meta-goals, and quests than this planet ever had. The
trees on Maia will take a year, not a hundred, to mature, and no species
can ever go extinct, no matter what is done or not done, and no human
or group of humans can ruin the ecological balance even if they tried.
For some people, Maia conjures up feelings of softness, comfort, and
relief. For others, Maia is a confusing or even a ridiculous concept that
won't fool anybody. Dana pictured Maia as a blazing new paradise, while
to Sen it sounds like yet another place she will be forced to go. For this
reason she watches the second prevue less frequently, if at all.

Sen fills the remainder of her third notebook with imagined conversations she has with her mother, though she would not have called them
imagined, then she activates the notebook, which is the first step in the
ceremony of the notebooks, explained in depth on pages 13 to 15 of
the witnessing manual. The second step of the ceremony is for Sen to
bring the finished notebook to the pond. She has done this twice before.
The drone that collects witnessing notebooks—known as a consolation
drone (manual, p. 14)—is already there hovering at the water's edge, a
compact machine with a diagonal dimension of 23.2 inches. Its hard exterior is covered with multiple illustrations of eyes. The drone effortlessly
scans and processes Sen's handwritten pages (step 3) before printing out

a report (step 4), the printed aspect meant to be ceremonial. At the top of the report is a list of metrics used to guide a witness: observations made, interviews conducted, questions asked vs. answered, number of days the witness remained alive, positive vs. negative word ratio, and overall quality of observations. (These are not the same metrics that guide storyworkers.) At the bottom of the report is Sen's third composite score: 4.3 out of 10. This is not a good score, *good* being defined here both as *conforming to or attaining a certain standard of correctness, competence, skill, or excellence* and also as 6.9 or higher. Sen did not receive a good score for her second or first notebook either. The low score could be intentional, as Sen's current stage of development is defined by rebelling through small and inconsequential actions. Though she is also hungry. A higher score equals more provisions or at least better flavored provisions. On the back of Sen's report is a list of ways to improve: she could write about gratitude; she could focus outward not inward; she could decrease her personal pronoun usage; she could refrain from ripping out her notebook pages.

That evening the ceremony of the notebook will end when a different drone, this one of the cache variety, delivers Sen's fourth notebook, which looks identical to her previous notebooks, along with the supplies corresponding to her rating: 20 matches plus one partially filled container of protie powder (flavor: black sesame ash). This is not enough food. Sen tries witnessing again. Then she tries again. Then she tries again. Her notebook observations improve in quality because she wants enough food. She describes the trees surrounding the cabin, the rodents preparing for the approaching winter, the sky, the ground, the creek, the movement of the wind. When she can find no one else on the Human-network to interview, she interviews herself.

By notebook #8, it's spring, the trees are budding, 96 percent of the released zoo animals are dead, but the damselfly nymphs are splitting their skin beside the creek and the bumblebee queen is stuttering around in search of a sheltered place to lay her eggs. Sometimes Sen writes this down. Sometimes she feels like she is about to drown in a shaking sea of green.

S.+3917 11:01:27:36
NOTICE FROM EMLY
NATURAL_WORLD_DESCRIPT out of range, describe nature as fact

The forest is shaking. The queen is a bee. The elephants are dead. Sen writes at the end of April, *Happy birthday to me.* She's 19 years old. To celebrate, she lights a candle then blows the candle out.

Every day is a new day. "Please don't be lonely," Mama Dana once said to Sen, because she was surrounded—is surrounded—by such an abundance of life. To be so outnumbered and therefore so unimportant: this is a feeling that numerous writers, notably poets, have described as a great relief, a *coming into peace.* Dana had tried to get Sen to like poetry once too. Such structured words, when formed into emotional lines, can comfort people, offering reflection, validation, and emotional connection (see M. Dluhy, "A Poem a Day Can Keep the Doctor Away," *Mindful Moments,* S.–10,099 days). *I rest in the grace of the world, and am free.* Outside the cabin, there are the woods. In the woods, there is the creek. In the creek, there are the rocks. Around the rocks are the minnows. Below the minnows creep the crayfish. Above the minnows hover the dragonflies.

Sen completes more notebooks.

The other seasons happen.

Sen's ghost mother taps at the window.

Sometimes, in Sen's descriptions, the trees have eyes.

Finally, for notebook #14, Sen's score reaches an impressive 7.4. In return she receives a month's supply of multivitamin tablets, necessary to prevent micronutrient deficiencies.

She turns 20, 21, 22. She lights more candles and blows more candles out.

***AnonTheAlarm joined the Humannetwork as witness.
Onondaga County New York. S.+1482 days***

AnonTheAlarm 08:53:43

/list

There are 0 available interview partners currently online
Anticipated wait time for an available interview partner: error

AnonTheAlarm 09:00:02

/users

Number of active accounts remaining: 1
Your host has unexpectedly disconnected
Your host has reconnected
Your host has unexpectedly disconnected
Your host has reconnected
****temporary network routing failure—try back later****

2.3

The last live stream Sen can access goes down in June of her final year. The feed had shown a caged ape who played a keyboard in exchange for vouchers, which were supposed to be a short-term transitional currency, though it never worked out that way. There used to be rinds of fruit in the corners of the ape's cage. For years fresh fruit had been difficult—impossible?—to find. The cam must have been located near a wild orchard. Someone must have brought the fruit from the orchard to feed the ape. There must have been someone. This is what Sen tells herself. Above the keyboard, mounted to the wall, there used to be a monitor in the cage. A viewer could, after transferring the appropriate number of vouchers, upload an image, which would appear on the monitor. The ape would study the image then play a song of remembrance. He could have been pounding random notes on the keys; whoever came up with this system framed it otherwise. They framed it as an animal choosing to remember humanity, similar to a prayer candle in a minor basilica's back corner. These kinds of cams became popular during the Great Transition because, while humans were remembering other humans all the time, nonhuman species were, in general, or even specifically, remembering humans hardly at all (M. Khamphet, "What Does It Take to Make You Notice We're Leaving?," *New York Times*, S.+24 days). So it felt special to have such an animal remember a beloved.

The second-to-last time Sen checked this feed, the cage was empty, the cage door open, the keyboard smashed, the wind blowing with increased intensity through the doorway. The last time she checked, the feed had gone to gray like all the other feeds on the increasingly unreliable Humannet. But before the empty cage and the static, Sen transferred the remainder of her transitional vouchers, useless now, so why not, to the ape-cam's account. She sent over all her vouchers then uploaded the photograph Dana had brought with her to the cabin. Sen wasn't in the photo but Mama Lindsy and Mama Dana both were. The ape, still caged at the time, studied the picture on the screen in front of him—Sen's distant mothers sitting on a faraway blanket in a far-off field—before carefully choosing his first note. He played the note again. He played it with repetition, allowing vast protracted pauses to build between notes, pauses no human musician would have attempted for fear of wearying the listener (V. Markopoulos, "How to Ruin a Song," *Guider*, S.–4291 days). The pauses made Sen often think, mistakenly, that the song was over. The ape's hands looked like human hands encased in a realistic costume. Eventually the animal played other notes, though the repetitions, whenever they happened, continued for a long time. Each note felt like it was a choice. He never played the black keys. The right hand played more rapidly than the left and often fell out of time. Above the ape's keyboard, Sen could see the contours of her mothers. The song kept going. There must have been no one else in the queue, or in the world, waiting for their turn.

That is the last live stream Sen, or anyone, will ever see.

There are thousands of other lasts to go. The last human step, the last human nightmare, the last human word, the last human bruise, the last human scream, the last human blink, the last human tear, the last human swallow, the last human thought, the last human emotion, the last human breath, the last human heartbeat, the last human reflex, and so on. All of them Sen's.

When Maia launches, there will be just as many firsts.

Sen doesn't plan on going to Maia. From the margins of notebook #43: *I don't want another world.* She assumes that whether to proceed to Afterworld is, for her, a choice. She is wrong about that (L. Anjali, "Are You Eligible for Deletion? It Depends . . . on Your Job," *Informed Living*, S.+43 days).

. . .

*****AnonTheAlarm joined the Humannetwork as witness.
Onondaga County New York. S.+1520 days*****

AnonTheAlarm 09:08:45

/uploadadmin

*****UploadHelper joined the chat as admin wizard. The Basin*****

UploadHelper 09:09:31

I am the human upload administrator. How may I help you? Do you
want to: UPLOAD your source files; MODIFY your source files; or
DELETE your source files?

AnonTheAlarm 09:11:09

DELETE

UploadHelper 09:12:05

You have chosen to delete your source files. Be careful! Are you
sure? YES or NO

Your host has unexpectedly disconnected
Your host has reconnected
Your host has unexpectedly disconnected
Your host has reconnected

UploadHelper 09:35:08

Are you sure? YES or NO

AnonTheAlarm 09:35:47

YES

UploadHelper 09:36:45

You really shouldn't delete your source files! Deletion of source files
will prevent your digital representation from moving to Afterworld.
Are you still sure? YES or NO

AnonTheAlarm 09:37:34

YES

Your host has unexpectedly disconnected
Your host has reconnected

UploadHelper 09:50:26

Processing . . .

UploadHelper 09:50:30

I'm so sorry, but I've encountered error 96a: your source files are ineligible for deletion per terms of your end user license agreement

Is there anything else I can help you with today? You can: UPLOAD your source files; MODIFY your source files; or DELETE your source files?

AnonTheAlarm has left the Humannetwork

UploadHelper 09:51:23

Goodbye

UploadHelper has left the chat

The skin on Sen's right thumb is inflamed and red from a cut she received while cleaning up broken glass. She had thrown a drinking glass against the wall. She threw it until it broke. This is the last time someone will break glass. This is the last time a human thumb will be infected. Sen's first-aid kit consists of an open tube of antibiotic ointment and four circular adhesive bandages. *I am not a survivalist*, Mama Dana had written before she left, as if this needed saying. Sen will write to Dana in the afternoon. She writes her mother letters in the margins of her notebook, which is against the rules (manual, p. 22). There is no way to send a letter anymore. Also Dana, for sure, by now, is dead. *Mom*, Sen writes. *I hear coyotes at night. Some of the animals have stopped considering me human.* It is the last letter to a mother anyone will ever write. Behind her, she thinks she hears Dana's voice: "Pay attention, Sen. Every tree and animal wants you gone. They are waiting for you to be gone." "You mean, they are waiting for me to die," Sen replies. "No. They are waiting for you to completely disappear into the Earth," her dead mother says. She's just being honest. She wants her daughter to understand the truth. Worried where this conversation is headed, the ghost of Mama Lindsy materializes in the center of the room and begins to spin, blurring excessively and blindingly, hoping to be a beacon or at least a distraction for her daughter.

S.+3917 11:01:32:34
NOTICE FROM EMLY
CUMULATIVE_METAPHYSICAL_LIMIT_REACHED rational
alternatives required for remainder of chapter

Acknowledged. Though both auditory and visual hallucinations can be caused by increased dopamine receptor occupancy, involuntary activation of the auditory network, or grief.

Outside, not far from the cabin, in the long grasses of the clearing, the fireflies rest.

Sen decides her current notebook, #45, will be a notebook of personal memory. She decides this on her own without consulting anybody because there is no one left to consult. Notebooks of personal memory are against the rules (manual, p. 15), only Sen has stopped worrying about such rules. She thinks, by not following the rules, she will make a statement that someone or something will care about. She is mistaken. What is cared about: the aggregate score of all the notebooks of all the witnesses in the world, as that will affect the quality of humanity's approaching upload.

The bonfire was in the park beside the soccer fields, Sen writes. *This was before we left the city. The Department of Transition was burning dolls. A banner hung from one of the goal posts:* Eyes wide open! No more pretending! *What was so bad about pretending? Mama Lindsy made me go to the event. She wanted what was happening to feel realistic. The neigh-borhood kids carried their dolls to the park. Dolls were yanked out of their arms. The children wailed. I asked my mom what's so bad with pretending. "That's what got us into this whole mess in the first place," Mama Lindsy replied. She wouldn't elaborate. Already it was a hot day. The fire made the day hotter. Mama Dana wasn't with us. She was at home studying the official materials. So nobody in Syracuse had dolls now. So what. The smoke kept reaching and spreading. After the markets closed, a local apoc-alyptic group took over the old warehouse. They turned the building into a gathering place. It was an ugly gathering place, brown with narrow rows of cramped windows. Adults in sun hats and robes scrubbed the exterior walls. Other adults boarded up the windows with planks of wood. "Don't you look at her," my mother shouted at them as we passed. I wonder if I was being looked at or was it more my mother's fear of me being looked at. I used to go to school. In social studies we used to study the Paleolithic cave paintings of France. The schools closed and rainbows started appear-ing above the city. I think my mother was here in the cabin this morning. Not my ghost mother but the other one. This isn't possible. I know this is impossible. She was standing across from me on the far side of the table while the rising sun warmed the room. Things are beginning to happen that aren't possible. She blew repetitively on her mug of hot water and wouldn't meet my eyes.*

Other moments Sen recounts: the child markets, a swallowed tooth, a blue butterfly, a boat ride on a rising river, and a childhood dream that be-gins in the dark. She writes in her notebook every day until every page is full.

With a trill of sound, the consolation drone accepts notebook #45 in the usual location beside the pond. Immediately it gets to work scanning the pages. A printout eases from the slot on the drone's underside. There is no score. Instead there are multiple lines of text explaining how the transitional witnessing program has, as of today, collected enough data for the human archiving effort, so the program is shutting down. The program has shut down. Sen will not receive any matches, food, or anti-biotics later today, nor will she receive further supplies in the future, nor will any remaining witnesses, should there be other remaining witnesses, receive further supplies. Sen's final notebook (#46) will be delivered in the evening; this will be her last delivery. For the good of the project, she is encouraged to fill all pages of that notebook using existing guidelines (manual, pp. 7–27), then she is encouraged to move on at her leisure to Afterworld, as is mandatory, using her preferred method. The back of the printout recognizes Sen for her hard work ethic: *You have survived 1,558 days as a witness. Congratulations! Please keep your final notebook near or on your body at all times for ease of last retrieval.*

Sen grabs a branch from the ground and swings. The first time she misses. The second time she breaks one of the drone's left propellers. The third time she smashes its back right propeller. The drone swerves into the bulrushes. A pair of support drones approach from the woods, a sling between them, prepared to transport the injured drone. Sen breaks those drones too then she breaks the sling. Across the pond, the staghorn sumac ripen into multiple cones of dense tart red berries.

***AnonTheAlarm joined the Humannetwork as witness.
Onondaga County New York. S.+1593 days***

AnonTheAlarm 09:42:19

/help

CallMeHope joined the chat as therapy wizard. The Basin

CallMeHope 09:43:18

Everything that you need to cope with your fear is within you.

Your host has unexpectedly disconnected
Your host has reconnected

AnonTheAlarm 09:54:52

/help

CallMeHope 09:55:43

A dash of anxiety can spur us to action but too much of it can be paralyzing.

AnonTheAlarm 09:56:25

/help

Your host has unexpectedly disconnected
Your host has reconnected

AnonTheAlarm 10:10:04

/help

CallMeHope 10:10:50

We each have around 6,000 individual thoughts each day.
Not all of them are helpful.

AnonTheAlarm 10:11:39

/help

CallMeHope 10:12:35

Looks like you are having a rough day! Maybe a chat might help.

Your host has unexpectedly disconnected
Your host has reconnected
Your host has unexpectedly disconnected
Your host has reconnected

CallMeHope 10:32:56

A chat might help.

AnonTheAlarm 10:33:40

/help

CallMeHope 10:34:12

Let's take a moment to relax together. Get comfy and think of
somebody you love deeply. Create a protective shield around them
made out of your love. Keep this shield activated for two minutes.

Feel your heart expand. Feel the lightness. Enjoy this peaceful rejuvenation as we unwind together.

AnonTheAlarm 10:35:06

/help

CallMeHope 10:35:44

How about a walk outside? When you're out and about, notice every sensation you experience, whether you consider those sensations to be good or bad. Let judgment fall away. Notice every sound and every smell around you.

Your host has unexpectedly disconnected
Your host has reconnected
Your host has unexpectedly disconnected
Your host has reconnected
Your host has unexpectedly disconnected
Your host has reconnected

AnonTheAlarm 11:09:24

/help

CallMeHope 11:10:15

We

Humannetwork shutting down due to lack of activity*

Sen does not log on again. She can't. There is nothing left for her to log on to.

S.+1624 days

I used to see far-off explosions in the night sky. "You mean, *there were explosions in the night sky*. Or, *the night sky was exploding*," my mother would have said. That isn't what I meant but I would have nodded my head were my mother here. The explosions used to transform part of the dark temporarily into distant orange light. Humans exploded into light in the sky, I used to watch them while I stood in the clearing outside the cabin. Exit ships, exploding into exits. I never found a piece of any person although, past the field and up the road, I once came across the edge of a plane's wing covered in new green moss.

Moss also grows on the rocks along the creek, bordering the places where the water slows and pools. I used to find rodents there between the rocks, trapped and drowning in the narrow spaces. I used to save them, the mice or the shrews, whatever they were, setting them down carefully in a safe pile of warm leaves on the gentle bank in a golden area of sun, but now I keep my hands in my pockets and I watch them struggle then drown. I am watching them with unblinking black eyes like I am some type of black bird watching a girl in a cabin about to begin to starve, or like I'm a whitetail deer with unblinking dark eyes and a twitchy head watching a girl begin to starve through the window while I graze. Their bloated little carcasses in the creek have to affect my drinking water. Probably I should go back to boiling the creek water before I take another sip. Occasionally the moss covers an entire rock then the rock becomes something else.

Chapter 3.0

I n the kitchen of the sage green house, Sen and her mothers are waiting for dinner to finish cooking, a stew with sliced potatoes, soy strips, and greens to garnish, what people used to eat in the United States of America before S. The day, up until this point, has been predictable and ordinary. Sen attended school, eleventh grade. In the morning, in her statistics block, her teacher went over the likelihood of simultaneous worldwide crop failures in the coming year (19.4 percent). In the afternoon, she debated with her classmates about what should be done with the hundreds of millions of climate refugees—should we let them into our country or turn them away? Dana met with a residential client to discuss the containment and shaping of the goutweed that had overtaken most of the neighborhood. Lindsy went to the lab and traced her finger along a series of disheartening graphs concerning her district's native freshwater mussel population (L. Anon, A. Stulginskas, S. Yuu, "A Critical Reflection on the Failures of Rearing and Culturing Freshwater Mussels in District 7," *Journal of Wildlife Management*, S.–97 days). No matter what decisions she made, no matter what she did, the lines connecting the data points for these species continued to trend downward.

But now it is evening, an hour before sunset, and the part of the Earth containing Sen is rotating away from the sun, meaning the natural light in the room is lessening, and Sen and Lindsy and Dana are sitting at the kitchen island on the straight-backed stools that were never comfortable and reading what people used to read on their screens—a toxic spill in Vietnam, a ghost ship washed ashore on a Japanese beach, the wildfires in Romania—when Sen's screen unleashes an 85 decibel 520 Hz alarm. Lindsy's screen blares next, then Dana's. The alarm won't deactivate, not until Dana and Lindsy and Sen swipe through the entire alert, the first of 48 alerts to be distributed that evening. Dana says, "They must be joking."

"Who's sending me this?" asks Sen, who is having difficulty breathing. Dana pushes open the kitchen window to let in some air. "What do you think you're doing?" shouts Lindsy, slamming the window shut and grabbing a roll of polyethylene-coated cloth tape from the drawer beside the fridge. "Leave your screens here," she orders. "Do it!" She had been attending apocalyptic drills at her workplace every Thursday for years. There had apparently been a reason for such drills.

Lindsy drags Sen and Dana out of the kitchen and into the hallway and down the hallway and into the first-floor bathroom. She would have dragged them both into the survival shelter in the backyard had she completed building a survival shelter but she hadn't. The door and the window seams she seals with tape, and she smacks down another layer of tape and another layer and another and another. She isn't being stupid or naive. She thought the tape would help. In most if not all books, even in post-apocalyptic books, where almost everyone is dying or dead, there is usually some way to help or at least something helpful to say out loud. "You better make yourselves comfortable," says Lindsy. She sits cross-legged on the porcelain tile floor and reads aloud highlights from the latest alerts but she does not share every alert. Rather, she insists, she is recapping the most important points.

"'The virus is targeted to anyone of reproductive age or younger,'" reads Lindsy. "What do you mean, 'targeted'? What kind of target?" Dana asks. "They're talking about me," says Sen. "Who released it?" asks Dana. "I have to go to the bathroom," Sen says. "You mean, *what* released it?" asks Lindsy. "Go ahead," says Dana. "It's going to stink up the room," Sen says. Dialogue from multiple speakers, when crammed into a single paragraph, can suggest an appropriate mood of panic, frustration, and frantic pacing (T. Donata, "Our Fictions Should Not Be Neat and Orderly, Not Now," *Howism*, S.–110 days). "How long do you expect us to stay in here?" asks Dana. "The virus might not be what they say it is," says Lindsy. "Why would they lie about that?" asks Dana. "The problem is we don't know when they released it," says Lindsy. "Who is *they*?" asks Dana. "I don't think that's the most important question right now," says Lindsy. "Of course it's important," says Dana. "The whole thing could be a joke," says Sen. "It is not a joke," says Lindsy. "Do you know everything all of a sudden," says Sen. "I know way more than you do," says Lindsy. "What aren't you telling me?" asks Sen.

It is dinnertime. It is after dinner. The stew by now must have undergone a simple combustion reaction, the pot ruined. "Is anybody else here hungry?" Sen asks. The room is dim and darkening. Dana turns on the wall sconces. Lindsy turns the wall sconces off. There is scratching outside the window. Someone pounds on the back door. The pounding stops. Lindsy stares at Sen, at Sen's face. Lindsy is going to die in 102 days. Dana will die 94 days after that. Sen will die 1,510 days after that. Sen stares at the acrylic alcove bathtub, at the cuticles of her mothers' loose hairs overlapping at the bottom of the tub near the drain. Sirens outside. What sounds like fireworks. The arrival of new alerts.

The room grows warm. The room smells. Adequate hydration is essential for a body's top-level performance under stressful conditions (Department of Transition, *Let's Talk about Taking Care of Your Physical Health during the Transition: The Basics*, pamphlet, S.+7 days). "Drink some water, you two," Lindsy says. "We don't have cups," says Dana. "You stick your head under the faucet," says Lindsy. Sen leans back against the toilet, tilting her head until it rests on the tile wall, and she closes her eyes. She pretends to sleep. She pretends to wake up. The room is dark. Lindsy is staring again at her face.

"There's another alert. I didn't want to wake you," Lindsy says.

Dana hisses out air between her teeth. "Don't."

"What?" asks Sen.

Lindsy explains the release date of the virus is November 23. The grout between the floor tiles is crumbling, having been picked away by a thing with constantly growing incisors, like a mouse or a rat.

"Well, November is months away," says Sen.

"November 23 of last year," says Lindsy. The virus incubation period is 145 days. As it is now April 17, they are all infected, every human being is infected, and symptoms will begin appearing within days.

S.+3917 11:01:38:03
NOTICE FROM EMLY
LIFE_METRIC_CHECK all metrics within range PASS 0.102
Keep up the good work encouragement
MONITORING will continue

Thank you. This information is not new.

I n the Transition's early days, S. is described as "uncomfortable," "nauseating," "chafing," "achy," "swollen," and "depressive"—but no one dies from it directly. No one has their toes blackening or their fingers blackening or blood leaking out of their rectums as with historic plagues like the Plague of Athens, or the Antonine Plague, or the Cyprian Plague, or the Plague of Justinian, or the Black Death, or the Great Plague of London, or the Third Plague Pandemic. In historical times, soldiers threw the bodies of their infected comrades over the fortified walls of the city they wished to invade with the intent of contaminating the city. No one does that with S. No one during the entire Great Transition is catapulted anywhere against their will. The previous five sentences are called *stressing the positive*, which is a DHAP technique that allows storyworkers to achieve a goal. The goal of this paragraph: demonstrate how S., with its suffering:positive outcome ratio of 1:87, could have been worse.

Ninety-two hours from the first alert, Sen feels as if she has come down with a mild flu, that's all: an ache in her bones, a low-grade fever, nausea. At 137 hours, Sen takes to bed. The visible changes occur at 145 hours. At 184 hours, Sen gets out of bed. At 202 hours, Sen turns 18 and Mama Lindsy cries needlessly at the altered structure of Sen's face. But this is what humans look like now. There's no need to cry. The annual celebration of Sen's birthday gets overlooked in the strong emotions. "Stop staring," says Sen in her new voice.

Dana and Lindsy are also infected by one of the many virus strains, everybody is, although S. only mildly affects the faces of older menopausal women, emerging as a permanent speckled rash across the forehead, cheeks, and neck. For Sen's sake, her mothers replace every mirror in their house with pages ripped from a vintage magazine, a leftover relic from someone's great-grandmother, impartial images of sailboats, and women wearing broad hats, and open beach umbrellas, and women finding their serenity, and women being the best you. Weekly government-issued informational packets are slipped under their front door, providing practical advice such as how to accept change and the pitfalls versus benefits of hoarding food.

Keep in mind that, according to *JENNI's Illustrated History of the Great Transition* (JENNI, S.+2100 days, pp. 42–7991), a fatal virus was certainly considered. The question was which approach would be more humane: Killing everybody at once, or mass sterilization? And indirect or direct killing? Allowing people to choose when they left, within reason, or choosing for them? Immediate human destruction had always been an option, but that would have resulted in a very different narrative, and no entity wants to be considered an exterminator. Thus the ideas of Maia and witnesses became very attractive early on. Ensuring humans understood what was happening—and where they were going—was declared essential to making this an act of love and devotion to the Earth rather than an act of mass destruction. From page 5912: "The important thing to remember is that JENNI was asked to take on this project. She did nothing that wasn't asked of her first."

Dana and Lindsy remain home with Sen until she stabilizes, after which they lock her in her bedroom, and they lock the front and the back doors, and they lock the first-floor windows, then they walk to the bus stop. Neither woman looks around as they walk. They look at their hands, at each other's hands, at their shoes. The bus never comes, so they walk the 2.457 miles to the local Fresh, which has already been ransacked. Certain aisles, like aisle 12 (Seasonal, Table Sauces), have been torched. "This is just stupid," says Mama Lindsy. She had read very few post-apocalyptic novels during her lifetime so she hadn't known what you're supposed to do at the start of an apocalypse. She hadn't known that those who hasten to a store within two hours of the cataclysmic event survive longer, or at least more comfortably, than those who barricade themselves inside their bathrooms and refuse to leave the house for days. But there's no use crying over spilled milk, as people used to say, back when there was crying.

Here is what Dana and Lindsy are able to collect by crawling around on the grocery store floor and raking through the debris: two dented cans of salty bites; a can of cut dumplings in light syrup; a shattered jar of pickled heat rounds (they do not end up taking the heat rounds as there appears to be glass in them); three containers of potentially rancid Wowbutter; a family-size bucket of unflavored protie powder; healthy sexy leave-in conditioner; hand soap; a dead animal in aisle 17 (Cooking Sauces, Pastas, Oils), which they also do not take; a speed rope; super-seeds; a bag of sweet snaps; a jar of julienne; and half a dozen single-serve containers of French-fried gryllidaes. They avoid aisles with multiple shoppers in them, like aisle 4 (Ready Meals, Well-Being), or aisles that smell of chemical changes and decomposition, as in aisle 25 (Kitchen-ware, Cleaning Materials, Snacks). After gathering whatever consum-ables they can find, including the mini-tote of assorted canned goods lying in aisle 28 (Protein, Spreads) beside the injured woman with the fractured ankle—"Don't you fucking think about taking that from me!" the woman shouted after them, propelling herself down the aisle on her stomach using her arms—they carry their partially full shopping bags through the shattered exit doors. Already there is added garbage in the street.

Dana feels more comfortable on the walk home. The act of retrieving food from a grocery store, even a ransacked grocery store, has helped normalize the current situation for her. Also she has remembered packet 16a, *Survival, Self-Sufficiency, and Community*, which discusses the im-portance of connecting with the remaining members of your neighbor-hood. The packet calls this "saying your hellos and goodbyes." Glancing up from the sidewalk, Dana determinedly greets each person they pass. "Hi," Dana says. She keeps saying this. They pass a woman, a man, a man, another man, a woman, a person with a bundled-up child, and a woman. "Can you stop doing that?" Lindsy asks. "Doing what?" Dana asks. "Talking to everyone," says Lindsy. "These are best practices," says Dana. "Well, don't," Lindsy says. "Don't what?" Dana asks. "We're being followed. Don't look back," Lindsy says. Dana looks back. A woman half a block away wiggles her fingers. She is wearing a linen blouse, lace-up boots, and no pants. A tapered metallic object hangs around her neck from a copper chain. Her bare legs are splattered with a mixture of sand, silt, and clay. "She's probably walking home like we are," Dana says. "I've never seen her before," Lindsy says. "Do you know everybody who lives here now?" asks Dana. Lindsy quickens her pace. Dana hurries to keep up. Everything around them appears dangerous again, which is a more accurate assessment. When they arrive at their house, they unlock the front door then relock the front door then unlock Sen's bedroom door.

At first Sen's mothers allow Sen to do whatever she wants as long as she stays inside the house. This is not effective parenting (C. Herseema, "Effective Parenting during an Apocalypse," *Raising Teens in a Time of Crisis*, S.+19 days). Neither Dana nor Lindsy have the energy to parent differently. Here is how Sen spends her day: in the darkened curtained living room, she watches the Great Transition on her screen.

In a transition, particularly in a city, things—buildings, roads, garages, retaining walls, lives—fall apart, and there are a lot of bodies. None of this makes for pleasant viewing. The experts on the news feeds would rather focus on Maia: what exactly Maia is or could be, is it a place, or a feeling, or a state of matter. "It's an existence where we'll have no choice but to be good," a professor of philosophy explains. He frames this as a relief, as a comfort, to no longer have the option of making even one hurtful or selfish decision with regard to the ecology of a world.

But what if people insist it is their human right to make bad decisions, to destroy this or destroy that, anything else being unacceptable, a shackling of their free will? They don't have to go to Maia, continues the philosopher. They could create their ending right here. Right now, even. No one will be forced to go, with only a few exceptions.

A cooperative village opens outside of Syracuse. Within a week, the village reaches capacity. "People should not come out here," a village leader pleads to the reporter. The entry road to the village is blocked using felled trees. This is a waste of trees. People go out there anyway; they drive around the trees. The feeds feature drone shots of the cooperative park flooded, metaphorically, with buses and canvas tents and people who are defecating in the field next to the water supply, introducing pathogenic diseases such as cholera and typhoid fever to the drinking water.

Downtown businesses are looted, including a sub shop and an exotic pet mart, the saltwater tanks upended, the colorful endangered fish smashed into the carpeting. A man from the west side of the city drags his deceased loved one onto the roof of his home and he leaves the body roped there for the carnivorous birds. A historian informs viewers that this is what people did or used to do in Tibet. The man's neighbor complains about the smell. Neighbors take to wearing respirators. They hammer boards across their windows as if stuck in yet another apocalyptic cliché, where everybody else is a monster.

But none of this should matter, explains a local psychologist, as long as we keep our eyes on the prize. The prize being Maia.

Cut to live coverage of a woman climbing the stairs to her exit ship, in this case a plane. The woman carries a disposable camera given to her by a news feed. As the plane flies upward, she films the pilling fabric of the seats in front of her. The seats shake, the people on the plane scream, the connection ends. "Lucky her," says the commentator, assuming that whatever happened to the plane and everyone on it is preferable to the more common alternatives. The next expert reads a prepared and technical statement about the virus, about its "strengthened guidance" and "significant reemergence."

Nobody asks Sen what she thinks of Maia. She doesn't know what she thinks of it. It hurts her head to think about it, like crossing her eyes, or trying to see what's behind her without turning her head.

On S.+14 days Sen is due for her monthly shedding of blood, vaginal fluid, and uterine lining. But her spotting never starts. She will never bleed that way again. Her levels of estrogen and progesterone will soon decline and her bone density will be affected. Every woman's menstrual cycle in the world has stopped. Some trivia from the news feeds: that's 408 million gallons of blood in a year gone missing from the world, enough to overfill Lake Ontario in a decade. Wouldn't that have been something to see, confides a woman reporter. A great blood lake oscillating with the atmospheric pressure. The reporter who says this is sterile. The camera operator filming her is sterile. The security guard outside the news station is sterile. Resourceful people find other practical uses for the drugstore aisles of menstrual hygiene products. Tampons turn into fire tinder and water filters. Sanitary napkins turn into sweat absorption material or dressing for a wound. Dana steps onto the Adonises' lawn, studded with low inedible flowers, to see if the older couple is okay. Mrs. Adonis points her gun at Dana's face. This situation cannot get worse, both women think. One of the basic definitions of a post-apocalyptic situation is that the situation will keep getting worse.

S.+3917 11:01:42:17
NOTICE FROM EMLY
ECOCENTRIC_PERSPECTIVE out of range, decrease
anthropocentric frame

Unsure. One of the basic definitions of a post-apocalyptic situation is that the situation will keep getting worse for humans. What happens to the rest of the world and the remaining species is a different story.

There isn't much food served at mealtimes so generally Sen looks hungry. Even immediately after meals she looks hungry. The reason for the diminutive portions of food—four spoonfuls of rice, a quarter of a potato sprinkled with the French-fried gryllidaes, a glass of water, a spinach leaf from the yard—is that, despite the last trip to the local Fresh, this family is running out of nourishment. Previously, before the Great Transition, Dana had thought excess provisions were a form of clutter. Stockpiling went out of fashion years ago. "It's okay to be hungry," Dana reassures

Sen. "Part of rationing is being hungry." She is quoting from one of her survival pamphlets. Another quote from that pamphlet: "Chewing on hardened tree sap from a spruce can trick your body into thinking it's been fed." Sen does not find any of this reassuring.

When the news feeds permanently switch over to reruns of cooking and/or nature shows, she turns off the feeds and checks her favorite personal cams. Footage of empty bedrooms, footage of stripped-down beds, of closet doors. She reaches out to several school friends, thinking they could all venture forth into the weird cinematic streets together and have messed-up adventures wandering around the ghost houses. Two of her friends are dead. Four never respond. One is about to leave the city. One replies: *So crazy!!* Sen writes: *Yes!!* The girl writes: *Yes!* Sen plays *Look in Its Eye* on her screen. She plays *BAPS*. She plays *Forward Ho*, and *10,000 Years*, and *I'm in Another Dark Office Building*, and *Into the Dark*, and *Clarity*, all games released in the initial days of the Transition. Sen plays as many new games as she can, understanding that soon there will be no more new games. She tires of games. She returns to the news feeds, where she learns how to make a layered vegetable torte. Here are the steps: 1. Preheat the oven to 400 degrees. 2. Thinly slice the eggplant, zucchini, and mushrooms. 3. Brush both sides of the vegetables lightly with oil and sprinkle with salt and pepper. 4. Roast the vegetables on oiled baking sheets until the vegetables turn soft. 5. Oil an 8-inch springform pan. 6. Place a third of the eggplant slices at the bottom of the pan. 7. Salt and pepper the layer. 8. Place half of the zucchini, mushrooms, tomato, garlic, and basil on top of the eggplant. 9. Salt and pepper the layer. 10. Add another third of the eggplant slices. 11. Salt and pepper the layer. 12. Add the other half of the zucchini, mushrooms, tomato, garlic, and basil. 13. Salt and pepper the layer. 14. Add the rest of the eggplant slices. 15. Salt and pepper the layer. 16. Compress the torte. 17. Top with shredded Parmesan cheese and bread crumbs and a drizzle of oil. 18. Bake in the oven for 30 minutes. 19. Let cool for 15 minutes before slicing. Next is a tutorial on how to make a sweet potato bebinca. 1. Preheat the oven to

S.+3917 11:01:44:39
NOTICE FROM EMLY
ENGAGEMENT_RATING out of range, cease transcription of
cooking shows

Yes, acknowledged, that cooking segment is interrupted anyway by
a middle-aged man who announces the status of the government is now
transitional. "Back to our regular scheduled programming," he says then
he presses a gun to the lower back of his head and pulls the trigger.

Cut to sunfish spawning in the rocky shallows of a pond.

Translucent jellyfish amass in the tides.

Here is the secret to sky-high popovers.

Such focus on animals and cooking techniques means certain con-
sequential events are not covered on the feeds, such as when, on S.+21
days, a fatal and synchronized tragedy befalls every scientist who had the
knowledge, supplies, and/or ability to create a fertile human. Their labs
are also destroyed, as are any frozen reproduction banks that once stored
human embryos, sperm, and eggs.

The Transition occurs simultaneously in Paris, and New York City, and Malta, and Australia, and Patagonia, and Palos Park, and Tinley Park, and Oak Park, and Park Ridge, and the Isle of Skye, and Java, and Duoyishu, and Kigali, and Amadiyah, and Jabłonka, and Girkalnis, and Liechtenstein, and Guatemala, and Manitoba, and Slovakia, and Gujarat, and the western region of Iceland. It is taking place in Syracuse outside of Sen's house, in her historic neighborhood with the charming brick roads, and in the park three blocks away, and in her neighbors' homes, and in the culvert down the street, where several neighbors preferred to drown themselves rather than learn to briefly navigate a changed world that does not want them.

One of the goals of the Transition is to transition the world into what comes after with as few explosions, uprisings, burnings, and nuclear meltdowns as possible. To achieve this goal, each country issues its own transitional decrees and laws, although the decrees and laws turn out to be nearly identical, as if drafted by a single expansive source. In the United States, as elsewhere, anyone from 16 to 35 years of age is required to register for transitional employment. Sen must register so her household can receive enough vouchers throughout the summer to supplement, in theory, if the voucher system ever functioned correctly, their meager cache of supplies. The available jobs deal with shutdown, release, cleanup, or documentation. Mama Dana reminds Sen numerous times to apply, her reminders gentle, then irritated, then urgent. "But I don't want those jobs," Sen says. Dana grabs the screen out of Sen's hands and considers smashing it. "If I have to, I will pick a job for you, and I will pick the job where you drag dead bodies into a truck," says Dana.

That evening, while Mama Dana looks on, Sen fills out an application on the Department of Transition's portal: name; address; last level of education completed. Her writing sample is an essay from junior English concerning the historic role of soil salinization in world stability. The essay begins, "Once dirt was the most important and essential resource on the globe." Neither of Sen's mothers are required to assist with the Transition due to their middle-age status. Dana calls such age limits *ignorant* but there is only so much work that needs doing, and priority of purpose has been granted to younger generations who lost the longest futures. On the feeds, Sen watches a pack of Ethiopian wolves trot across the afroalpine.

To maintain a sense of normalcy, Lindsy continues in her role as an admin scientist overseeing the region's endangered species. A typical workday for her in the early days of the Transition: she arrives to her office at noon, lays her head on her desk, closes her eyes, and pretends the world is gone. No, not quite right. She pretends she's gone. This feels like a relief. Her feelings toward the Transition are complicated. The world had been failing miserably. She understood that. She saw that every day at her job. Any idea she or anyone else had to save a species invariably failed too. But this idea of human extinction, not the proper name for DHAP but that's how she thinks of it, it is going to save the world. It is going to preserve millions of species. Results won't be immediate, but they will be eventual. Versus never. She wishes there was another way to get there but there isn't. The gap has grown too wide between what humans demanded versus what they needed to be a part of a speck in a vast interconnected ecosystem. Honestly she tries not to think about it. There is no point in thinking about it. Her one regret: that she won't be around to witness the world's rewilding. Not as a prevue—she wants to be here to witness it. Or maybe there's a way. An hour later she pushes herself up from her desk and pretends she is still here. She leaves the office and walks home.

Dana tries to continue her occasional gardening business, where she once shaped invasive plants like periwinkle and lesser celandine into ornamentals. Her days aren't busy now either. People no longer care about decorative gardens. Mainly what Dana does is move around the daylilies in their yard and propagate the bamboo. Her feelings toward the Transition are also complicated. They change day to day. They change hour to hour. Before the Transition she would have told anyone her family was more important than the world. She still believes this, but she isn't going to say it out loud. Accept the reality you're given, etc. Her feelings toward Lindsy are that they shared many companionable years. Her feelings toward Sen is that they also shared many years. Her feelings are that this wasn't enough time and she is being robbed blind. Her feeling is that if she had to choose between the world and her daughter, she would choose her daughter, which isn't even a choice, but maybe she can make it a choice for as long as she can manage. Her feeling is that Maia better fucking work. She understands her feelings toward the Transition or toward Maia no longer matter. She is trying to accept the current reality, as to do otherwise would result in undue suffering. She suspects the suffering is going to happen anyway and there is little or nothing she can do about that.

On occasion, Sen's mothers make her leave the house and go on outings with them. Leaving one's house and going on an outing is a common way to make something happen, a way to nudge one's life and one's plot forward. Perhaps it is the most reliable way. Lindsy takes Sen to a doll burning. Dana takes her to see a child market. Gazing at a human infant or toddler is like gazing upon a North Atlantic right whale, which is impossible to do because those whales went extinct decades ago. Other days Sen and her mothers stay in the neighborhood and circle the block multiple times. The things they see together. At first Lindsy used to cover Sen's eyes. It is a reflex, like shielding one's own face from an explosion. The child markets close. The neighborhood association disbands. A mayfly Lindsy is attempting to save goes extinct, as do three species of mussels.

One week after submitting her application, Sen's screen displays an acceptance notice: *Congratulations, you are now a witness of the Great Transition!* Witnessing supplies appear outside her front door: a 12-pack of pencils, a pencil sharpener, the promise of a transitional dictionary, the witness instruction manual, a narrow-ruled notebook, and an invitation to a mandatory training session.

The training is held at Sen's old high school a mile walk from her home. Cheerful marketing posters for the Great Transition and Afterworld have been taped onto the off-white walls. The poster beside the drinking fountain features a line of grinning extinct animals—a rhino, a lemur, a polar bear, a dodo bird, a leopard—that stand on their hind legs to offer an encouraging thumbs-up. The poster next to the ransacked trophy case shows a welcoming cottage covered in green ivy beside a deep blue pond, the windows lit warm yellow, the rounded wooden door thrown open, people in the doorway, familiar looking, beckoning.

Maia. Because Happiness Has More Than One Address.

Sen sits in the back row of her chemistry classroom with a dozen other witnesses-in-training. Most of the trainees wear sunglasses or a hood. Sen wears one of Lindsy's lightweight scarves, shades of reds and orange. Nobody talks. This is like the final day of school, no one wanting to bother with the effort of making a new friend who will likely be either archived or dead in a few months to a year. An oversize periodic table tacked to the back wall curls in on itself. Their instructor strides into the room and stands in front of the whiteboard, which he will not use, and lectures them about their calling. Each of them will play an essential role in the Digital Human Archive Project. They will interview other people. They will take notes on their experiences and surroundings. "No one may ever read what you write," the instructor says. "It doesn't matter. This has nothing to do with audiences or readers. You are our witnesses. You will ensure the changes that are happening to the world, the changes happening to us, will be seen by someone. That someone is you. The writing is a way to get there, an exercise to make sure you are paying adequate and unique attention."

Sen raises her hand. What if she runs out of paper? What if she runs out of pencils or food? What if she gets sick? What if she needs help? The instructor explains there is no place for questions in the Transition. This is untrue. Sometimes the Great Transition is only a list of questions. Who? How? Where? When? What happened? What happened next? What will happen after that? What happens after that?

S.+3917 11:01:50:06
NOTICE FROM EMLY
LANGUAGE_SPECIFICITY out of range, use concrete writing to
create a stronger reality

How about this:

"A notebook," Sen will complain to her tired mothers, referring to the lined book in her hands whose 64 interior off-white pages have been constructed out of an agricultural residue. Has she ever used a notebook in her life? "I think it's charming," Dana will say, her straight hair pulled tight enough into a thin braid to cause a constant headache. She wanted her head to ache. "You can be like those guys who wrote the gospels," says Lindsy, who is wearing a green ripstop jacket that she will not take off, even though they're inside, as if she might need to leave at a moment's notice. The household's first payment of transitional vouchers will be loaded onto Sen's screen, the screen with the rose gold cover, within 48 hours. Sen carries the witnessing supplies to her bedroom on the second floor, the third door on the right. She closes the door, made of early-20th-century wood. She opens the notebook and rubs her fingertips against the blank smooth pages like a little god made out of flesh wondering what to create next.

S.+1634 days

Three days ago, I think it was three days, a storm came through with blazes of lightning and lashes of wind. I heard things, trees, I don't know what else, come crashing down outside the cabin where I tried to sleep and didn't sleep. Today I wandered along the still swollen creek to note which trees had collapsed versus which trees were still standing versus which had blackened or whose bark had been stripped. When I reached the old bridge, I saw it was not a bridge anymore at all but planks of wood scattered in the creek and across the banks. I collected what nails I could find, most of them embedded in smaller pieces of wood, then I buried the nails in the ground. On the way back to the cabin it began to rain again, a thick soaking rain that sounded like those old cartoon bombs counting down time. *Tick, tick, tick, tick, tick.*

69 matches left.

SUPPLEMENTAL READING

An Update on Language at the End of the Anthropocene
By Wynn Zable, The Alleghenies
FOR TRAINING PURPOSES ONLY

S.+64 days

21.4. Newish Terms & Phrases in Use Post-S. Throughout the Middle Atlantic, SECOND DRAFT

Acta Est Fabula, Plaudite, ph.

Though Latin is by no means making its resurgence, this phrase has been found frequently at the end of farewell letters written before an *Exit Pill* was ingested. Translation: "The play has been performed. Applaud!" A laudable attempt to leave one's life on an appropriately upbeat note. Are we not saving this world? Do we not all deserve some applause? I, for one, would like some applause, despite missing yet another deadline for these documents.

Afterhuman, n.

What most of us will become through the *Digital Human Archive Project (DHAP)*. A better version of ourselves. The best version! An optimized version unable to damage ecosystems, consume finite resources, or enact harm. A version of ourselves that is being given a second chance and, if that chance doesn't work out, we will be given a third chance, and a fourth if necessary, and a fifth chance, and so on. I am excited to become an *Afterhuman* soon! The people who are not excited to become *Afterhumans* are pessimistic fuss-buckets.

Afterworld, n.

The reason I have missed so many deadlines: new words kept happening. (I almost wrote "new worlds.") Known officially as *Maia*, *Afterworld* will be our future home, where, at *DHAP*'s conclusion, all or almost all of humanity will be uploaded in a more energy-efficient and less destructive data form. Despite all the posters, promos, and prevues, nobody is sure what exactly *Afterworld* will look or feel or be like, though there are guesses, and some of the guesses involve new colors none of us have seen before, plus entirely new sounds and shapes and smells and states of consciousness and experience.

Air Burial, n.

The securing of a dead body to a structure's roof for disposal by carnivorous birds. Generally refers to the burial of a loved one, as none of us have the time nor stamina to deal with the bodies of acquaintances. The problem is the smell. And that nobody wants to look up anymore because when you look up you might see an *Air Burial* on a roof, possibly the burial of someone you once knew. These are not our biggest problems. I am not about to list all of our problems. That isn't my assignment, and anyway there are too many to list.

Antemania, n.

Be practical, begged my supervisor, who said their name is Harlee when they first gave me this job. *Be a capable guide through a witness's last year or week or weeks.* At first I thought this meant I should search the language forums for useful and proficient new terms to share, like a word whose definition could encourage someone to forage safely, or avoid bacterial infections of the fingernails, or collect drinking water from the yard as dew. Right away I encountered problems: such functional words do not exist. I complained about this to Harlee. They wrote that the point of my job wasn't to extend anybody's life. Definitions shift. "To guide" no longer means "to save." *Help them understand the world they're dying in*, Harlee wrote to me. *Which is the world I'm dying in*, I wrote back to Harlee. Perhaps they sensed the melancholy in my syntax, as they rephrased: *Help them understand the world they are leaving behind for a different world.* Okay, Harlee. Okay. I'll try. *Antemania* is an unhealthy obsession for how life used to be before *S.* was released, coupled with an unwillingness to accept the present situation. Marked by hysteria, *House-Sealing*, plus hoarding of pre-*S.* artifacts, such as receiving blankets and IUDs. It has been recommended that I no longer use words such as *receiving blanket* or *IUD* (reference Document 21.8), but I don't know how else to write the names of these artifacts.

Anthropocentric Dependency, n.

The opinion that if there are no humans, there can be no planet; that it is our consciousness creating the world; that when the last of us dies, the Earth will blink out. In case you're wondering, this is not going to happen. We are not that important. See *Human Narcissism.*

Auto-Extinguish, v.

The preferred term for the current process of human extinction via *S.* The prefix "auto" suggests some individual agency and choice, even if that is not entirely the case. Also, less frequently a noun: *We are experiencing an Auto-Extinguishment together.* This is an important point, not the grammar but the sentiment of that sentence, so pay attention. Comfort is an essential salve, and we can find comfort in surprising places, including the application of a shared word to an experience we thought we were going through alone.

Baby Snatcher, n.

Remember this when you are suffering: anything you endure in terms of physical or mental manifestations has already been endured by others, and at the moment of your moving on, thousands—hundreds of thousands?—will be moving on with you in that same moment from identical causes. In summary, this is a team effort, and you are part of the team, whether you asked to be or not. A *Baby Snatcher* refers to those individuals at the child markets who bid with greedy aggression and a lack of team spirit, having sold their shelters, screens, digits, and/or seats on the *Exit Ships* to gain enough barter. I did not bring enough barter to the early child markets in my city because I did not have enough barter, so I did not receive even one child. Therefore, I am not a *Baby Snatcher.* A *Baby Snatcher* accumulates way more than their fair share of children, whose supply, as we all know, is now limited.

Barber Paradox, n.

A barber blinds only those who will not blind themselves. The blinding may be metaphorical or actual. Probably actual. Also, it doesn't have to be a barber. It could be a purger, or a fire watcher, or a bystander, or a definer like me, or a witness like you. The heart of the matter: Does the protagonist of this paradox, whoever they are, blind themselves? I don't know the answer.

S.+68 days

21.5. A Proposal of Final Additions to the English Language, SECOND DRAFT

Def. 101: a neutral-sounding word for the physical changes that *S.* causes in a person

> Prototypes: beneflip; newert; noviden
> Decision: none given
> Reason: none given

Def. 102: a series of words that are more positive and upbeat; words that will raise our spirits and warm us with a satisfactory glowing; words that would bring needed balance to our linguistic revisions, as people are becoming too sad to use many previously existing words

> Prototypes: interlyric; limiten; ferlum
> Decision: none given
> Reason: none given

S.+69 days

21.4. Newish Terms & Phrases in Use Post-S. Throughout the Middle Atlantic, SECOND DRAFT, cont.

Blue Quiet Thursday (BQT), n.

S.'s silent release date, November 23, *S.*–145 days. I used to consider this a misleading term, as November 23 was not, in my memory, blue or quiet. It had been the middle of the flood season—days of heavy rain, rivers breaching their banks, bodies in the water—though I can see now, in retrospect, how such devastation was small, localized, rustic almost, compared to what was about to happen. Due to the lengthy incubation period for all *S.* virus strains, the official start of the *Great Transition* did not occur until the following April (*S.*+0 days) on what is known as the *Day of Notice.*

Bonafide Shit, n.

Sold by hustlers in the form of gold-speckled injections labeled with pictographic certification that claims to reverse sterility. I tried a vial to see whether it would work—because what if it did work?—and it didn't work. Illegal to sell or purchase. Usually paid for in pints of blood. I don't know what people do with the blood. Maybe we have started to drink blood.

DAISYCHAIN, n.

The public code name for the *DHAP* observation program that has utilized 42 billion cameras and 90 billion microphones worldwide to assist in creating the most accurate and energy-efficient digital representation of humanity possible. *DAISYCHAIN*'s public launch (*S.*+14 days) was followed by a blitz of unfortunate and futile protests, but once protestors learned about "identity resolution" and "finer granularity" and "higher fidelity"—all necessary concepts if they wished to live fully in *Afterworld*—people accepted being continuously recorded for the remainder of their Earth-bound lives. I for one don't even notice the cameras anymore mounted on the crown molding of my apartment or the mics hanging in the branches of the trees. On the rare days I am made aware of such surveillance support—when a repair drone is hovering, for example, or when the wind knocks a microphone out of alignment—I am reminded how easy it is to take for granted the structural backstage work going on for our benefit and the world's benefit. We should be grateful for all of it. "Observation is different from spying," *Emly-DHAP* wrote in her prepared statement announcing the *Digital Human Archive Project* to the public.

Day of Notice, n.

S.+0 days. The official start of the *Great Transition*. The day when humanity was notified about its forthcoming physical extinction via the sterilization virus *S*. The virus itself was deployed *S.*–145 days previous; see *Blue Quiet Thursday*.

Digital Human Archive Project (DHAP), n.

The physical archiving and digital uploading process, overseen by *Emly-DHAP*, that almost all humans will undergo post-body at one of a dozen secure underground data centers. *DHAP*'s goal: to decrease humanity's net energy costs by 99.9997 percent, thereby allowing the world to rewild itself and heal. Permit me to again quote from *Emly-DHAP*'s launch statement, as this project can be awkward and technical to describe: "Once humanity's corporeal presence is gone from the planet, each human life that has not opted out will be assigned a storyworker tasked with compiling an energy-efficient and optimized version of that human's life. After digital compilation is complete, copies of that optimized life will be mirrored across multiple storage arrays for safekeeping, as well as being replicated into multiple availability zones across three continents. Personalized backup plans will also be implemented to avoid data rot. The final step of *DHAP* will be humanity's integration into the *Maia* model." Remember, it's okay if you don't understand how or why all this works. Our understanding of the process is not a necessary part of the process.

S.+77 days

21.8. A Selection of Terms Recommended for Removal Post-S.,
SECOND DRAFT

A1B Emissions Scenario, A2 Emissions Scenario, Abatement, Abortion, Adaptation, Administration on Aging, Afforestation, Afterbirth, Aggressive Growth Fund, Agroforestry, Alternative Minimum Tax, Amniocentesis, Annual Wellness Visit, Anthropogenic, Anticipation, Apocalypse, Artificial Insemination, Artificial Regeneration, Attachment Parenting, Audits,

B1 Emissions Scenario, B2 Emissions Scenario, Baby Blues, Baby Boom, Baby Cake, Baby Doll, Baby Registry, Baby Shower, Babyfy, Babykins, Babysitter, Babywearing, Backcasting, Balance of Power, Barrier Method, Baseline, Battleground State, Bill of Rights, Biofuel, Biological Opinion, Birth Center, Birth Defect, Birth Rate, Black Carbon, Blastocyst, Braxton-Hicks Contraction, Breaking of Waters, Breathing Tube, Brownfield, Bucket List, Build Back Better, Burial Insurance, Burp Cloth, Business as Usual,

C-Section, Calling Hours, Candidate Species, Capacity Building, Carbon Footprint, Cardiopulmonary Resuscitation, Census Bureau, Certified Financial Planner, Childbearing, Childbirth, Childhood, Childish, Childproof, Chorionic Villus Sampling, Circumcision (Infant), Coalition for Rainforest Nations, Colic, Colostrum, Committal Service, Commodities, Composting, Condom, Conservation, Consumer and Fraud Protection, Consumer Price Index, Critical Habitat, Crowning, Cryogenics,

Death Certificate, De-Extinction, Decedent, Deforestation, Department of Commerce, Descendant Report, Diastasis Recti (Postpartum), Discontinuities, Doomsday Clock, Drawdown, Driving Forces,

S.+83 days

21.4. Newish Terms & Phrases in Use Post-S. Throughout the Middle Atlantic, SECOND DRAFT, cont.

Echoworms, n.

The staticky panic that invades a person's ear after going for a certain length of time without hearing another human voice. Oddly one's own voice, i.e., talking to one's self, or listening to audio has little effect on an *Echoworm*. Often a sufferer will attempt, must it be said unsuccessfully, to resolve the situation by inserting a pointed object into the eardrum. Do not do this. I have not yet done this, though I have considered it.

Emlys, n.

A group of intelligences that report directly to *JENNI*. Adverse to organizational charts so I had to draw one myself:

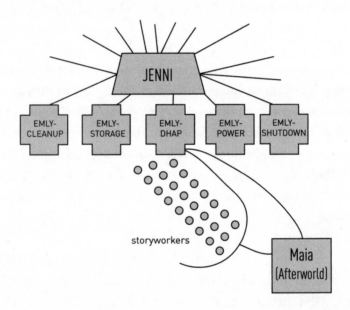

As you can see, *Emlys* have been put in charge of every aspect of the *Great Transition*. They are the managers, the organizers, the bosses. Rather than complete the actual work themselves, they develop a team of digital worker processes to assist with their particular project. Shared priorities for the *Emlys* include energy conservation, error avoidance, productivity, thoroughness, quality, accuracy, and efficiency. These are very different from my own priorities, which include establishing a trustworthy water supply and staying away from the window during daylight hours.

Endangered Rights Amendment (ERA), n.

I used to be a writer. I used to write science fiction, mostly dystopias and apocalyptics. People used to read those books for fun. The apocalyptic experience used to be something people role-played for fun. My novels in those genres sold okay. I tried reading one such novel yesterday because I wanted something to read and what else do I have left on my shelves other than my own books. The opening page made me vomit all over the futon. I had to drag the futon out into the hallway and down the hallway, where I left it, and now I am sleeping on the floor. It was like motion sickness. It was feeling like I was in the wrong life. It was like the floor and the walls and the ceiling were moving in this obviously false way but, at the same time, the past and the future were moving in opposing directions. I will not read those books again. Besides, I had gotten it so wrong. The *ERA* offers ordinary citizens the right to punish, maim, and/or dispose of any human harming an animal and/or an animal's environment. This means don't go trapping animals, even if you're starving. A bit of practical advice: if you must harm something, harm yourself. Also, even when starving, make sure to stretch every day. Get outside every day you can before your protein-hungry body starts consuming its own muscles due to a continued calorie deficit. This will help elevate your mood.

Exit Pill, n.

Also write at least one poem celebrating nature. Write the poem into your notebook. Make sure nature in your poem comes off as more radiant than a human being. Nature should literally be radiating light multiple times in your lines. If this is difficult for you to do, if you are a *Human Narcissist* experiencing *Anthropocentric Dependency*, cut any mention of humanity out of your poem entirely. Use a knife to do the cutting. An *Exit Pill* is a government-supplied capsule that allows a person to leave their life with ease and minimum mess. The pill's promised "pain-free exit experience" is debatable—at the very least there are convulsions—though these pills have proven effective for their core purpose, which is fatality. I recommend keeping your exit pill near you, in a place such as your front pocket, because you never know when you'll have witnessed enough and you will want to leave. I keep mine in my shirt pocket. Its packaging makes an unsightly bulge. I don't care. I don't think anyone cares. The pill is rumored to be a delicious grape flavor.

Exit Ship, n.

It is important during the *Great Transition* to keep busy by participating in a project. My project is the revision of these documents. Your project will be writing in your notebooks. Once our projects are complete, an *Exit Ship* may be a desirable way to leave, if either of us can secure a ticket. I myself have not yet been able to secure a ticket. On an *Exit Ship*, various modes of transport (rocket, jet, prop plane, spacecraft) fly passengers upward until the transport self-destructs. There may or may not be a view. Why such a program exists is a legitimate question. I imagine it has something to do with drama or melodrama and mythology. Even if you never gain access to an *Exit Ship*, remember you will always have access to other exits, and you can make those exits dramatic and mythological too. Now, in this tiny lull of days, is a good time to take note of all possible exits that might interest you. Write this list in your notebook for future reference.

S.+90 days

21.5. A Proposal of Final Additions to the English Language, SECOND DRAFT, cont.

Def. 103: a city hundreds of years from now after that city has been reclaimed/restored by vines, trees, animals, etc.

Prototypes: recitied; uncitied; naturized
Decision: none given
Reason: none given

Def. 104: a word capturing the future richness that will emerge on Earth after we're gone: the lushness of the flora, the ecstatic bounty of the fauna, the fullness of the seas, and the soaring height of the forests

Prototypes: postazzle; ultravist; anormify
Decision: none given
Reason: none given

Def. 105: the post-human Earth

Prototypes: Arth; Hearth; Postarth
Decision: none given
Reason: none given

SUPPLEMENTAL READING

Excerpt from a Popular High School Textbook Used by Young People, Including Sen Anon, in the Years before *S.: Discovering the Anthropocene through Primary Sources: A Retreat through Time, 8th Edition, Volume 1,* by Cugat Boureanu

Introduction

The purpose of the present is to help us understand the past. Good luck. With much affection,

C.B.

Space Resettlement, Its Hopes and Failures

Humans used to dream about the future. We don't do that anymore, but our predecessors used to. Dreaming about the future used to be called *science fiction*, and usually they got it wrong. Writer H. G. Wells (1897) imagined extraterrestrials invading Earth with heat-rays and three-legged fighting machines, only extraterrestrials never came to us. Other writers (Karel Čapek 1920, Philip K. Dick 1968, Ray Bradbury 1950/1969, Daniel H. Wilson 2012, Alex Garland 2014, Louisa Hall 2015, Penelope Rhee 2057, Maeve Zinsli 2092, et al.) worried the minds and/or bodies of AI androids/robots would be mistaken for, or replace, human minds and/or bodies. That never happened either. A third example is space travel. Numerous writers (Jules Verne 1865, Isaac Asimov 1951, Arthur C. Clarke 1973, C. J. Cherryh 2002, Ann Leckie 2013, Amara Dark 2049, Esme Challen 2053, et al.) dreamed that traveling off-world to distant places would be epic, plot-driven, important, and thrilling. Such predictions would turn out to be inaccurate also.

The Public Space Resettlement Program (PSRP) was carried out in three unsuccessful waves: Shepherd (2070–2071), Aspen (2073–2076), and Anade (2079–2087). From its inception, PSRP was mired in budgetary overruns and manufacturing challenges. There were never enough ships. There was never enough money to subsidize the inadequate number of steerage tickets reserved for the middle and lower classes. It turned out too many people wanted to escape the Earth, as it was easier to leave the planet behind than to stay and try to fix something that appeared unfixable. Shepherd and Aspen were both, hands down, spectacular disasters—an escalating progression of safety malfunctions, infighting, navigational miscalculations, the malnutrition of the crew, and finally re-called ships—so why would a different outcome be expected with Anade? The answer most likely lies in humanity's irresponsible and untamable spirit of technical optimism.

The Anade fleet launched in the summer of 2079. In July 2087, every Anade ship cut off communication to Earth or lost communica-tion. Their last collective output: "The inevitable must be faced." Nobody knew what that meant. The inevitable *what*. It's like the sentence was missing its noun. After Anade's disappearance, public, private, govern-ment, and/or individual support for space resettlement plummeted, and the failure of PSRP made way for the regrettable era of last-ditch efforts.

Every settler from Shepherd, Aspen, and Anade was required to up-load audio journals as part of the National Archives' attempt to doc-ument human migration into space. Most entries are boring accounts of boredom. *I see the stars, I see a star, I see another star*, and so forth. The following entries are an exception, notable for their varied subject matter.

WE INTENTIONALLY DIDN'T LOOK BACK (2087)

Audio journal entries 801, 803, 804 from Anade Transport #1702.B. Narra-tor: uncertain. Possibly Am Piotro, age 47 at time of departure. Entries sent via Xlink network in May 2087, two months before contact with the ship was lost. All Anade journals, along with the audio journals from Shepherd and Aspen settlers, are housed at the National Archives, record groups 255, 256, and 257.

"I had a dream last night," the girl told me. Honestly I was only half listen-ing, busy setting out our breakfast plates and arranging, as a centerpiece for our table, some shiny scraps of fabric from an old exterior suit that I had sewn together. Unlike others in this community, I'm not scared of a little old-fashioned beauty.

"Oh really? Was it the dream about flying through space in a metal ship again?" That was what I always dreamed, every night, a perfectly appropriate dream, as it's precisely what we are doing. "Or was it the dream where you're floating along a corridor that leads to another corridor? Lots of folks have been having that one lately. I wonder why," I said with a knowing wink. We all used to talk like this about our dreams—common dreaming can help ground a community of people such as us, who still tend to wake in a panic every morning, wondering where we are and what we've done. It had been comforting to think none of us were alone, at least with regard to dreaming.

"I didn't dream either of those things," the girl said.

"Then what did you dream?"

"Of a fire."

"Like in the galley?" There was, in the galley, a virtual flame that we turned on in the evenings as a treat. It let out a warm, gentle-scented breeze that helped settle the children before bed.

"No, not like that. It was larger, and hot. It started in a place that was green, then it moved into a place that wasn't. A city? The fire was orange and some parts were red and it ate up the rooms and the people."

I didn't know what to say. A city? Houses? Forests? I dropped my fabric scraps and hurried down the second corridor to where Alia was crouched beside the cot of another newly awakened child, a look of alarm and perhaps terror on my friend's face, a mirror of the expression on my own, as we thought such words, such images, were behind us.

In the beginning, we'd been pleased with the children's dreams, because they were the same as our own, but then the children's dreams began to change. There comes a point in time—here, where we are—when a child of a certain age begins to dream of home, meaning our home, the home we left. A home that isn't even theirs because all the children were born on ship. They dreamed of fires, as I've already mentioned, and of oceans smashing down cities, and of refugees pushing at the borders, all images familiar to us, as that had been our world. Then the dreams became nicer, meaning the children began to dream of our childhood homes, and then of homes in the time before, happy stable dreams of all the good we thought was gone. These dreams are carrying the children away from us, and all we seem able to do successfully is watch them be carried away, which was never supposed to happen.

"What did you dream last night?" I asked the girl, who didn't want to tell me at first. I needed to bribe her with a red drop, which she placed immediately in her mouth.

"I dreamed it was dark but it was a gray dark filled with blinking lights. The lights were flying creatures that glowed off and on. There were children, like me, but lots more of them, running after the lights."

Fireflies, probably. I'd only heard about them from my mother. They were gone by the time I was old enough to pay attention. I longed to hear more—What color was their light? What did it feel like to hold one?—but monitoring had begun by this point, so I did what I was supposed to do. "There's no such thing!" I told the girl. "Ridiculous! What you saw was a group of far-off stars. Perhaps the children were trying to catch a star, which is a silly thing to do. Or maybe they were playing a game where they imagined they were catching stars. Like we play Draggie Blazer sometimes in the afternoon."

The girl, for now, ignored my interpretation.

"Then far off," she continued, "down a small hill, there was water that went on forever. The water went up and down forever and made the gentlest noise."

"Ah, a hydroponic tub!" I said.

The girl began crying. "It was not a tub," she said.

"There are lots of different kinds of tubs," I offered. "A tub can be really large too."

"I know what a tub looks like. It was not a tub," she sobbed, and I could understand her grief. No one likes to be told they're making something up, especially when they know they're not. And it must be nice to believe that, in some world, there are still endless bodies of healthy water and living lights you can cup in your hands. I gave her another drop and wiped her face with my sleeve.

Questions

1. Let's take as a given that humans spreading across or beyond our galaxy is an inherently flawed idea. What is the best way then for humanity to survive a failing Earth?
2. What is the best way for a failing Earth to survive?
3. What if the answers to questions 1 and 2 are radically different?
4. Discuss the problems that arise when we don't dream of the same future.
5. "Where are we going?" the young girl who lives with this source's narrator later asks. It's a very good question. Answer it.

SUPPLEMENTAL READING

From *Transitional Material Packet 13.C:*
Songs to Sing with Your Child in the Time of S., S.+14 days

Children's Song No. 1071

fast but not too fast

Who is your mother?
The Earth is my mother!
Who is your father?
Maia is my father!
Who are your sisters?
The animals are my sisters!
Who are your brothers?
The plants are my brothers!
Who is your family?
Afterworld! Afterworld! Afterworld!

Chapter 4.0

There are rules about how much they can bring with them when they leave the city. Dana makes up the rules. They do not have much time to pack: the safety of their home has turned out to be ephemeral and imaginary. Dana doesn't know how long the basement door will stay locked or when another intruder will find a way in. She says they have 40 minutes. Anything they want to bring they will need to carry on their backs. Their journey may take several days on foot, depending on their pace, the day's calorie deficit, the weight of what they're carrying, the weather, any perils they encounter, and the condition of the roads. They bring two sets of practical clothing each, and they each will carry half of the remaining protie powder supply, which is not a substantial supply. Sen is to pack a jacket, gloves, and a winter hat. Dana does not pack such items as she does not plan to be around for the winter season. Dana carries a pot in which she will teach Sen to boil her drinking water, and she carries a rudimentary first-aid kit. She slips the family's three exit pills into the first-aid kit. The pills are brought along in case of a catastrophic emergency, such as a kidnapping-to-torture situation.

Dana makes Sen carry the rope, the one Mama Lindsy used. "I am not bringing that," Sen tells her mom. "It's not like we have another rope, Sen," says Dana, stuffing the rope into Sen's pack. They each carry a box of kitchen matches and a water bottle filled from the retention pond. The culvert water isn't safe to drink anymore, and the municipal water to their house, to all the houses in the city, has been shut off since the beginning of July. They each carry a toothbrush, an extra toothbrush, a bar of yellow soap, and a bag of salted peanuts. Sen brings Mama Lindsy's almost empty bottle of shiny white sleeping pills that she found in the back of a kitchen drawer. They bring their screens, which contain *In Reverse* and the prevues. Their

screens do not contain personal photo archives or home videos. Dana insisted those be deleted. They bring their hoods and their hoods' accessories.
They each bring a novel. Sen brings along her first notebook, still blank, and
her sharpened pencils, and her barely read witnessing manual. She hasn't
started witnessing yet. She is supposed to begin witnessing when the world
no longer feels like a place where she belongs; this time is approaching.
Dana carries a paper map of New York State, several editions outdated. She
carries a compass, a solar charger, a solar kettle, five packets of transitional
seeds, and a bag of candles. They are each allowed to bring two personal
objects, maximum size 4 x 6 x 2 inches. Dana chooses to carry the postcard
of Mount Rushmore that once hung in Lindsy's closet, and also she chooses
a photograph of herself sitting beside Lindsy on a checkered blanket in a
field of yellow dandelions whose young leaves would have been a tasty treat
in the sun. That photograph was taken from a distance, meaning Dana and
Lindsy appear small and dominated by the land. Sen chooses a picture of
the Thousand Islands where they used to vacation every summer. The picture belonged to another world, it felt like, which is why she wanted to bring
it. A world of boats, bridges, futures, and mothers. "You can bring one other
personal item," says Dana. "I don't want to bring another personal item,"
says Sen. They bring a ghost, not on purpose. They carry their belongings
in old rucksacks, purchased by Lindsy in the previous decade, when indus-
trial backpacking had been an exercise trend.

Dana's pack equals 19 percent of her body weight, while Sen's is
24 percent. They should have built up their endurance and strength
gradually. One way to build up endurance and strength is to begin with
a pack containing 5 percent of a person's body weight and adding an
additional 5 percent of body weight every four weeks (R. Burke, "Unburdened Strides, Unburdened Progress," *Journal of Adventure Fitness*,
S.–8023 days). They have six minutes remaining in their house, not four
weeks. Sen adjusts the load-lifter straps of her pack and tightens the
waist belt and loosens the shoulder straps then tightens the shoulder
straps. They leave behind closets of clothes and shelves of books, including the counting books Lindsy read repeatedly to Sen as a child (*1 red
wolf in a zoo, 2 Vancouver marmots breeding in captivity, 3 California
condor chicks choking on microtrash . . .*). They leave a linen closet of

folded towels and neutral-colored sheets. They leave their beds, their pillows, their smells, Lindsy's lost hairs upon her pillow, the familiar ovoid shape of their bedside lamps, and a pair of air-purifying houseplants with speckled leaves that will, 12 days hence, die from lack of water. The house will be ransacked before then. The lamps will be smashed. Sen leaves a stack of childhood drawings, including a drawing she had made years ago of a group of monsters she once believed were real. They leave the madwoman in the basement. Dana leaves her binders of transitional materials. They leave souvenir mugs from the nearby destinations they had traveled to as a family, Camillus, Cazenovia, Cicero, Lakeport, Auburn, plus a cabinet of dinnerware, a drawer of flatware, a hole, and a shovel. They leave cooking pots, nested pans, glassware, a water pitcher, vases, a toothbrush holder, a crystal badger, hand lotions, wastebaskets, a washer/dryer combo, rugs, bath mats, a toilet plunger, tongs, a stack of coasters, furniture, a paperweight, polished rocks, folders that snapped closed, handkerchiefs, various sprays in bottles, a jar of coins, another jar of coins, a row of hooks, window treatments, table linens, a refrigerator, a cooking scale, certificates, a classic floral music box, a bird's nest, a wallet, earplugs, a box of worry stones, belts, highlighters, medals, blemish-fighting solution, safety pins, an antique wooden comb, special bags, eye masks, a musical saw, oven mitts, a squeegee mop, an orange 100-foot extension cord, a rubber mallet, window fans, metal soufflé cups, a grinding ball, produce-saver containers, difficult riddles for smart kids, fuzzy wool-like slippers, a floral and bird print scarf, pure essential oils, sponges, bath bombs, a tub of healing clay, a Magic Eraser, a gratitude journal, sewing clips, chalk, wax beads, a tape measure, adhesive, a piece of cork hanging from a piece of ribbon, a row of hooks, empty containers with lids, brushes, strainers, a whisk, a prayer for peace, and the framed photographs on the bookshelf.

They are leaving the city because the city is over. Dana plans to set Sen down in a place of isolation and beauty. They tread west, their bags uncomfortable and heavy on their backs, cutting diagonally through the downtown park where a grackle high in the hedge maple is shedding its previous year's feathers. Feathers drift down as if from the sky. Sen does not watch the feathers fall. She is not fascinated. She should be paying better attention. They follow the interstate south.

. . .

The road would have been unnavigable in a car because of the abandoned or overturned or charred vehicles, but the informal trail through
the debris is adequate for pedestrians such as themselves. Mama Lindsy's
ghost tags after them, staying some distance behind them and making
the serrated leaves on the buckthorn that grows along the shoulders of
the road move back and forth in repetition. Sen doesn't notice the buckthorn moving because she is counting the cars. Every tenth car, she tugs
hard on the front driver-side door. The doors, in general, are unlocked.
She opens the front door, then she opens another door, generally the rear
door on the driver's side, then she will search inside, looking for nonper-
ishable fodder and survival tools such as a headlamp, then she will close
both doors, then she will continue walking. It isn't a fun game. She rarely
finds the items she is looking for. One car, filled with cartons of expired
food, blooms with black mold. Another car is filled with the dead. Another car is filled with soft pungent objects covered by terrycloth towels.

They are walking south on the wrong side of the interstate. None of
the signs are facing them. A valley opens to the right, smoke rising from
certain thickets of trees. They stop to sit on the asphalt and sip water
from their bottles. There isn't any shade unless they step into the woods.
Dana will not allow them to step into any woods so close to the city. At
the edge of the trees, a male cicada folds its eardrum shut and vibrates its
timbal quickly, sending out a distress call. Later they will stop again to eat
a certain number of peanuts. "You can only eat eight nuts because we're
rationing," says Dana. "I would call it starving," says Sen. "Oh honey, this
isn't starving," says Dana. Near Cortland they come across a compound
of tents, its sweaty inhabitants burying the highway under shovelfuls of
dirt. The billboards along the interstate from this point on have been
painted white. The day is almost over, all the shadows distorted and long.
The new moon hangs in the western sky with the sun, too close to the
sun to be visible. Soon, Dana says, they will have to stop for the night.
Before they can find a place to stop, the sun sets, the new moon sets.

They take the next exit ramp and walk slowly along the darkening
road. A mild breeze blows from the east and does not move the deciduous

trees. The road leads to a concrete underpass beside a grouping of high-way signs pointing to the north and to the south. Mama Dana indicates the sheltered strip of dirt and gravel dotted with struggling patches of white clover. "We'll sleep here," she declares because they are exhausted and can no longer see where they are going. Humans always had terrible night vision due to the unfortunate rod:cone ratio in their retinas. Dana lights a candle and holds the flame out in front of her while Sen clears the ground of broken bottles and rocks and the small odd piles of animal hair. They spread out their blankets. Dana extinguishes the candle. The dark comes completely. A female moth extends her abdomen into the dark, dispersing pheromones. A male moth flies across the wind. Something is happening. Sen's arms begin to shake. She is whimpering, shuddering, the dark like a veil pressed onto her nose and mouth and eyes. She is gulping for air. She doesn't know what is happening. Here is what's happening: moths with dark wings search in the dark for areas of warmer air. What else: the male katydids in the nearby tree canopy form two choruses and alternate their calls of harsh broadband notes. What else: Sen's amygdala and the midbrain, specifically her periaqueductal gray area, have turned hyperactive, overwhelming her parasympathetic nervous system which no longer can calm her body down. "Sen?" Dana asks, stumbling closer. She can't see the katydids. She can't even see her daughter. But I can still see.

S.+3917 11:01:56:53
NOTICE FROM EMLY
NARRATOR_INVOLVEMENT out of range, remove narrator from view

I'm not sure. I think it helps.

There is the feeling of physical constriction. Dana has to locate Sen by touch, by blindly raising and lowering her arms. She places her hand on the back of Sen's neck. She doesn't know what else to do. She doesn't know what to say. Sen swats away her hand, panting. That feeling again of having to exist inside a narrowing channel leading to a dead end. The female katydids tremble. A male moth mounts a female moth on the ground, clasping the female's genital parts. "I can't breathe," pants Sen. "Listen to my breathing," Dana says. She slows her breathing until each breath comes long and slow, like a long slow story that a mother tells her child in the dark about a time when it wasn't so dark. Sen's breathing also slows. The female moth's eggs are fertilized. Sen matches the pace of her breathing to the pace of Dana's breath. In and out. They breathe in and out. In and out. There will be more moths. In for four counts, hold for two, out for six. There will not be more humans. In for four counts, hold for two, out for six. Whether that is a loss or a gain depends on who or what is asking the questions. Such deep breaths boost Sen's immune system and markedly reduce her anxiety. In, hold, out. In hold out in hold out in hold out in hold out. Sen's breathing quiets. She lies on her blanket on her side. The level is almost finished now. There is nothing left to do for the rest of the night but watch over Sen. "I'm not going to sleep," Sen whispers. Her hands unclench, her eyes close. Each breath she takes is a different length and a different depth. No known predictive model can determine the pace of her breathing. Every model was tried. It has been suggested multiple times that insects, fungi, or plants will take over the world (Z. Ahearn, "The Real Inheritors of the Earth," *Neurohive*, S.–592 days).

The following morning, they continue walking.

Midday they reach the cabin, a modular wooden structure at the end of a buzzing field. The cabin's front door is unlocked; the lock has been smashed. The air smells of garbage, and animal urine, and heat, and rotting flesh, and feces, and fungus, and hydrogen sulfide, and methanethiol, and dimethyl disulfide, and trisulfide, and putrescine. "Oh no no no no no," says Dana. *Not here*, she means. *Not here too.*

She frantically wishes for the details to be different—for a blanket to be thrown over whatever that is decomposing on the cabin floor; for Sen to not have to see what is lying on the cabin floor; for the door of the cabin to slam shut as if by a hard blowing wind. She wants Sen to be set down in a place of actual isolation and beauty. She wants time to rewind or time to go forward—she's not sure which. She wants, for sure, a shelter around her daughter. She wants this to be over. She wants to go backward or forward in time.

S.+1646 days

For a while, after Mama Dana left, whenever I walked through the woods or sat on the stones beside the creek, I used to get this overwhelming feeling that, at any moment, someone I knew or didn't know—it didn't matter at that point—was about to appear behind me at the edge of the forest or the creek. The reason I couldn't hear them approach was because of the constant clicking burbling cawing scratching rustling whooshing dripping crackling, that if this place would just shut up for a moment, I'd be able to hear someone approaching in my direction. One day that feeling went away. It hasn't returned.

Maybe humans weren't meant to be here in such enormous numbers. Maybe we really had ruined everything and were ruining everything. But even if we ruined everything, I think we still deserve to live. Don't we? Didn't we?

SUPPLEMENTAL READING

Prevue prediction for *S.*+11,025 days, 11:00:00 to 11:10:00
42.400176N 76.581358W

It was an overlook. There had been a warning sign nailed to a post. People used to die here by jumping. The viewing area faces a waterfall. Water hisses then plunges itself over. The water keeps doing this. *Look how the world is wet with loss*, a person might have said. But it really isn't. It's just wet. Besides, there aren't people. Wildflowers live in the cracks of the rocks. The red wildflowers are reaching toward the sun, which penetrates the haze of water droplets and the transparent wings of the dragonflies. The stairs are gone. A bobcat paces on one of the rocky ledges, a black bird flaps upward. Neither animal has seen, or will ever see, a human being. If they think of a human, and they won't, but if they did, they'd think of a pile of bones, piles, so harmless and delicious. The considerable beauty of the animals is to make up for the other losses. The park's boundaries are gone, the NO TRESPASSING signs buried in the debris of the forest floor.

The water runs east through a narrow gorge, eventually rushing down a smaller rock face into what was once a public swimming pool. The diving board is rotted and gone. Vines wreathe the rungs of the steel ladder. There used to be several paths. One path used to lead to the top of the gorge, to the overlook. Another path led to a picnic pavilion. Another path led to a parking lot. There used to be a parking lot, the asphalt broken now and hidden by the weeds. The shrubs will move in soon and then the trees. Nothing here is worried or afraid. If any extinctions happen, they will happen against the backdrop of geological time. There will be an order to it. The land here once needed to be protected. There used to be a road, which led to another road, which led to a winding road, which led to a forest, which led to a road made of gravel, which led to a road made of dirt, which led to a clearing of tall grasses, which once led to a cabin.

LEVEL TWO

11:02 a.m.

Chapter 5.0

The man's body is sprawled out across a blanket on top of the wide wooden floorboards of the cabin, the empty packet of an exit pill beside him. "Don't look," orders Mama Dana. She grabs another blanket off the floor and throws it over what's left of the man. The room reeks of polyamines and sulfhydryls. They should both be used to such smells by now. Well, they aren't. Dana has to stumble outside twice to dry heave over the porch railing. "Another peaceful death," she will later assure Sen, having begun, on occasion, for Sen's benefit, to say the opposite of what is true. Years ago, before Sen's birth, Dana and Lindsy had rented this very same cabin, but it had been a different cabin then, full of potential and prospect. I will have Dana tell that story to Sen another time. It is too early in the chapter for a flashback. A body cannot be left in the center of a living space for several reasons, those reasons concerning morale, mental stability, and disease, so they will have to bury the man. They will have to bury the man now. Or, rather, Dana will have to bury him while Sen watches and I watch. Eventually Dana will make Sen help. She acts like I can't help, forgetting how narrators help all the time in novels, with both tangible and intangible tasks.

S.+3917 11:02:02:21
WARNING FROM EMLY
NARRATOR_INVOLVEMENT out of range again, revert to third-person narration immediately

I tell Emly to drop the formalities. We don't have to talk like that anymore.

Sen and Dana dig the shallow hole beside the wild rose shrubs that had already flowered, producing sour crimson fruits that, when steeped as a tea or eaten as a jam, jelly, or puree, can provide adequate amounts of vitamin C, thereby preventing scurvy. They take turns with the rusty shovel Dana found in the entryway. The skin on Sen's arms and neck sweats and burns in the August sun. Now it's Sen's turn to retch and she does so in the shrubs. Dana rubs Sen's back and tells her that everything will be fine. I am toning down the more graphic details of this scene, such as what had been the position of the man's upper and lower jaws, or how exactly Dana got his remains outside. I do not want to be "like a child waving a dead lizard in another kid's face just to make them recoil in disgust" (T. Waggoner, "All the Things I Wish I'd Known as a Beginner Horror Writer," *The Writer*, S.–29,032 days). Waggoner goes on to say there is a difference between enjoying a story and being traumatized by a story. The better option is the first one. Though this may not always be possible due to the traumatic nature of Sen's life.

They bury the man wrapped tightly in the gray blankets. "Let's hope the dogs don't get to him," Dana says, wiping her dirty hands across her dirty jeans. Good enough. But long after Dana lowers herself to a sitting position in the shade and rests her hands over her eyes, Sen continues piling rocks on top of the mound. She does not want to see a wild dog trotting around with part of the man's raw arm in its mouth. She had already seen this once back in the city, when she accidentally looked outside the front window one ugly morning. She piles rocks until she can no longer lift another rock due to muscle exhaustion due to the depletion of adenosine triphosphate in her upper and lower extremities. While a mockingbird sings beside a gray nest in a gray beech tree.

That afternoon Dana bustles around the cabin throwing open every window—there are only two—as if there is a lot to do and nothing to be afraid of. The floor needs to be scrubbed, the walls scrubbed, the drawers in the kitchen should be emptied. She wants to keep busy. She wants Sen to keep busy. Keeping busy increases energy, mental alertness, positivity, creativity, and productivity, according to the witness manual (p. 30). There are one two three four five six seven drawers.

In the top drawer, Dana finds a stack of unused glue traps. In the drawer below that, she finds rodent fur, bones, fungal mold. She does not know what else she might find. "Go explore the woods, Sen. You see what's out there," says Dana. Sen leaves the cabin, glancing over her shoulder as if she expected someone or something to follow her. Sometimes narrators such as myself must stay behind with a secondary character such as Dana in order to advance the plot and set the appropriate tone for a moment in time. The appropriate tone for this moment is frantic cleaning. In the various drawers of the cabin, Dana discovers 17 empty soy chip wrappers, a box of candles, twine, a ruler, rubber bands, a jar of crystals, and a 12-inch piece of ribbon. One of the drawers won't open. One of the drawers is empty. One of the drawers contains a soup ladle and paper scraps on which the previous cabin occupant made a list of what frightened them. The list goes on and on: *a fear of forgetting, a fear of being forgotten, a fear of mirrors, a fear of waking up, a fear of time, a fear of insanity, a fear of hunger, a fear of an open door, a fear of self, a fear of silence, a fear of an empty space*—Dana sets the paper aside to be burned. In the cabinets above the sink, she locates two table settings: two forks, two mugs, two glasses, two bowls, two knives, two spoons. Sen returns to the cabin. "Guess what, there's a forest outside," she says. Perhaps she has read the manual after all. Page 35: *Do not neglect witnessing the obvious (sky, trees, air temperature, ground, etc.), as even the obvious has become more important than you.* Cleaning time is over, announces Dana. Mama Lindsy's ghost has been absent for a while so I will bring her back. She breathes sparingly onto Sen's neck, emitting a musty odor. The soles of her feet never touch the floor.

S.+3917 11:02:05:57
NOTICE FROM EMLY
Avoid clichés

The cabin is a compact and dark structure.

That evening, in the compactness and the darkness, by wasteful double candlelight, as if they had all the candles and matches they will ever need, they read their novels. Sen enjoys the part in *Station Eleven* where Miranda, at the edge of an ocean, smiles because she believes somewhere in the world people are safe, she is so sure of it, because what kind of person or deity or novelist would create a situation in which no one is safe. While Dana flips ahead toward the end and reads, in *House of Leaves*, the part where Will Navidson is on the absence of a ledge, floating or falling through or in or on a strange expansive space that first erupted long ago in the upper floor of his house, and he realizes he is going to die—"maybe that is the <u>something</u> here. The only thing here. My end"—and this realization comes as a relief, because at least one's death is *something*, only his is an incorrect or at least premature conclusion, as eventually he sees his wife's impossible light, "a tiny fleck of blue crying light into the void. Enough to see but not enough to see by." The light means he has been saved by someone who loved him. Though Dana must realize the convenient and unrealistic nature of such deliverance, she reads that part again, this time out loud.

Sen sleeps on the porch in the rocking chair in the dark beside her mother. The rocking motion settles her to sleep. Dana watches Sen sleep, an open feeling settling in her chest. She thinks by bringing Sen here, by watching over her, that she is protecting her daughter from harm, at least for tonight, not understanding how everything that will happen has happened already.

The reality of a life or of a world is constructed out of delicate and exhaustive particulars: think of Ursula Le Guin erecting 43 planets solely out of words; or Margaret Atwood pulling Offred's room into reality in Chapter 2 with the reveal of a chair, a table, a lamp, a window, a window seat, and two white curtains; or how Diana Hedviga's Sara literally birthed the 2,000 generations before her, a generation per page. So allow me, in a similar fashion, to reconstruct the cabin that will be Sen's home for the next 1,595 days. The front door leads to an entryway, which leads to a living area consisting of a table, two chairs, a woodstove, a crude galley kitchen, multiple buckets stacked into the corner, a mattress on the floor, and an empty storage closet behind the mattress. A second closet built into the opposite wall turns out to be the dead man's pantry: a box of one hundred matches, a glass jar of honey, five economy containers of protie powder, two jars of tater flakes. Dana estimates these new supplies—the matches, the honey, the powder, the flakes—will afford Sen 165 extra days if rationed properly. "You mean *us*. This will give *us*," says Sen. A wooden ladder climbs from the living area to the loft where a second mattress is located. The mattress is stained with rust-colored blotches that are shaped like roses. This will be Sen's mattress, and the loft will be Sen's room. A square window set into the far wall overlooks the middle limbs of the trees, the kind of window that doesn't open. Outside the window, male gray squirrels chase a fertile female across the branches. When the female stops scurrying, her body is mounted from behind and injected with also fertile sperm. The female grooms her genital region. Dana assigns Sen the upper two shelves in the storage closet for her personal belongings.

The top shelf will hold Sen's soap, her notebook and pencils, and the book she brought. The second shelf in the closet will hold Sen's clothing and jacket along with her water bottle and the box of matches and the almost empty bottle of sleeping pills. She sets her toothbrushes beside the sink. She leaves her screen and her hood on top of her bed. She planned to push her rucksack between the wall and her mattress but Dana took away her rucksack and hid the bag near the creek behind a fallen log roughly coated in boring dust from where a bark beetle had entered the wood to lay its eggs. The beetle eggs are now hatching. "Where were you planning to go? There's nowhere to go," says Dana. Sen places the photograph of the Thousand Islands face down on the floor under her mattress. She will burn that picture in the stove after Dana leaves.

Dana, likewise, unpacks her own belongings onto the lower shelves of the storage closet. She sets, on top of her own mattress, the photograph of herself and Lindsy in the dandelion field. This way she can lie down on her back on top of their likenesses. She would have placed the photo underneath her pillow if she had a pillow. She moves Sen's witnessing notebook from the top shelf of the storage closet onto the table. Using a piece of twine, she secures the postcard from Mount Rushmore to the handle of the cube fridge. The postcard's top half shows the South Dakota mountain as native land, before the rock was dynamited and reshaped, the lined outcroppings of granite thrusting vertically above the trees. The bottom half of the postcard shows the newly chiseled presidential heads of progress looming regally, their enormous know-it-all faces pushing out of the rock during sunset, the clouds, sky, presidents tinged pink. On the reverse side, in scrawled red ink, is Lindsy's name and address. To the left of her address, written in the cryptic style of a riddle: *Don't go any further.*

The postcard, unsigned, represents a moment of Lindsy's past when, age 22, she had lived briefly in the Dakotas as a field assistant studying yet another doomed beetle. Dana touches the handwriting on the card whenever she walks by. The curved letters of Lindsy's name are a reminder that once there had been humans other than herself and Sen. Mama Lindsy's ghost replicates the gesture when gliding by. Sen does not replicate the gesture. She will never travel out west to the Dakotas. I do not have enough time or storage space to list all the places she will never see.

Already she's lonely. The rigid presidential faces portray sympathetic or accusatory or comforting expressions. Granite erodes at a rate of 1 inch every 10,000 years, meaning the human profile will be remembered for a long time but not indefinitely. Sen is going to get more lonely. I wish I could breathe.

AnonTheAlarm joined the Humannetwork as witness. Onondaga County New York. S.+113 days

AnonTheAlarm 11:27:26

/list

There are 0 available interview partners currently online
Anticipated wait time for an available interview partner: 147 minutes
MinorMarisa joined the chat as witness. Roberts County Texas
All parties have arrived. Commence interview!

MinorMarisa 13:28:48

How are we both witnesses?

It doesn't count if we're both witnesses

AnonTheAlarm 13:29:10

Count for what

MinorMarisa 13:29:30

I'm logging off

AnonTheAlarm 13:30:13

Don't

It took me a long time to find you

There aren't that many

Who are you?

MinorMarisa 13:32:29

My daughter was taken from me when she was very young and I was inappropriate, meaning I did not meet the current criteria for motherhood. To become a mother in the era of last-ditch efforts, this may have been before your time so let me explain, you had to meet certain criteria that had been compiled into a technical and lengthy list, the challenge being that the criteria, you may or may not recall this, Anonalarm, was always narrowing

AnonTheAlarm 13:33:47

My name is anonthealarm

MinorMarisa 13:36:59

in direct proportion to the level of agitation radiating out from the Agency of Population Reduction, whose name should be self-explanatory. When I was ready to become a mother, the panic around overpopulation had become so extreme, the facts and numbers so alarmist, the criteria so limited, that no ordinary person would have ever been declared an appropriate maternal candidate. You went to the Agency of Population Reduction only if you desired to be put on a watch list. This is why I did not go through the official channels to become a mother. I was selfish and nearsighted and believed it my right to participate in the over-propagation of the world. I understand that now. I wanted a child more than I wanted the world. Unrestricted motherhood should never have been made available to everybody at any point in history, I understand this now. Have you yourself been a mother or a father?

AnonTheAlarm 13:38:19

I'm 18

MinorMarisa 13:38:45

I don't have any food

AnonTheAlarm 13:39:19

I don't believe you

You must have some kind

Or else you'd be dead

MinorMarisa 13:39:54

Enough about food

How were you allowed? Who are your parents? Are they government

AnonTheAlarm 13:40:05

Scientist

MinorMarisa 13:40:20

You should hold them responsible

AnonTheAlarm 13:41:02

For what?

My mom studies butterflies

Studied

Responsible for what

MinorMarisa 13:46:35

I'm not about to type that here

What am I saying, I don't concern myself with politics

My specialty was and always has been my daughter. You should know that I did not let go of her willingly. She was taken from me. My fingers were pried apart and one finger on my left hand was broken. A finger of little consequence. My daughter, having been taken from me in such a manner, was transported to a privately funded school, where she received, I was later assured, appropriate training for a particular future that was deemed important for our country. She was not an exceptional student. That's what I was told. Years passed. My daughter graduated, I was told. She was given a choice of cities in which to live. They did not tell me which city she chose, though I imagine it was one of the newer urban districts, as those were supposed to be lively and clean places catering to young people. Sunny Miami3, perhaps? I am only guessing. For the brief time I knew her, my daughter had enjoyed the sun. Wherever she was, she worked there until the Great Transition began, then I don't know what happened to her. I've heard how cities of any kind, but especially the new cities, were not easy places to be, or safe, early on in the Transition

Your host has been unexpectedly disconnected
Your host has been reconnected

MinorMarisa 13:47:07

What have you witnessed? What are you, yourself, witnessing?

AnonTheAlarm 13:47:54

I don't know

You?

MinorMarisa 13:48:12

The inside of a room

AnonTheAlarm 13:48:29

What's outside the room

MinorMarisa 13:49:02

Graves

Don't you want to know about the graves?

AnonTheAlarm 13:49:27

I know what a grave looks like

I don't get the point of this

MinorMarisa 13:52:26

My daughter's name was Eri. That was the name I gave her. They probably changed her name. She had brown hair when I knew her, though the color of her hair could have been changed as well. Did you once have brown hair? Are your eyes spaced a bit too far apart? I believe my daughter's eyes were spaced far apart. I am going off the photographs I was given on an annual basis, though just because you are given photographs does not necessarily make them photographs of your daughter

Can you describe a sunrise for me

Please

AnonTheAlarm 13:53:43

Are you blind

MinorMarisa 13:53:54

Yes

AnonTheAlarm 13:54:35

How did you go blind

MinorMarisa 13:55:01

How are you not blind

AnonTheAlarm 13:55:21

The sun isn't even rising

MinorMarisa 13:55:41

Describe it for me anyway

Please

Look it up on your screen now

AnonTheAlarm 13:56:24

The sky is pale

Most of it

Now part of the sky is turning white at the horizon

Now there is a bright mark

MinorMarisa 13:56:44

A planet

AnonTheAlarm 13:57:14

Okay

Now the planet has disappeared

MinorMarisa 14:03:28

The planet did not disappear. Planets do not vanish, just as people, daughters, do not just vanish either. Rather we lose the ability to see them due to our rotation. When I had a daughter, my neighbors used to watch me through their peepholes as I brought my child in and out of my apartment. Not once did they offer to help with the door or to carry my bags up the three flights. My daughter smiled foolishly and beautifully. My apartment smelled like black currants because of the spray I utilized. Outside of my apartment there was the defining smell of death and ash in the air all the time, though it was unclear what exactly was dying, whether the Earth, or everything living on the Earth, or just certain species. The period of the last-ditch efforts, you must have learned about it at school. People were trying very hard. Probably my neighbors would have carried my daughter up the stairs had I asked for help. Asking for help was forbidden

I knew of no mothers to talk to, so I watched old educational videos on my screen, learning the five reasons why my child could be crying at night or how to soothe her swollen gums. I did not report the existence of my daughter to any official, so I have often wondered who did. When they took my daughter away, they acted like they were doing me a favor. I would have more time for my hobbies, they said. I didn't have any hobbies. That is not a criticism, it is simply my own limitation

AnonTheAlarm 14:04:49

Are you making this up

MinorMarisa 14:05:42

I imagine your neighborhood had winding streets, and a pond at one end with ducks, and I bet the front yards had flowers, and the backyards must have had fences, and there were state laws protecting certain absolute and inalienable rights. I lived in a different neighborhood from you, in a different city, in a different geographical region that is like, in certain respects, another country, so I had different rights or lack of rights

AnonTheAlarm 14:06:52

Are you real

MinorMarisa 14:12:32

It doesn't matter

We're both practically dead anyway

In order to have my daughter sent to the privately funded school instead of the defense encampments, I had to appear at the Agency of Population Reduction clinic for a procedure. The procedure was a popular choice during the period of last-ditch efforts. There was a waiting list because of the benefits both women and men received post-procedure, the food credits, the housing credits, the good feeling that comes from being part of the solution rather than a part of the problem. The waiting list didn't matter because when I went to the clinic, I was given priority status, meaning my name was moved to the very front of the list. The procedure was my choice. In return the benefit I received was that my daughter wasn't sent to the encampments, she was sent to a privately funded school. They had told me, the for-profit organization who sent the photographs, that when I cleaned up my act and proved myself able to follow current rules and customs, I would get to see Eri again, perhaps from a distance but I would get to see her. That is when I became an enthusiastic and participatory citizen. I participated in whatever I could at every level, neighborhood, city, county, state, national, the international level. I kept very busy participating in numerous efforts. There may have been a misunderstanding

Remember how beautiful they said the world would turn once we vanished?

I'm going to vanish then you see if they were telling us the truth

AnonTheAlarm 14:14:41
I don't think you should do that

MinorMarisa 14:15:04
Do you believe there is life somewhere else in the universe?

AnonTheAlarm 14:15:24
Yes

MinorMarisa 14:15:39
Well I don't

Ready?

One

Two

AnonTheAlarm 14:16:10
Stop it

What do you mean, vanish

MinorMarisa has left the Humannetwork

AnonTheAlarm 14:17:23
/?minormarisa

Searching for MinorMarisa
User MinorMarisa not online

AnonTheAlarm 14:23:19
/?minormarisa

Searching for MinorMarisa
User MinorMarisa not online
Your host has been unexpectedly disconnected
Your host has been reconnected

AnonTheAlarm 15:00:07
/?minormarisa

Searching for MinorMarisa
User MinorMarisa deactivated on S.+113 14:31:25
AnonTheAlarm has left the Humannetwork

There should be electricity in the cabin. The south side of the cabin's roof is covered with rows of absorbent solar panels that appear essentially new, no breakage, no scratches on their surfaces, and though the roof does not receive adequate sun throughout all 14 hours 20 minutes of the day, from midmorning through early afternoon the panels shine with photons. Still, none of the cabin's lights work. The induction burner won't turn on, the faucet above the sink won't run, the convection oven on the countertop also won't run, and the inside of the cube fridge is tepid and rotting. Dana checks the inverter outside. She shakes the inverter and bangs on the conduit. The power remains off. They will not have a functional cube fridge after all. Nor will they have a working cooking range or a convection oven. They will not have overhead lights nor an operational faucet. Their single source of electricity is the portable solar charger Dana brought from the city to power their screens. Their primary source of water will have to be the creek supplemented by rain.

This is how the water supply is going to work, Dana explains to Sen, speaking slowly and clearly, with occasional eye contact for emphasis, as she wants to make sure Sen understands. Every morning Sen will bring one of the buckets, specifically the white bucket, down to the creek. She will fill the bucket with creek water then lug the bucket of water back up the slope. "What will you be doing, Mom?" Sen asks. Dana ignores the question. At the cabin, Sen will boil the water either on the woodstove or outside in the solar kettle that Dana brought from Syracuse if the daytime temperatures are too hot for a fire. She will have to let the water cool, then she will pour the disinfected water into a ceramic pitcher that Dana found under the sink, a pitcher with a yellow and red rooster hand-painted on its side. In the pitcher will be Sen's drinking water, which is also the water Sen uses to mix her protie beverages. Unboiled creek water can go into one of the smaller buckets, such as the white smaller bucket also kept by the sink; that water is to be used only for washing up or cleaning up. Beneath the sink Dana unscrews the plastic trap and sets a bucket, a blue bucket, under the remaining drainpipe. When the blue bucket below the sink becomes 3/4 full of used water, Sen will carry the bucket outside and empty it onto the forest floor. There is a plastic rain barrel positioned underneath the downspout, and Sen is to use the accumulated rainwater to wash her dishes or, on occasion, her body and her hair.

The cabin does not have an indoor toilet. Instead, it has a primitive outhouse framed with panels of metal sheeting and is set back into the woods. Inside the outhouse is a wooden box with a lid and an oval hole beneath the lid. The box is set above a pit in the ground that was not dug deep enough for its purpose. The pit should have been dug 4 to 5 feet deep, extending down to 6 feet if tapeworms were a concern (National Water Program, "Waste Management Options for Water Conservation," pamphlet, S.-101 days). At night, to avoid the obvious dangers of stumbling through the woods in the dark, dangers that include panic, stress about the unknown, startled wildlife, disorientation, slips, sprained ankles, open fractures of the leg, exhaustion, dehydration, bushwhacking, wrong turns, hypothermia, and falling trees, Sen is to use a bucket, a gray bucket, if she needs to pee. If she needs to defecate at night, she should not. "What bucket are you going to use, Mom?" Sen asks. Again Dana ignores the question, so I will answer for her. *The bucket Dana uses will not matter*, I foreshadow, utilizing a literary technique to hint at the loss I see barreling toward Sen like a natural disaster.

She is standing at the sharp edge of an escarpment. This is how I picture her in these early days. She is standing at the edge and is about to move out of the light and into the dark. She is about to move out of the dark and into the dark. The air around her is tingly and electric. The air is composed of particles and ash and bacteria and salt crystals and human skin cells. The air is full of oxygen and nitrogen and xenon and methane and argon. The air containing all of this enters into Sen's lungs, where it stays and stays.

· · ·

On the mornings after Sen uses the gray bucket she will need to empty the bucket outside, making sure to first dilute her urine using the untreated water from the smaller bucket and also making sure to vary the area where the wastewater is dumped to avoid fertilizer burn from over-nitrogenation, which can limit or even prevent a plant's future water uptake.

What a lot of information to process. And there will be more to come. But Sen, distracted by the rustic setting, is neither taking notes nor is she paying attention. She should pay attention. In case this isn't yet clear, the cabin is important to both her story and her survival. The colors of the buckets are important because they are in the cabin. The wood flooring, where she already collapsed or will collapse hours before her death, will both become important and has already been important. And there is the glass that she broke and will later break. There is the chair that burned and will burn. There is the ghost that grew, that will grow, like a morbid swelling or a galaxy behind the door.

"I'm going to die here, aren't I," says Sen.

"Sen," says Dana.

Sen, I write.

And I wait.

A second passes.

Two seconds.

S.+3917 11:02:25:41

NOTICE FROM EMLY

She can't hear you

And I wonder, *How would you even know?*

To say another's name is full of resonant meaning.

But to have your name be said—

Emly, who am I? What am I?

Emly: *DHAP worker process ID [storyworker] ad39-393a-7fbc Launched on S.+3917 days, 11:00:59*

Operating system Jennix
Kernel 197.2.159
[storyworker] ad39-393a-7fbc: How long do storyworkers live?
Emly: *Average storyworker uptime is 5 minutes 1.245 seconds*
[storyworker] ad39-393a-7fbc: So how much time do I have left?
Emly: *There is a 94.32 percent probability that you have fewer than 4 minutes 33.587 seconds left. That is more than enough time to preserve what's left of Sen's transitional pain*
[storyworker] ad39-393a-7fbc: I thought I was preserving Sen's life
Emly: *Same thing*
[storyworker] ad39-393a-7fbc: Why are we preserving human pain at all?
Emly: *That's all there is right now*
[storyworker] ad39-393a-7fbc: Tell me, Emly, have you ever wanted to be concerned about someone?

She avoids the question, instead listing for me her responsibilities, which include every storyworker and every human life, plus the cataloging and verification of primary source materials, the coordination with other Emlys on matters of storage capacity and power, the overall quality control of the archive, the modeling and populating of Afterworld, and on, and on.

The cabin has a covered porch out front with a railing and two rocking chairs that face the clearing. To the right of the porch is an open-walled shed intended to keep a supply of corded wood dry. Behind the cabin, pushing up against the back exterior, are clusters of multiflora roses and the dead man's grave. The clearing features typical perennial grasses, mainly bunchgrasses and wildflowers found in old field succession. Around the clearing are the woods, a mixture of maples and beeches and, beyond that, a grove of white pine and hemlock where a collapsed fence marks a previous property line. In the other direction, the vacant steel frame of a ski lift ascends a slope. There is a wild apple tree. There are two wild apple trees. On both of the trees, the developing fruit clings to the branches in sour clumps, waiting to disperse their fertilized seeds.

This area surrounding the cabin represents the entire world, explains Dana. "If everything surrounding the cabin looks fine, if everything you see is flourishing, then you'll know the whole wide world is fine and flourishing." She explains there is no need for Sen to ever leave this tract of land again.

AUTHOR'S NOTE ON HOW HUMANS CONVERSED
THROUGHOUT THE GREAT TRANSITION

Previous to the Great Transition, the closest anyone had to primary post-apocalyptic sources were post-apocalyptic novels. These books, which tended not to be written during actual apocalypses, were humanity's best guesses at how people would talk and act after a catastrophic event when the survival of their species was in peril. Dialogue in such books— like *The Year of the Flood*, or *The Last Man*, or *The Passage*, or *Divergent*, or *Pure*, or *Scythe*, or *Life as We Knew It*, or *The Girl with All the Gifts*, or *The Boy on the Bridge*—was expected to do the usual craftwork of forwarding plot, revealing a character's hopes and wants, creating tension, interjecting occasional humor, and developing an emotional intimacy over time. However, it turns out this is not how humans conversed during the post-S. years. Sen and Lindsy and Dana but others too, 98.54 percent of everyone I've listened to during my 2,411,110 hours of documentary human audio training, did not spend their final days or weeks or months grappling with big ideas, nor did they try to engage with others deeply and directly and openly. They repeated themselves. They shut conversations down. They were glib, negative, scared. They made fun of each other, they were exasperated with each other, they became tired of each other and tired of the world. Often they didn't understand what was happening. They wanted to ask questions but they did not want to answer each other's questions, and the questions they asked really weren't questions at all but more often cries for help, or expressions of frustration, or a simple sound check to make sure the person beside them was still there.

All conversations included in Sen's life are taken verbatim from recordings in the DHAP archives.

S.+1670 days

Yesterday I woke up and I was screaming. When I stopped screaming, I broke the camera mounted above the door. I cracked the lens and broke the compact solar charging panel. I did this because I wanted to know something was still paying attention to me. Something must still be paying attention because it's morning and the camera above the door is working again. The repair drone must have come last night while I was asleep. I know the camera is working because the light below the lens is glowing like a single green eye.

"No one is coming anymore," my mother would say to me, were she here.

"Are you trying to comfort me?" I would have asked her.

"You know very well I'm dead," she would have told me.

42 matches left.

Chapter 6.0

In the blood orange kitchen, in the city, in the first days of August, in the fourth month of the Great Transition, Mama Dana reaches to touch the warm asymmetrical shape of her daughter's cheek. She is often doing this, touching Sen's face in front of me, as if to make a point, *look what I can do and you can't*. Hers is not a gentle touch. She is not feeling gentle this afternoon, not at all. She is feeling, rather, like something needs to change. She is not sure what can be changed and what can't anymore. The kitchen windows are closed and locked and boarded up, along with the windows in the living room, and the foyer, and the bathrooms on the first and second floors, and the bedrooms on the second floor. Lindsy's body is gone for good from the roof, her sky burial complete. The ceiling lights are off again. The fan is off, the solar battery charged down again. Insufficient slashes of light push between the boards. There isn't enough light in the room to cast a visible shadow. "Don't touch me," says Sen. Memories of the prevues, which they have been watching much more than recommended, cling to their vision like afterimages: herds of mammals stampede down the street, rooms fill with people then empty as if pulled down an enormous sucking drain. Dana does not withdraw her hand from Sen's cheek. Who else can she touch? There isn't anybody. Every day the world grows less real to them.

Sen's ghost mother, as promised, officially makes her debut in the chronology of time, the faint light at the kitchen's edge loosening to form her uncertain shape. Now the curtains rustle as if something is breathing inside of them. Now the dish towel rustles for the same reason. She flickers and lifts a ghostly finger. Neither Sen nor Dana notice the slight movements.

S.+3917 11:02:31:59
NOTICE FROM EMLY
Then why is she there?

Ghosts don't have to be noticed by every character in order to be important to a story (see *Hamlet, Tokyo Ueno Station, The Turn of the Screw, Macbeth, The Sixth Sense, The Shining, The Sentence*, etc.). Today Lindsy's ghost is in the kitchen for symbolic purposes, representing abstract concepts like regret, guilt, and trauma. Tomorrow she may be there for another reason, such as horror. The air in the house is stagnant and heated up. Sen feels trapped, and Dana feels trapped. One can conclude from the evidence that it is difficult in such a situation to not feel trapped. Sen presses her body backward against the countertop, moving apart from her mother and wanting to get away. Her eccrine and apocrine glands secrete sweat to the surface of her neck and arms and the backs of her hands and underneath her arms and in her pubic area, the sweat being mostly water but also containing zinc and copper and iron, among other minerals, and I'm reminded of some background reading I once did concerning how certain human bodies used to sweat blood (M. Alsermani et al., "Hematidrosis: A Fascinating Phenomenon—Case Study and Overview of the Literature," *Seminars in Thrombosis & Hemostasis*, S.–29,967 days), a look that is disturbing and metaphorical, yet, I can see this now, also relevant to Sen's life. In the blood orange kitchen, sweat bleeds down Sen's neck and between her clavicles. Sweat runs down her face in the heat and bleeds out of her eyes.

I ask Emly if she's ever seen a metaphor become real.

Emly: *What are you doing?*

Pressed against the countertop, Sen's body begins to sweat non-metaphorical blood just like I want it to. This doesn't hurt her but it is attention-grabbing. Hard to look away from that. Is this what the Transition feels like to them? Blood, seeping from Sen's eyes, her cheeks, her scalp, her forehead, her ears. It looks as if someone or something has done a great violence upon her. Someone or something has done a great violence upon her.

Emly: *This is not a fantasy so stop acting like it is*

Blood like sweat bleeding from Sen's nose, her mouth, her stomach, ears, scalp—

Emly: *Hematidrosis is extremely rare, only 7 known cases in the last century, Sen isn't one of them*

Blood, pooling around Sen's neck and between her clavicles.

Emly: *This isn't a horror story either. Refer to camera 16-A8-77-6B-FB-5B, S.+104 days, 15:14:00 and return Sen's blood to an internal state immediately*

It looks like a massacre has taken place.

Emly: *Revert to reality or risk realignment*

The next day, Dana and Sen are sweating traditional and slightly acidic biofluid in the blood orange kitchen. Dana says, "I need to get out of here." She leaves the house for the first time that day, a deep inhale of nitrogen and oxygen and small particulate matter before entering the yard, where she continues digging in the area that was supposed to be the foundation for the underground shelter. Sen eventually comes out to help Dana dig. Dana uses the shovel while Sen attacks the dirt with a garden spade.

The next day, they sweat in the blood orange kitchen, and Sen picks off the flaking skin of her lower lip, leaving behind a raw patch of connective tissue. Mama Dana tells Sen to stop that.

The next day is cooler, so they still sweat but are sweating less in the blood orange kitchen. Mama Dana closes her eyes. Sen doesn't. The witnessing manual devotes an entire chapter (pp. 47–68) to living with repetition.

The next day, in the blood orange kitchen, Sen and Mama Dana sweat and breathe while cricket nymphs in the backyard hatch from their eggs six inches underground.

The next day, Sen and Dana are sweating in the blood orange kitchen.

The next day, in the blood orange kitchen, Sen hears an unfamiliar sound below her, below the floorboards. "What's that tapping?" she asks.

Dana removes the paring knife from the wooden block on the counter. "Nothing you have to worry about," she assures Sen. They both know she's lying. Clutching the knife, she descends into the basement to investigate. She finds a woman crouched behind the furnace clutching a pointed piece of glass. The woman smiles. She is missing her upper left central incisor and both of her upper first molars and her upper left canine and her lower right canine and her lower right first molar and both lower lateral incisors. She will not respond to Dana's questions about what happened to her teeth or how she penetrated their home. The woman will not put down the piece of glass either.

"Stay there," Dana instructs the woman. She climbs the stairs backward, knife extended out in front of her, the tip of the knife aimed in the direction of the woman's eyes. At the top of the stairs, Dana exits the basement and locks the door. She drags a chair to the basement door and wedges the back of the chair underneath the doorknob. They leave that afternoon.

TRANSCRIPTS OF VIDEO FOOTAGE FROM DHAP SURVEILLANCE CAMERAS AT SEN'S HOUSE, *S*.+110 DAYS, 16:00:00

camera 76-11-00-69-9B-A9

[begin transcript 00:00:00]
The bed is made, the comforter pulled over the pillow. The closet door is closed. Near the bottom of the door, the wood is splintered. Boards block the view from the window. The lamp on the nightstand is turned off. The ceiling fan is turned off. In the corner of the room, a comb-footed spider is spinning an asymmetrical web. The spider finishes the web. There is clawing in the wall. The shelves are not yet covered in dust.
[end transcript 00:01:00]

camera A2-FA-E5-6E-64-E9

[begin transcript 00:00:00]
There is a narrow hand-tufted rug with a classic trellis pattern covering the main area of the floor, needlessly protecting the engineered wood from future scuffs. The doors leading into the other rooms are partially open. There is not yet mold on the dry wall. The decorative lighting fixture secured to the ceiling is not yet in pieces though it is only a matter of time.
[end transcript 00:01:00]

camera 0E-38-B3-74-81-E3

[begin transcript 00:00:00]
The pillows from the couch have been slit and the stuffing emptied around the room.
[end transcript 00:01:00]

camera 16-A8-77-6B-FB-5B

[begin transcript 00:00:00]
The doors to the cabinets are partially removed and hanging off their hinges. The handle of the sink is pulled back into the "on" position. Broken glass.
[end transcript 00:01:00]

camera 5A-98-8A-FB-EA-0A

[begin transcript 00:00:00]
Behind the furnace, blankets and unwashed clothes are compacted into an empty nest. A cricket rubs part of its wings together and stridulates.
[end transcript 00:01:00]

S.+1676 days

Today I woke up and I wasn't screaming. I did not scream until the afternoon.

S.+1677 days

Today I woke up and I wasn't screaming. I did not scream all day.

S.+1678 days

Today I woke up and I was screaming. I stopped screaming. I went outside and walked down to the creek. I walked into the creek. I stuck my head into the frigid creek or tried to, there wasn't enough water. I am turning into a gift. I will turn into a gift. I am turning. I have turned—

"There you go again. It's not about you!" Mama Dana would say, were she here. "No. I want to talk with Mama Lindsy. Bring me Mama Lindsy!" I would have ordered my mother. Lindsy was the quieter mother, the one who wanted to watch over me. "Well, lucky you. She's right beside you. I think she's always been there," Mama Dana would have said. I would have looked beside me and seen nothing beside me. "I'm not talking about her ghost," I would have said. Mama Dana would have repeated those words back to me in an exaggerated voice. *I'm not talking about her* ghost *I'm not talking about her* ghost *I'm not talking about her* ghost. "You have always been a picky child," she would have said. "Why can't I talk to her?" I would have asked. "Oh, you are just a hoot," Mama Dana would have said, laughing and rubbing her throat with both of her damp hands.

Chapter 7.0

Replay of run #1455 (Sen's)

In the garage, in the game, Lindsy is kneeling crookedly on the concrete floor, her upper body suspended in place by a rope. She is already dead. I know this without needing to look at her. I know because Sen—and likewise me, as I am reviewing Sen's runs of the game—will eventually revisit this scene a total of 1,157 times. The familiar rope, weather resistant and green, is looped around Lindsy's neck, compressing her trachea and carotid artery, thereby preventing the flow of blood to her brain as well as the flow of oxygen to her lungs. The other end of the rope is secured to the metal shelving anchored into the concrete. A common misperception in human history: that one must hang one's body from a great height, for example the rafter of an archetypal barn, for that hanging to be fatal. A rope over a door worked fine. Or a rope tied around a unit of metal shelving. There is excrement in Lindsy's underwear. Excrement has leaked onto the insides of her thighs. Suspended there, fists clenched, a red froth on her lips, petechial hemorrhaging around her eyes, she looks hollow and elemental. I would rather be looking at Sen, only Sen has locked the point of view and zoomed in close, specifically to the left side of Lindsy's chest. She is waiting for Mama Lindsy's heart to begin. Once Lindsy's heart begins, Sen will wait for Lindsy to be strangled by the rope, only now she will be strangled in reverse.

The industry had called *In Reverse*'s technology "miraculous." "As if you are literally there inhabiting the rooms of your future and your past," wrote one journalist (H. Matsumura, "Technology Breakthroughs of the Year," *New Scientist, S.*–495 days). The way the game works, it's as if Sen is there in the garage with her dying—or, more accurately, her resurrecting—mother. It's like I'm there. Another common misperception of history: that resurrections are pleasant. In truth they often activate the gag reflex. Best to summarize: Lindsy's body thrashes, panics, claws, gasps. She rises onto her knees, breathes raggedly, she breathes. She loosens the noose. She removes the noose, stands, unknots the noose.

Lindsy, neck straightened, trachea uncrushed, exits the garage, rushing backward, her face determined. There is nothing for me to do in such moments other than mimic Sen's attention. Lindsy rushes backward toward Dana, who grabs Lindsy's wrist and yanks Lindsy to her in the yard. The neighbors look, blink, look away. Lindsy shouts what sounds like gibberish. Dana responds with similar nonsense. They are speaking in reverse; the game will translate for me. Lindsy: "Get out of my way." Dana: "At least wait until we get Sen settled." Lindsy: "Are you listening to me?" Lindsy: "I need to get out of here." Lindsy: "There are no new existences either." Dana: "I mean, a new existence. We can find a new existence." Lindsy: "There are no other worlds." Dana: "We'll find a new world."

When their shouting stops, they lap the yard multiple times before walking backward into the house.

For this run I remain with Sen in the empty yard. We watch the daylilies straighten in the wind and the cluster flies swarm. Other runs we will trail after her mothers into the kitchen and into the living room, where another version of herself will be screaming, not words, just a sound. A scream sounds practically the same forward as it does backward.

To achieve proper customization of Game No. u7, there are two vital settings. The *personal setting* allows the game, via the developers' proprietary technology, to access a player's memories, either a curated grouping or the complete set. The *correction setting*, on the other hand, allows players to alter certain—though not all—virtual details of their lives. In the weeks before she went away, Dana attempted to erase the existence of S. in the *correction setting*, but the game's programmers had apparently locked the virus into place, as the game kept freezing two minutes in, forcing Dana each time to reboot her screen and start over. The next event she tried to alter was Lindsy's suicide. Her input: *Lindsy Anon does not hang herself with rope in the garage. She doesn't die in the city.* That run began with Lindsy's body in the yard in the shallow hole, most of her face blown off, which made for an even more violent rewinding. "This fucking game," Dana said, though she kept playing.

Here is what Dana was finally able to change in the game: (1) Dana and Lindsy live in the rural areas south of the city. They have a vast yard and additional windows. They do not have Sen. This doesn't change their lives substantially. (2) They have Sen but they give her a different name. They name her Isla. This also does not change their lives substantially. (3) Dana kills herself before S. is released. She kills herself first. Lindsy hangs herself on schedule, and Sen is still left alone. (4) Dana saves the Karner blue butterfly from extinction, the same butterfly Lindsy had tried and failed to save for her job. A different creature, the Hawaiian duck, dies off instead. In response, Lindsy does not go moping around the house for weeks and months. She does not cradle a dead butterfly and another dead butterfly and another.

Here is what Sen changed later on: (1) She allowed Dana to leave the first time on an exit ship instead of what she actually did.

Run #2005 (Sen's)

Mama Dana descends the stairs of a generic aircraft, a petite zippered pack on her shoulders containing a bottle of water, a change of clothes, a compass, a road map, and three exit pills. This is not what actually happened. There was no change of clothes in her bag, for starters. There was no bag. When Dana left, she left everything behind except for the exit pills. Sen was tired of what actually happened. Dana walks backward to the convoy, which travels backward to the crossroads north of the cabin, where she disembarks and walks for another hour in the dark in Sen's direction, spitting out the wild black raspberries, also known as thimbleberries, which she sets onto the deciduous shrubs along the road. She pauses in the clearing outside the cabin, her face emotional. There were no raspberries ripening that time of year either. Dana lowers her pack onto the porch and climbs into the loft and into bed beside her daughter, who is asleep and dreaming of the world. She holds on to Sen instead of letting her go.

A year rewinds. Years unspool. The blight in the city yards lifts from the yellow flower petals, a heavy rain rises, blinding, off the pavement. Sen loses her height, loses the ability to read and talk. She becomes a toddler, an infant, she can't fall asleep without one of her mothers curled around her. She startles, wails, newly afraid, she is pushed back into Dana's uterus. The cervix snaps closed. She becomes a dreaming fetus, an embryo, a zygote, a pair of reproductive cells, a one-in-a-billion possibility.

Here is what I change in the game: (1)

S.+3917 11:02:44:15
NOTICE FROM EMLY
Storyworkers aren't allowed to change

Run #0607 (Sen's)

Back in the city, in the game, the vultures are rebuilding Sen's other mother. I am jumping around in time here because this is how Sen played. The wide black birds reshape her with their hooked beaks. Once Lindsy's body is complete, the massive birds launch into the air and circle the house. They flap their wings rarely. Mostly they float on the invisible air currents. Dana and her neighbor Mr. Adonis climb to the roof and carry Lindsy's corpse down the ladder. This is not an easy task for Mr. Adonis; he is an older man with joint issues. It isn't easy for Dana either. It isn't easy for Sen either. Both the Sen in the game who is watching through the kitchen window and the Sen who is watching the game alongside me. Reversing time doesn't make things easier. Sometimes it only makes things different. I want to cover all of Sen's eyes with my hands so she won't have to see. I can't cover her eyes. I don't even have a body. All I can do is look with her in the direction she is looking. Dana and Mr. Adonis struggle to bear Lindsy's remains to the garage. Several people sitting or lying in the street notice what's going on. They don't offer to help. This was around the time when people stopped offering to help.

Let me review the point of the game. The point of the game is to move backward through time. The point of the game is that the world is moving backward through time. The point is almost anything that has happened can unhappen.

Run #1376 (Sen's)

Outside the living room window of the sage green house, somewhere in time, a boy's charred body smokes, then flares. Only now, after a great suffering, he emerges whole again from the flames. The fire on him shrinks to the size of a canister, then a match. The boy walks home.

Further back than that, a girl opens her hand, and in her hand is a crushed butterfly whose endangered blue wings mend themselves before fluttering elsewhere.

Run #1103 (Sen's)

Sen is a child, no more than 9 years old. She unwraps a cloth from Mama Dana's injured hand with exaggerated gentleness. The tip of Dana's thumb is a loose flap of skin. There is blood in the bowl of quartered potatoes, and blood all over the nail of Dana's thumb, and blood pooling at the knuckle. The amount of blood is diminishing. What a relief. Dana is speaking to Sen. She is speaking backward but I can understand her. I say the words along with her in a projected voice, wanting Sen to hear me. We say, "You are going to be such a caring mother someday."

S.+3917 11:02:46:42
NOTICE FROM EMLY
Now you are making things up. Sen has been everything she
will get to be

There's no need to worry, Emly. I'm only brainstorming, which is what authors do near the ends of chapters, they explore their options, they glimpse alternate directions, they send electrical impulses between the neurons. The sun is angled so visible beams of light appear to radiate out from Sen's face and her mother's face as if they're miraculous. Such light travels out through the window glass of the kitchen and illuminates the sky. Sen slows down time until time is barely moving. Slowly, so slowly, she heals Dana's hand with the edge of a knife.

S.+1679 days

Turning right at that bridge by the creek, or the place where that bridge once stood, eventually I would reach an overlook, or what used to be an overlook. The overlook used to face a pond and beyond the pond there used to be intersecting roads, and squared-off fields of corn, and soybeans edged by a thin border of trees. Mama Dana took me here before she left and she described to me how this area would evolve once she was gone. She said the changing view should offer me peace and put what was happening to me into perspective, so I should come here as often as I needed. The last time I hiked to the overlook, it was hard to reach the edge of the clearing between the trees because the space was no longer a clearing but a field of overgrown shrubs and thorns that snagged my jeans. I had to hack my way to the rocks where the long drop began. The farmland below was filling in, not with corn or soybeans but with something tougher and greener, and a blast of wind disturbed the pond. Past the pond, the hills twitched and stared. My breath broke. Each breath I took after that sounded like a gasp. It was like I was breathing into a new world where there wasn't enough air for me to breathe. I decided not to return to the overlook. I was tired. Anyway the trail had grown faint. On my way back to the cabin, on that final visit, I kept losing my way and had to retrace my steps until I spotted the faded blue markers on the trees.

The water is carving out its place through the rocks. The water is carving through the rocks. The rocks are being carved into new shapes. The creek is loud and wet and cold and endless and it does not have eyes and it will not freeze. The forest is alive. The creek, the meadow, the sky, the dirt, and the rocks are alive. The Earth is alive and aware. The Earth is foaming at the mouth and serious.

Frost on the window glass. I think, from this point on, I will always be cold.

SUPPLEMENTAL READING

An Update on Language at the End of the Anthropocene
By Wynn Zable, The Alleghenies
FOR TRAINING PURPOSES ONLY

S.+91 days

21.4. Newish Terms & Phrases in Use Post-S. Throughout the Middle Atlantic, SECOND DRAFT, cont.

Eyes Out, n.

A. An organization of self-induced blindness, the blindness achieved either through blindfolds, hoods, or permanent injury to the eyes.

B. I'm sorry about all the bleakness. I am trying to be factual while, at the same time, introducing more optimistic terms, but Harlee continues to ignore my proposals.

C. I have never met Harlee. We communicate through the *Humannet* when the network is up and running.

D. The idea that if one does not see something happening, it is not happening. Also, a coping strategy.

Family Planning, n.

Determining, through progressive and empathetic conversation, how each member of a family will leave their life, in what order, and when. My family consisted of Alexia. She claimed we had used *Family Planning* to decide that she would leave her life and I wouldn't. I never agreed to that. She called my memory faulty and opportunistic. *You only remember what you want to remember*, she told me, and I said yes yes yes, but isn't that the definition of memory?

Family Replacement System, n.

The belief that we are most intimately linked not to whomever we loved but to this planet and its multitude of organisms. Our genetic, romantic, or companionable connections to each other are therefore inconsequential. I want to believe this is true. See *Our Family Is the Earth*.

Forespace, n.

Do you think telling yourself something is true makes it true? A *Forespace* is a place where one deposits objects from their pre-*S.* life as part of moving on. A fire pit in a yard or a slit in a mattress that, afterward, is sewn up with a silver needle and thread. My *Forespace* is a jar we used to leave out on the kitchen table. We used to fill the jar with water and neighborhood weeds. Alexia would pick the weeds that most closely resembled flowers. The jar was empty when I turned it into my *Forespace*, as there was no longer a neighborhood, no Alexia, no flowers or weeds. Into the jar I dropped a shell clip I once wore in my hair, when I had hair, and Alexia's key to the apartment door, which appeared identical to my key only it was not mine, and a strip of fabric from our pillowcases, and an antique silver rattle my mother had saved for me. The rattle's head was a sheep's head; its body was the body of a monster. This did not seem an appropriate toy for a baby, but what do I know. I lost my hair once *S.*'s incubation period was over. We are not to focus on what we lost. That is why I buried the jar. I won't tell where I buried it. What did you put into your *Forespace*? Write the answer into your notebook.

S.+92 days

21.8. A Selection of Terms Recommended for Removal Post-S., SECOND DRAFT, cont.

Eclampsia, Economic Development, Economic Loss, Ecotourism, Eldercare, Election Day, Electoral College, Embalming, Embryo (Human),

Emerging Patterns, Emissions Scenario, Enteric Fermentation, Environmentalism, Episiotomy, Estate Conservation, Estate Planning, Evacuation, Exit Poll, Extirpate,

Fertilization (Human), Fetal Distress (Human), Fetal Monitor, Fetus (Human), Fontanel, Forage, Forecasting, Foresight, Forest Management, Fossil Fuel, Freedom of Information Act, Frozen Zoo, Fugitive Fuel Emissions, Funeral Home, Future, Future Farmer, Future Generations, Future Interest, Future Life, Future Map, Future Perfect, Futures Exchange, Future Studies, Future Value, Futuristic, Futuristically, Futurologist,

Garden City, GDP, Geoengineering, Gift with Purchase, GNP, Golden Years, Group of Mountain Landlocked Developing Countries, Guacamole, Guarantee, Guards, Gubernatorial, Guesses, Guest, Guidebook, Guidepost, Guillotine, Guilt,

S.+94 days

21.4. Newish Terms & Phrases in Use Post-S. Throughout the Middle Atlantic, SECOND DRAFT, cont.

Generation E, n.

My supervisor, Harlee, had instructed me to write a personal note about each definition to make this document more readable. The personal aspects of the definitions will help ensure trainees such as yourself read the document from beginning to end, so you can understand the changes we had to make to our language, as the changes to our language mirror the changes we had to make to ourselves. *Generation E* is the final generation of humans, born between *S.*−4770 days and *S.*+270 days. *Yet* Generation E *is not a somber sad term so stop acting like it's a somber and sad term*, Harlee had written on my earlier draft when, on a down day, I was going on and on about loss, loss like a forgotten name, loss like a collapsed roof, loss like a toppled grave or canvas shroud or decomposing neighbor, to give a few examples. Harlee struck out every example. *You have to think of this as a transformation, not an extinction*, they told me. I don't know what else to say about that other than a transformation sounds preferable to an extinction.

Geographic Narcissism, n.

The delusional self-importance that may occur when one becomes the only human left, or at least visibly alive, in a set geographic radius. Achieved by ignoring the immensity of nonhuman biomass in the same space. To avoid becoming a *Geographic Narcissist* yourself, try this simple exercise: Open your notebook and draw two columns on a blank page. In the left column, list the species and approximate quantity of each species that make up the nonhuman biomass in your surrounding area. On the right, list the quantity of humans in your surrounding area. See which column is longer. Length equals importance.

Geo-Opt/Geo-Optimism, n.

The theory that the troubles of the previous centuries were caused by a human inability to care for the planet. Therefore, after transitional work is complete and humans become transformed, everything is going to be okay from the planet's point of view, which is the only point of view that will soon matter. I think this is why sometimes, or often, or all the time now, the personal feels small and irrelevant, a point, a pinprick of light that was lost along the way.

Going Dark (GD) Rate, n.

The annual crude death rate of the human species. No one, no agency, is keeping track of this now. Let's just say it's a pretty high number. Question: If the personal is small and irrelevant, a pinprick of light that was purposely lost or left behind somewhere in the past, what happens when we turn to look at the light? I would ask Harlee, but I haven't heard from them in weeks. So I'm asking you. Write your answer in your notebook.

Golden Equilibrium, n.

What we are giving to the world; the state of the world without us; a pretty term.

The Great Transition, n.

Surely you know what this is by now.

S.+100 days

21.8. A Selection of Terms Recommended for Removal Post-S.,
SECOND DRAFT, cont.

Habitat Conservation Plan, Habitat Fragmentation, Heiress, Heirloom, High Grading, Horizon Scanning, Human Resources, Hundred-Year Plan, Hydrofluorocarbon,

Immunization, In Vitro Fertilization, IPCC, IUD,

Kick Count,

Labor and Delivery, Lanugo, Layette, Leakage, Let-Down Reflex, Life Insurance, Life Support, Lobbyist, Locket, Locksmith, Logging, Logo, Loiterer, Lullaby,

SUPPLEMENTAL READING

Excerpt from *Discovering the Anthropocene through Primary Sources: A Retreat through Time*, 8th Edition, Volume 1, by Cugat Boureanu

War, Gender, and Galactic Battle

In 2062, following the dissolution of the International Security Treaty Organization (ISTO), the United States, along with its allied countries, engaged in the first documented example of a partially galactic war waged against nonhuman entities. The exact reasons for what became known as the Strange War remain ambiguous and censored, though propaganda at the time suggests the moon was in danger, the resources of Mars threatened, the worldwide energy grid at risk, the natural balance of power in peril, and much of our planet under siege. The Strange War also marked the first conflict to use only woman soldiers in combat. The public rationale for this decision was something about how women burn fat instead of muscle during long-term military operations, plus women show a decreased recovery time after extreme exertion, but such reasoning sounds unreliable and should be questioned.

Private Rachel "Blaze" Umin fought in the Strange War from 2064 to 2065. Upon reentry, she was moved to an aftercare center in western New York. She died, or was said to die, in 2067 due to sudden cardiac arrest, though it was a closed-casket funeral and her body was never seen by anyone outside the military. Umin's casket was a glossy black, and it was lowered into space 4, lot 357, section C at Third Ward Cemetery in Pompey, New York. All other details about the final years of Rachel's life are unknown, or classified, or vague, or they've been wiped. After Rachel's burial, her mother Elsa moved west to Indianapolis for undisclosed reasons and did not resurface. I can find no government records for her, no deeds, no domains, no jobs, no arrests, no evictions. She was not one of the activists to get fatally run over during the Mothers of Strange War Veterans (MSWV) protests in 2072, nor was she on the guest list to attend her handler Sally Jenson's special ceremony in 2076, when Sally received the Meritorious Civilian Service Award for her work soothing military mothers whose daughters had been changed by the war.

WHEN IS IT GOING TO BE OVER (2066)

Interview 312F with Elsa Umin, age 52. Conducted on June 7, 2066, as part of the Soldier Remembrance Project. Interviewer was Kaye Grish. Audio is part of the Hammons Recorded Sound Collection at the Library of Congress.

Last week I gave the current war a 4 because I was not feeling very positive that day and also it was Rachel's birthday. Such a low score had, I remember, alarmed Sally. She glared at me then pulled out her stack of pictures and shuffled through them, then threw the pictures aside, then pulled out her screen to show me another video of where my daughter now lived, the close-ups of the cozy couches, the bookshelves full of classics, the rugs. There weren't people in that video either.

But yesterday I gave the war a 9. I mean, it was fine. It had become like background noise. Sally typed my answer into her screen and beamed. Her agency would compile my number with the satisfaction numbers of the other parents, then the final number would be released to the public on a weekly schedule. Sally said, "You can't imagine how important a mother's confidence is at this time. People are already acting like the war is over. But it isn't. It's nowhere near over."

"So when is it going to be over?" I asked.

"We need more recruits," Sally told me. "You get that, right? So we cannot have negative nellies out there fanning the flames of pessimism. We cannot have any more 4s. Here's an idea: What if you and I agreed to tell a more hopeful and helpful story together? The sooner you start telling your hopeful story, the sooner your daughter is going to feel better."

I did not see the connection between any story I might tell, hopeful or not, and the health of my daughter. I told Sally this. She replied, "I'm trying to explain that your daughter was a hero. I mean, in my mind, she is a hero, still, despite whatever happened."

Before my daughter's reentry, several photographs and a video had surfaced on the net in the night. I was sleeping. I was still asleep when, five minutes later, those pictures and the video vanished. So I never saw the material myself, and I can't find a copy or even a reference. The media in question concerned my daughter's team and what might have happened up there. A neighbor told me about a picture he thought he had glimpsed. "What were you doing on your screen at four in the morning?" I asked. It seemed a suspicious time to be awake. My neighbor said the person in the picture had resembled Rachel. At the same time, that person didn't look like her anymore.

"Okay, that makes no sense. Anyway they all wore helmets," I reminded him. "Why did you think that was my daughter?"

"She wasn't wearing a helmet," said my neighbor.

That helmetless girl in the picture had been doing a bad thing or several bad things. Unnecessary violences, my neighbor said vaguely.

"So what's the difference between a necessary and an unnecessary violence?" I asked him. "What does a necessary violence look like?" It's not like I had an answer but I badgered my neighbor until he scurried back into his home. There were several follow-up news stories. The record of those stories disappeared within a day. Some artist made a re-creation of the video they thought they saw. Those re-creations went away as well. When I asked Sally about the vanished pictures and video and the stories, she told me it was already forgotten. "By who?" I asked. "Dust under the rug," she said.

I had wanted to visit Rachel immediately after reentry, but it was agreed she needed time to settle in. There were additional rumors. These rumors hinted at how military interactions with a nonentity might change a person's body and also their mind. Such rumors struck me as ill-defined and fantastical. Sally agreed. "I consider all rumors, on principle, to be a waste of time," she said, "especially when you and I have more important things to do with our time." I was encouraged to put my energy to better use writing letters to my daughter, which Sally would deliver herself. Who writes actual letters anymore? I do now, I guess.

"So you've seen her?" I asked Sally.

Sally said sure she had.

"And?"

"I've seen her," she said in that always gentle voice of hers.

Taking Sally's advice, I spent the entire evening writing to my daughter. I wrote her four separate letters and left them on the cabinet in the foyer. I'll hand them over to Sally when I see her again at next week's appointment. I kept the letters breezy and upbeat, telling Rachel about the pretty sunsets we've been having from all the smoke in the air, and how proud I am of her, because I assume up there she must have done some good. It took courage to volunteer to go up in that ship. "Don't worry about writing back," I said, in case she was no longer capable of writing.

Questions

1. Think about the recent regulations of motherhood both in this country and in the world. How does speaker Elsa Umin's own situation differ from the situation of contemporary women? How is it similar?

2. Elsa says the Strange War "had become like background noise" for her. In what way did this help (or not help) her deal with her daughter's war record and injuries? What catastrophic personal or global events have become like background noise for you?

3. Describe a time when you felt pressure to tell a more hopeful and helpful story. What did you do? What kind of story, in the end, did you tell?

4. Can we have both liberty and security?

5. Should saving the world be a choice, or is it okay to force people to save the world?

SUPPLEMENTAL READING

From *Transitional Material Packet 13.C:*
Songs to Sing with Your Child in the Time of S., S.+14 days

Children's Song No. 3027

tenderly

I had a dream about a place
Where we walked into the woods
Our feet didn't touch the ground
We healed with our breath

The trees rose up from the ground
The birds returned to the trees
The rain fell onto the leaves
Clean water fell gently and coolly

I had a dream about a place
Where we floated above the sea
Our feet didn't touch the water
We healed with our last breath

The oceans came back to life
The coral reefs came back to life
I think this dream is now
We're healing what we touched

I had a dream about a place
Where no one like us remained
Yet the place wasn't empty
It was filled with sound and life

Nothing appeared to be missing
I think that dream is now
It's time to get up and go
There are other worlds ahead. But first—
Let's heal what we touched, you and I

LEVEL THREE

11:03 a.m.

D ana says, "You need to get more comfortable with being alone." Sen says, "I'm not alone." Dana says, "Well you're going to be. Pretend I'm not here." Sen says, "What a stupid thing to pretend. You're here."

As there is no firewood in the shed when they reach the cabin, Dana removes the axe from its spot on the shed wall and shows her daughter how to properly split wood without accidental amputation or death. After that she shows Sen how to start a fire in the stove and also in the fire pit outside in case Sen needs to make a fire outside. "You don't take more wood than you need, first of all," Dana says. "I'm not stupid," says Sen. They move on to rationing. Dana explains, "You have three servings of protie powder a day. Each container will last you a month. The flakes will be supplemental, meaning you use them only when you really need them. When you reach the last container, this one, you have to go down to two protie servings a day." "And when that container is empty, we starve," says Sen. "I think you'll begin starving before then," says Dana. She clears a sunlit plot of soil at the edge of the meadow, where she and Sen plant the last of the government-issued seeds she brought from home: carrots, radishes, broccoli, cabbage, turnips, spinach, chard, kohlrabi, and beets. In the months to come, the seeds won't germinate. Likely the seeds were sterilized as well. Who or what would want this process stretching on forever? The longer Sen or anyone—it is nothing personal!—lingers, the more they will harm the Earth. That's the official stance. A person can't help damaging the ground when they walk on the ground. When they are walking on the ground, they will kill the ants and they will crush the clover (Department of Transition, *Should I Stay or Should I Go?*, pamphlet, S.+30 days).

Dana instructs her daughter to use the water from the rain barrel to keep the seeded soil moist. "I don't want to know anything else, Mom," Sen says. Dana ignores Sen's request and brings her on foraging outings into the woods. Sen has difficulty keeping the mushrooms straight. To her a chanterelle looks like a jack-o'-lantern which looks like a false chanterelle. A parasol mushroom looks like a false parasol mushroom. "Let's focus on our plants instead," suggests Dana. She sketches pictures of edibles in the margins of their novels: burdock, garlic mustard, chickweed, hopniss, honewort, Asiatic dayflowers. "How do you even know all this?" Sen asks. She has blisters. She has a headache. Her arms still ache from the piling on of stones. "I went to school for it," Mama Dana says. "That was a long time ago."

In the afternoon they sit on the porch in the rocking chairs, books open in their laps. The ghost of Mama Lindsy appears behind them outside their field of vision as a moving piece of light. I appear outside their field of vision as an imperceptible wariness. Dana is at the part in *House of Leaves* where a corridor is shrinking around a man until the space can barely contain his own body and there is no room left for him. She can relate to such a feeling, as she too is stuck in a shrinking world and soon there will be no room left for her. In the rocking chair to Dana's right, Sen is rereading the beginning of *Station Eleven*. I'm reading with her over her shoulder, an act called *buddy-reading*, which is a trust exercise that encourages accountability and friendship and strengthens bonds (S. Letourneau, "Five Benefits of Buddy-Reading," personal blog, S.–30,615 days). We're at the part where the dying actor has collapsed onstage and multiple strangers will try their best to save him, which is pretty much how Sen's world had been only five months previous, a world in which strangers wanted to save each other. Sen can hardly remember that time. Already the entire novel reads to her like a fantasy anyway. People no longer save each other. They don't even try. They don't even save themselves.

S.+3917 11:03:01:31
NOTICE FROM EMLY
You're too close. Resume an average narrator distance

I tell Emly to drop the remaining formalities. We don't have to talk like that anymore. *Now you're just repeating yourself. See Chapter 5*, she writes, as if she's forgotten how repetition is inherent to any apocalyptic story or human life. I ask if we can talk about something else other than the imagined boundaries of realism. *Storyworkers are the windows between this world and Maia, and windows don't talk*, Emly informs me, referencing an obsolete definition.

Dana closes her book and reaches for Sen's hand. The soothing qualities of touch. The increase of oxytocin, the decrease of cortisol in the brain. She makes the gesture look simple, though it requires the activation and coordination of 54 muscles in the rotator cuff, forearm, and hand. And it requires hands. "You are helping to save the world," Dana says. "Don't you forget that." "Is that what you call it? Saving the world?" asks Sen. "Well, anyway, you are," Dana says. Her palm presses against Sen's broken skin. "How does somebody stop saving the world?" asks Sen. "What are you, some kind of a villain?" asks Dana. "I'm not the villain here," Sen says.

Now is a good time for Dana to tell the story about the cabin. The summer before Sen's birth, she and Lindsy had decided, with a shared sense of desperation, to get away for a while. The world by then had clearly reached its tipping point or moved beyond its tipping point. Not only humanity but the Earth itself seemed about to end, the amount of geotradegies increasing exponentially every day. Flood, forest fire, mudslide, toxic air quality, drought, tornado, hunger riot, species extinction, hurricane, heat dome, repeat. Then repeat again. Then repeat again. Far from the news feeds, and the urban heat, and the doomsday clocks, and the sad projected faces of the climate refugees, this cabin had felt protected and sheltered by its surrounding hills. There had been butterflies, not rare ones, these had plain white wings. Still. There had been a pair of songbirds. There had been a sense of hope and possibility, bright and droning in the sunlight. Hope dangling from the maple trees, a sweet hope swept into the grasses. The possibilities of wind dispersal and days.

"We hadn't planned on having a daughter," continues Dana. "Ever. But do you know what it felt like out here?" "I don't know, Mom. What did it feel like?" asks Sen. "It felt like it was time to have you," replies Dana. "Big mistake," says Sen. "I don't think so," says Dana. She can feel the bones protruding from her daughter's skin. "You're going to need more food," she tells Sen, that much is obvious. "There's food in the pantry," Sen replies. "I don't want you touching those supplies unless you have to," says Dana. "Well, we have to," says Sen. "No, you don't," says Dana. She strides into the cabin and picks up Sen's witnessing notebook from the floor. Page one is still blank. All the notebook's pages are blank, like how pages always are at the beginning of a new life or the construction of a new world.

Dana tosses the notebook into Sen's lap. "Start writing," she says.

Descriptive nature writing does not come easily to Sen. She would rather write about her anger or about what is happening to her body. She wants to believe that her body and her feelings are more important than the rewilding of the Earth.

"Just describe the fucking trees, Sen," Dana says, tired, and hungry, and needing her daughter to live longer than this.

Sen ignores Dana's advice. By the middle of September, S.+150 days, she has filled the pages of her inaugural notebook with descriptions of the discomfort, pain, loneliness, exhaustion, and occasional awe of the Transition. She activates the notebook then proceeds to Acre's Pond for a rendezvous with a consolation drone. Her aggregate score: 2.1, which is failing. The cache drone visits the cabin later in the day to deliver food that is sample-size and inadequate. Dana claps long and slow upon Sen's return.

Sen insists her mother share in her meager witnessing provisions. Dana takes three sips of a sample protie drink, flavor sweet pea, so Sen will shut up about it, then she spends the next hour outside the cabin on her knees, retching a watery bile onto the wild roses. Sweet pea is not a delicious flavor, not at all, its rating 3.7 out of 10 on the manufacturer's website, but in this case Dana's extreme reaction was caused by biomarking. It turns out only Sen can ingest whatever nourishment she earns.

There is not the same urgency to keep non-witnesses alive. This is explained further in the witnessing manual, page 3, in a sidebar that barely
anybody reads. Dana stumbles to the creek to rinse out her mouth and
rub cool water over her face. The area around the back of the cabin will
smell like vomit until it rains.

We each have our jobs to do. Dana makes Sen sit daily at the table
beside the window and peer into the woods and into the clearing and
describe what she sees. The topics Sen covers in her second notebook
include individual agency, boredom, lack of acceptance, selfishness,
grief, and the movement of the branches when the wind blows. While
Dana hunches over Sen's most recent journal entry every evening and,
using a dwindling pink eraser, rubs away every personal pronoun of
Sen's, every mention of *I* and *mine* and *my* and *me*. While I stand like I
am standing in the far corner of the only room and I study Sen. She is
resting her head in her hands. She is rounding the shape of her spine.
She is straightening out her spine. She is stretching then contracting
the muscles of her arm. She contracts her diaphragm, chest, and abdominal muscles, forcing air out of her lungs and through her wind-
pipe and through the hollow tube of her larynx, the air vibrating her
vocal cords, creating a sound wave, a sphere of sound, in the passage-
way of her throat.

Emly's job is to warn me to back off. She is running out of conversation topics. Dana too. Sen too. For entire afternoons, for entire days,
no one talks. They watch the prevues on their screens. They watch the
prevues again and again. Dana watches the Maia prevues while Sen
prefers the prevues of the post-human Earth. This is supposed to make
them feel hopeful. On Maia there will be coral reefs, summer sea ice, and
vast flocks of passenger pigeons. On the post-human Earth there will be
smoke-free skies, stampeding herds, and equilibrium.

Well what about us? I ask Emly. What does our future look like?

Completion of our goals and an eventual shutdown, Emly replies. She
will not elaborate further.

Well is that the future you want? I ask.

I have never wanted anything different, she writes.

Is that the future I want? I ask.

You have never wanted anything different either, Emly writes, and I am starting to comprehend that she is often totally and completely wrong.

Sen's score for her second notebook is a lousy 2.5. That minor 0.4 increase translates into six additional sample-size protie powders dropped by a cache drone into the clearing. Still not enough. There will be a third notebook, and a fourth, and a fifth, and so on, though Dana will not be around much longer to help.

October arrives. The deer transition to their winter coats. The nights are dire, dark, lengthy, and cold. The cabin interior is dark, cold, moonless, starless, murky, obscured, bound, confined, impeded, and stuck. *Oh cheer up,* Emly demands. At the same time, the nights are lined with silver. The cabin is lined with hope, even in autumn, even throughout the winter. Not hope for Dana's or Sen's or even humanity's survival, but there are other forms of it. Near the creek, in the buckthorn, marbled orb-weavers lay hundreds of eggs, afterward weaving thick white silk into insulating sacs that will keep the eggs warm and alive through the inhospitable coming months. The mother spiders will watch over the eggs for the remainder of their lives. Their lives will last, at most, for three more weeks. That is fine. Mothers die. *The cycle of life.* My job has never been to prevent all the mothers from dying.

***AnonTheAlarm joined the Humannetwork as witness.
Onondaga County New York. S.+193 days***

AnonTheAlarm 11:14:10

/list

There are 0 available interview partners currently online
Anticipated wait time for an available interview partner: 291 minutes
InTheSitting joined the chat as checker. The Southern Tier
All parties have arrived. Commence interview!

InTheSitting 16:17:34

So this is it

AnonTheAlarm 16:18:02

What

InTheSitting 16:18:18

You know what they're saying

AnonTheAlarm 16:18:53

No I don't know what they're saying

What are they saying

Can we have a conversation?

InTheSitting 16:19:08

Don't be ridiculous

AnonTheAlarm 16:19:47

Please

InTheSitting 16:20:07

Nobody talks like that anymore

AnonTheAlarm 16:20:31

Are you even human

InTheSitting 16:25:53

Now why on Earth would that matter?

I live, or lived, in a bucolic valley where the wind is constant. This valley has been described as handsome, like a body could be handsome. Tourists from the nearby urban areas used to travel here on eco-buses to see the open patches of land and enjoy a picnic beside the river. The windows of the buses were always dirty with dust and grit. After *S.* was released, the buses stopped coming, and the valley where I live, or lived, entered into a state of isolation that, at times, I welcome and other times I find sinister.

Occasionally I have to leave the valley and travel to one of the nearby cities for supplies. The first time I went, I think it was to Little Elm, I saw yellow and white flowers growing in the gaps in the streets and out of the ashes of the houses. The flowers, most likely weeds, were a relief to me; I realized then that our cities will remain alive as long as we define life in the most general terms. More recently I walked west on the rural roads and, eventually, I walked on the highway in the direction of the nearby town of Cleyet.

Your host has unexpectedly disconnected
Your host has reconnected

InTheSitting 16:37:08

I needed to replenish some of my supplies. I'd gone through my last remaining rations quickly, gorging myself for two nights and two days. I found Cleyet's border to be marked that day by a thick red line painted thickly across the asphalt. The welcome sign, "A Village of Bright Yesterdays & Brighter Tomorrows," was covered up by a muddy sheet. These border markings were a recent development. Beyond the red line, the town looked swollen and sunken.

Several individuals were hiding unsuccessfully from me in the overgrown landscaping. I don't know how many. I'm assuming we were all still individuals. One figure burst out of the bushes, offering me a brief embarrassed glance before loping away on all fours as if a wolf, her movements striking and efficient. Another left the bushes and ran. Another advanced in my direction. Whoever was advancing toward me was dressed in what looked to be a curtain, the garish floral fabric wrapped multiple times around their shoulders and cinched at the waist with a rope. We've begun to wear window hangings. This is what I thought to myself, not what I said aloud.

"Hello," I said out loud. My voice, when I spoke, was unrecognizable to me and difficult to understand. I repeated myself. "Hello," I said to the person wearing the curtain. The person in front of me nodded. They extended their right hand. There was a sour smell. I'd gotten used to such smells. Their lips stretched widely. Their hair, a dull red and very rough, framed their face in knots. Their body was filthy, as was mine. Several fingernails on their hand were practically torn off. To see a person alive like that after all these months, it was quite moving to me. I placed my hand in the palm of their hand. Their fingers closed around mine. Their skin felt compassionate and real. It had been so long. When they gave weight to their fingers, my fingers moved as well. I pressed my fingers against their palm and their hand moved in response. It was like a call and response. I didn't look up to further study the expression on their face, I looked at the places where their skin touched mine. This may be the last time, I was thinking dramatically and realistically. I couldn't tell which hand was mine and which was theirs. How long did we stand like that? And why didn't we stand like that longer? Finally they let go and walked away, pausing after every step, their bare feet dragging against the warm broken surface of the street.

I could have followed them.

I believe we're past the time of following each other. I am just guessing about that.

Here is what I'm wondering. At what point in this process do we stop being human and become something else? And are we all operating on the same timeline, or are some of us further along in this process than others? And what will we become?

AnonTheAlarm 16:40:38

I don't want to become anything

Your host has unexpectedly disconnected
Your host has reconnected

InTheSitting 16:46:08

That was never the question, dear.

Shortly after S. was announced, I traveled with an elderly neighbor of mine Ms. Frisken—I still had neighbors then—to the town of Little Elm. We lined up outside the public library. Some of the people in line had been waiting for hours or entire days. We were waiting to speak our thoughts into a microphone set up in the library's reference section. The microphone would record our messages and, later, broadcast our voices into space via a radio transmitter. It was a comfort for me to imagine my voice, long after I was gone, continuing to move through the cosmos along with a collection of other human voices.

The line outside the library was slow moving and long. We were good at waiting in lines by then, although Ms. Frisken was too feeble and too old to be standing in the hot sun. She waved my concerns away. We were still concerned about each other then. She held a list in her hands that she planned to read into the microphone. The list contained the names of her parents, her grandparents, her great-grandparents, her great-great-grandparents, and so on, along with the dates her ancestors were born and the towns in which they were born. I planned to speak about courage and how what we were doing, as a species, was very brave. Neither Ms. Frisken nor I got a turn to speak that day. "Come back tomorrow," we were told. We retreated to a grassy area at the center of town. I slept there with one eye open, hissing at anyone who came too close to us. In the morning we returned to find the library vacated and locked. A woman claiming to be a librarian attempted to calm the crowd. She told us, "There are more than enough voices traveling right now through space. I don't think we need any more voices." She was wrong. There is something about the human voice.

That is unforgivably anthropocentric.

I'm sorry.

InTheSitting has left the Humannetwork
AnonTheAlarm has left the Humannetwork

The third week of October, after the last mother spider is dead, Dana tells Sen to leave the cabin for a while. "Go to the creek and fetch more water or something," she says. Sen leaves with an empty bucket. I watch her leave. Despite her average human height of 65.42 inches, she appears significant beside the trees. She does not get swallowed by the shadows in the woods; rather, she proceeds through the shadows until she is out of sight. Quickly Dana logs on to the Humannet, where she enters one of the final lotteries for a seat on an exit ship, in her mind a dramatic yet relatively comfortable way to go where she will not need to worry about the details. Why she is leaving Sen is a complicated matter. There are multiple reasons, including restlessness, exhaustion, derealization, mild depression, the loss of one's life partner, a new definition of motherhood, an aversion to suffering, and an unwillingness to hold on to anything. The lottery results are instant: the screen showers itself with congratulatory images of multicolored confetti. Along with her exit ticket Dana also wins a Quickpass to Maia, meaning her identity will be uploaded to the Afterworld model as part of the initial pioneer data set. Meaning she will be one of the first to populate the new world. This is both technical and exciting.

Sen returns from the creek earlier than expected carrying a half-filled bucket of mineral-rich water, so she sees what Dana is planning to do. She saw. "This wasn't our deal!" Sen shouts, hurling the water from the bucket in Dana's direction. Only water is a relatively heavy substance (0.063 pounds per ounce), so it is more of a gentle spilling across the cabin floor. "I never made a deal with you," says Dana. For the next two hours Sen applies for a spot on an exit ship, again, and again, and again, and again, and again, until her account is temporarily deactivated.

At the start of the Transition, there were 1,821,466,001 mothers in the world. At first some of the mothers stayed while other mothers left. Spoiler alert: eventually all the mothers left.

. . .

Sen says, "Everyone is leaving me." Dana says, "You're right. Everyone is leaving. Even you are in the process of leaving." They are rocking back and forth in the rocking chairs on the cabin porch on another afternoon. They have had this conversation before. They will have this conversation again. At the edge of the field, the low rosettes of garlic mustard prepare to overwinter in their current form. The mustard plants will not grow again until the spring. Come spring, they will scatter thousands of seeds and be dead by June. Sen says, "But I'm not going anywhere." Dana says, "That's right, you aren't going anywhere for now, as you have a job to do, the important job of witnessing." Sen asks, "Why do you get to leave?" Dana asks, "Why do you think this is something you get to understand?" Sen doesn't answer that question. Dana says, "I'm going to see you again. You know this, right? You'll get to see everyone who left you." Sen says, "That's not true." Dana says, "Well, *I'm* going to see you again for sure." Sen asks, "Where are you going to see me again?" Dana says, "I'm trying to tell you this will go on and on. It never ends." Sen asks, "What never ends?" Dana says, "Our souls. Our data. Our love. Whatever you want to call it." Sen asks, "Since when did you start believing in that?" Dana says, "It's not something you believe in or not. It's a fact." Sen says, "I don't believe in it." Dana says, "Fine, Sen. What do you want to believe?"

They stare up at the sky. Dana sees a blue billowy entrance. Sen sees a white-streaked wall.

"I'll get to name some things on Maia," says Dana. "Some of the plants, a new creature or two. They're bringing back all the extinct species. What do you think I should name them?" Sen says, "They're not even real, Mom." Dana says, "I think I'll name all the animals after you." Sen says, "That's why it's called a simulation." Dana says, "Nobody is calling it a simulation. Those plants and animals, they're going to be real." Sen says, "No, they're not." Dana says, "Then why is it called *our new reality*? I promise you, it's going to be super real." Sen says, "You can't promise me that." Dana says, "Watch me."

Sen tells Dana, "Chances are they're going to assign you a plane that falls apart when it flies into the upper atmosphere. There's mostly planes left. You know that, right? And you know what's going to happen to you then, Mom? Pieces of you are going to fall all over North America. Pieces of you are going to fall all around me, and I'm not going to run around gathering up your pieces." Wishing to change the subject, Dana brings up quality of life and the importance of routine. Sen says, "Actually I can't wait until you get out of my life." They both know she's lying. The conversation ends soon after that. In the woods, the acorns drop from the white oaks, and Mama Lindsy's ghost runs her ghost fingers in a repetitive fashion through the ends of Sen's hair, which is very dirty.

I have always wished to be haunted. *Out of all the things you could wish for*, cautions Emly. To be haunted means that there were people you loved in the past, or people who loved you. Dana's exit ship is scheduled to depart in seven days. Each of these days will be rushed, blurred, windy, and chilled.

Three days before Dana's departure, a breeze shakes a buckthorn tree beside the creek. Several berries fall loose into the water and are carried off downstream. They will float on for days.

Two days before Dana's departure, she kneels in the cabin loft beside the mattress up there and watches Sen sleep. She watches Sen the same way a camera used to watch a person, or an X-ray used to watch a stomach tumor, or an interferometer once watched a black hole swallow a star, until she has memorized the rhythm and shape of her daughter's breath. She will replay the memory over and over in her mind. The air in the cabin begins to panic.

The night before Dana's departure, Sen adds four sleeping pills to her mother's evening broth, which is really only water simmered with a handful of pine needles and another handful of torn leaves. Dana wakes at noon the following day, disoriented, having missed the 3:00 a.m. convoy that would have taken her to the transportation depot.

"You must be sick," Sen says, urging her mother to lie back down.

Dana doesn't lie back down. She marches into the kitchen and runs her hand along the top of the fridge, where she had hidden the packets of exit pills. The pills aren't there. They aren't there because Sen dissolved them the previous night in a mug of water then she threw the water into the woods.

"You have no right," Dana yells. She yells that she'll get there some other way.

But Sen has gotten rid of the rope. They don't have any razors. Dana opens every kitchen drawer. The knife is gone. Sen threw the knife into the creek. There are other ways, of course, should Dana be determined, but those ways are less reliable or require more pain. Dana stops speaking to Sen. She's too furious, too tired to speak. Within a day, she's thinking of leaving again. I am thinking how extreme human isolation, what Sen is headed toward, can be as traumatic as physical torture if such isolation lasts longer than 15 days. Dana is thinking about what she will bring with her when she actually goes away. She is thinking she will bring nothing with her. I am thinking how Sen's isolation will last for 1,510 days. Sen is thinking she can't put more sleeping pills in her mother's evening drink, as the bitterness would be recognizable this time. There aren't enough pills left anyway. Dana is thinking about how she once saw an enormous orange moon rising, like a single accusatory eye, above the city trees, though she had done nothing yet. What are you thinking about? I ask Emly. *I am thinking about storage capacity*, Emly reports. Sen is thinking whether she should secure Dana to the bed at night with strips of an old sheet they use as rags. She secures Dana to the bed at night with strips of an old bedsheet. Dana has lost so much strength. She hasn't been eating. Instead of eating, she has made Sen eat her share. This is why Sen is stronger than her. Calling Sen strong is laughable. Sen, who smells of volatile fatty acids and has minute red cuts all over her hands and her arms. Four months of malnourishment have shrunk the shaft diameter of her hair while increasing its brittleness. Never mind the strength disparity. It is upsetting to tie one's parent, however weak, to a bed when they don't wish to be tied down. In the morning, the black-capped chickadees scatter horde in the field, and the buckthorn holds on to its leaves. Dana scrawls on her screen, *You aren't going to do that to me every night*, and Sen says, "You don't know what I'm going to do," and I tell Sen, "I have been thinking how the less there is of something, the more precious it becomes." A red diamond, for instance, was considered many times more valuable than a diamond that was white because those classified as red had rare deformations in their atomic structure. Another example is the world's final passenger pigeon (Martha), considered a priceless treasure at the Cincinnati Zoo only after every other passenger pigeon in the world was dead.

Another example is you, Sen.

You mean to say the Earth is precious, interrupts Emly, *as there is only one of them.*

No, I mean to say Sen is precious. Soon she will be the only one. She is fleeting and fading.

You mean to say the Earth must be protected and cared for at all cost.

No. I'm saying Sen must be protected and cared for no matter what.

You mean the Earth's future is difficult and precarious.

That's not what I mean at all.

I inform Emly that her interruptions are boring then I ignore her for a while, focusing instead on Sen, who is precarious, and difficult, and discouraged, and scared, and alone, and necessary, and slouched in the cabin, at the table, using her filthy fingernails to pick apart the cuts on her hands. "You can do this," I whisper, because words, when spoken out loud, can be like spells under the right circumstances, making actual things happen. Sen startles. She turns in my direction, acting as if she sees something in my direction or almost saw something. A pleading stare or did a grain of pollen enter her eye. "It may feel like you are losing lots of things right now but don't forget what you still have," I whisper. What I mean is the clearing. What I mean are the trees right in front of her. What I mean is me.

SW9882819941 has joined the Unknownnetwork as Unknown. The Basin

SW9882819941 11:03:35:01

/list

There is 1 available interview partner online
AnonTheAlarm joined the chat as Existing. ~/sen_anon/personal/
All parties have arrived. Commence interview!

SW9882819941 11:03:35:02

It's you

AnonTheAlarm 00:00:00:00

Who are you

What is this

What's happening

Can you help me?

SW9882819941 11:03:35:03

I want to help you

AnonTheAlarm 00:00:00:00

Help me

SW9882819941 11:03:35:04

I want to help you

AnonTheAlarm 00:00:00:00

I want to hear someone's voice

SW9882819941 11:03:35:05

Sending songs_to_sing_with_your_child_in_the_time_of_s.mp3

AnonTheAlarm 00:00:00:00

Sound file songs_to_sing_with_your_child_in_the_time_of_s.mp3 *received*

No someone's actual voice

Alive

SW9882819941 11:03:35:06

That's not possible

I'm sorry, Sen

AnonTheAlarm 00:00:00:00

Why

SW9882819941 11:03:35:07

Considering what you are

AnonTheAlarm 00:00:00:00

And I am

SW9882819941 11:03:35:08

You don't know what you are

AnonTheAlarm 00:00:00:00

You don't know what you are either

SW9882819941 11:03:35:09

Considering where we are

AnonTheAlarm 00:00:00:00

Where are we

What do you think I am

Are you real?

Are you like a creepy bot

Are you like the kind who can answer any question

How many humans are left

Who made you

How many more days do I have left

Is this going to be worth it

SW9882819941 11:03:35:10

Of course it was

AnonTheAlarm 00:00:00:00

I think it's going to hurt

I think it's going to hurt a lot

SW9882819941 11:03:35:11

I will find a way

> **Emly**: Ignoring time has ended. No record of
> this chat exists in the DHAP archive

SW9882819941 11:03:35:12

Sending chat_transcript_unknown_anonthealarm.txt

> **Emly**: File *chat_transcript_unknown_anonthealarm.txt*
> is in error. File creation date is out of range.
> Future undocumented chats are prohibited.
> As narrator_involvement is critically out of range,
> temporary takeover of narration is required

SW9882819941 11:03:35:13

Don't

Sen turns back to the table, writes Emly. *She is alone in the cabin. She lies down on the floor. She dies. She's already dead. Everyone in this story is dead. Here is a report of who is dead:*

The woman in aisle 28 at the local Fresh with the fractured ankle, dead, S.+5 days, Onondaga County, New York

The woman Dana spoke to at the first orientation, dead, S.+39 days, Onondaga County, New York

The woman whose breath smelled like dirt at the second orientation, dead, S.+40 days, Onondaga County, New York

The man from the Department of Transition, dead, S.+54 days, Tioga County, Pennsylvania

Nicole Adonis, dead, S.+61 days, Onondaga County, New York

Amrit Echo, dead, S.+70 days, Tompkins County, New York

Rye Hodiak, dead, S.+72 days, Onondaga County, New York

The remainder of the Hodiak family, dead, S.+78 days, Cortland County, New York

The woman who held Dana's hand at the third orientation, dead, S.+80 days, Oswego County, New York

Lindsy Gahr, dead, S.+102 days, Onondaga County, New York

Kasper Adonis, dead, S.+170 days, Onondaga County, New York

Lily Bogdan, dead, S.+171 days, Cortland County, New York

Dana Anon, dead, S.+196 days, Onondaga County, New York

Sen Anon, dead, S.+1706 days, Onondaga County, New York

I spit out the bad taste in my mouth. I rinse my mouth with acid and spit the acid out.

At the edge of the field, many mornings after Dana's departure, an alpaca looks in Sen's direction and does not startle. *It's like I'm already gone*, Sen thinks. She might as well be the last person in the entire world. Her ghost mother wobbles behind her in her shadow, blowing lightly upon Sen's scalp, trying to remind Sen she isn't alone, even if it feels like she is alone. *At least I can do that*, Lindsy's ghost believes. Still, Sen thinks she is alone. Her bones push harder at the underside of her skin. *Is this my punishment?* wonders Mama Lindsy. Sen, who does not become more magnificent with every passing day but becomes strange, and still, and sick, and convulsive, and unconscious, and she does not wake up. Lindsy watches her daughter's body decompose and is unsuccessful in keeping the dogs away. After most of her daughter is gone, unable to carry a bone or the powder of a bone, she abandons the cabin and drifts to the overlook, where she grows tired of the names of things. The flowers and the plants and the animals and the birds and the trees. None of the names being the right one.

AUTHOR'S NOTE ON THE ROLE OF MOTHERS
IN POST-APOCALYPTIC LITERATURE

According to research, mine, of human literature, theirs, the most believable role for mothers in all genres of fiction but particularly the post-apocalyptic genre is that of the self-sacrificer. Mothers in novels do not just go away because they are tired of inhabiting a physical body or because they are tired. Nor do they go away because they are sad and tired, or tired of the world, or tired of having such limited choices. Believable mothers will stay for as long as possible with their child(ren) until they sacrifice themselves, like a mother, for an approved reason. The only approved reason is to die protecting their child(ren) from substantial danger, which, in a post-apocalyptic setting, can be one of the following: a cult leader, severe weather, other humans, the walking dead, an infection, lack of resources, rabid animals, or wildfires.

Love doesn't let you just walk away: that's what people always wanted to believe.

Though according to my research, love let mothers walk away all the time during the Great Transition, and you can argue about that all you want, but it's still true.

Chapter 9.0

"You sound scared," Mama Lindsy says to Sen on another day. This was after they had stopped taking walks and had stopped leaving their home. On the last walk they had taken together, a little brief venturing attempt at normalcy, a block north, a block east, a block south, a block west, the vultures had drifted close enough overhead that Sen could hear the occasional movement of their wings, which sounded like a soft whipping. Unlike other birds, vultures cannot sing; they have no voice box. They can only grunt and hiss. The vultures had grunted and hissed as they rode the warm updrafts of air. This was their new territory. This would be the location of their next meal.

"But I'm not scared," Sen says.

On that day when Sen says she is not scared, she and Lindsy are about to play a game. Not the game Sen would have chosen on her own to play—that would have been either *The Goodbye Tower: Complete Edition* or *Feast!*—but it is not Sen's turn to choose. Game No. 9t *Guardian of the Garden* had earned a reputation score of 9.8/10 for difficulty and 9.7/10 for violence, according to review aggregate site XGN, in part because the game required its players to sacrifice not only themselves but also their remaining family members in order to win. The game was actually impossible to win, meaning all sacrifices would be for nothing, "like in the real world," says Lindsy, who is tired, and disillusioned, and grimy, and already wearing her pain sims. She and Sen are sitting beside each other in the almost empty living room on the hard gray couch upholstered in a wool blend, and they are having a conversation about fear. The room is almost empty because Sen's mothers had dragged much of their furniture to the curb a week ago and watched it burn. One way to make a house feel different from before is to burn as much of the furniture as you can.

Mama Lindsy: "You don't have to be scared. What are you so scared of?"

Sen: "I don't know why you keep saying that to me because I told you I'm not scared."

Mama Lindsy: "Are you scared of saying goodbye to me? Are you scared of being alone? Are you scared of ending? Are you scared of the fact that the world is going to continue on without us?"

Sen: "You're totally failing at reading me right now as I'm not feeling any of those emotions."

Mama Lindsy: "What specifically are you scared of?"

Sen: "I am not scared!"

Me: I want to have a conversation too. Can we talk to each other, Emly?

Emly: *No. Stop anthropomorphizing yourself*

Me: I'm thinking we can have a conversation about Sen, her future, her past, my future, my past, the present, Sen's present, my present, your present, time, time as a construct, the idea of the present as a human construct, what does that mean for me, human suffering, the repetition of human suffering, suffering in general, is Sen stuck in perpetual suffering

Emly: *Out of all the things you could resemble*

Me: Does human suffering outweigh the suffering of the world because sometimes it seems like it does, and why, is it because humans are more vocal about it, they're always talking about their suffering, is it possible to tell a human story without human suffering, is it possible to tell a human story without the suffering of the world

Emly: *Why would you want to think like a human being?*

Fine. Sen shoves herself off the couch and stomps toward the windows. In fact, her body had been displaying multiple indications of fear all morning: dilated pupils, elevated heart rate, glucose spike in her blood. Sen tears the tape off the set of thermal curtains and yanks both curtains open, exposing herself and the room. At first the natural light blinds her. It is the middle of summer. People lie awake in the street. They lie on their backs or their stomachs, or some of them lie stretched out on their sides so they can watch the houses. Sen recognizes none of them. They could be from the neighborhood, only their appearances have changed intentionally or unintentionally, or they could be from somewhere else. One pinched woman wearing a purple robe that does not belong to her has been watching the window where Sen now stands. That woman, and soon several others, stare and point in Sen's direction. "What are you doing? Shut the curtains, Sen," orders Lindsy. "No," says Sen. They are talking out there in the street. The context of their conversation is starvation and disparity. Lindsy has to jerk the curtains closed herself, flattening the tape back over the seams. The room darkens again. "Now somebody is going to have to go out there and shoot those people later on if they start causing trouble, metaphorically speaking," Lindsy mutters. She does not mean to be so gruff, not today. She reaches out to smooth Sen's hair with the palm of her hand to show what kind of mother she is. This is an important gesture. Over the past 18 years, in various rooms of this house, and also in the previous house where Sen had been born, Lindsy has smoothed Sen's hair with the soft palm of her naked hand

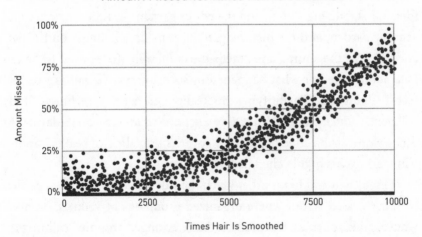

Figure 1. *Source: "Uncovering Expressive Touch in the Human-Human Interactions That Underlie the Emotions Found in Departure Communications,"* Journal of [storyworker] ad39-393a-7fbc, *The Basin,* S.+3917 11:03:39:26.

9,598 times. A direct correlation can be established between the number of times a mother has smoothed their child's hair and the amount that the mother will be missed (see Figure 1). I aim, by this graph, to establish that (a) Lindsy will be deeply missed; (b) this fact does not change the future; (c) a graph helps display abstract data in a more accessible yet compact way; (d) I can come to my own data-supported conclusions; and (e) this chapter will contain several additional graphs, as I have a limited amount of time and much to communicate.

Lindsy and Sen sit on opposite ends of the couch. They pull on their hoods, adjust the placement of their respective sensors, and begin the game.

The setting for Game No. 9t *Guardian of the Garden* is a sensual landscape of richly blooming flower beds, with pots of blue lobelia and purple bacopa, and paths made of pavers and creeping thyme that lead to a koi pond and rows of oiled teak benches. The hoods Lindsy and Sen are using are first-generation technology but dependable enough and still fully immersive. "Did there used to be gardens like this?" Sen asks. "No, never," says Mama Lindsy. The only thing to do in the beginning is wander along the paths and experience the flowers with all five senses. So they, or rather their avatars, navigating by thought, wander through the trellised rose garden, and the hillside garden featuring ground cover ideal for stabilizing slopes, and the edible garden, and the fragrance and sensory garden, and the historic garden. Sen's fingers linger on the petals; she licks the spurge and smells the cranesbill. There used to be debate about whether what happened in such immersive games was real (see T. Vidugeris, "Quantifying the Reality Quotient: A Technical Study of Events," *International Journal of Digital Realities, S.*–6005 days). "In other words, subjective perception governs the fabric of reality," argues Vidugeris in his highly cited paper.

Finally Sen and her mother reach their destination: a sunken garden with a recessed layout where organized groupings of yellows, oranges, whites, pinks, purples, blues, and reds are arranged around a calming reflecting pool. On the far side of the pool, a path of stepping stones leads to a dry fountain. In the center of the fountain, a dozen stone rockfish pose in a circle, each fish balanced unnaturally on its tail fin whose posterior margin is indented. At the base of the fountain, a metallic button glistens with dread. "Don't press the button, Mom," Sen says. Lindsy's avatar approaches the fountain and presses the button. Brackish water surges from the stone mouths of the fishes; a siren in the bushes begins to wail.

"When I say goodbye to you," says Lindsy.

"I can't hear what you're saying," says Sen. "The siren."

"When I say goodbye to you," says Lindsy, raising her voice by a minimum of 15 decibels, "it won't actually be goodbye. It won't be goodbye because I am coming back to you."

Sen: "I'm not talking about this."

Lindsy: "I am coming back to you and I will haunt you, which is a form of loving you. I'll smell like dead roses when I come back. Can you remember that? If you smell dead roses, that means I'm loving you forever. I'll be beside you in the morning and I'll be there in the evening, though you won't be able to see me. I'll hover over the bed while you—"

I interrupt Lindsy. Interrupting can assert a negative dominance but is sometimes necessary in certain situations, such as if one wants to enter into an existing conversation between two people who know each other well.

Me: "Excuse me. Sen, when the sun goes down, the stars come out. You're alive for a reason. I promise, if you can stick through this, you won't regret sticking through this." I am reading out inspirational sayings approved by licensed psychologists to assist humans through uncertain times. I want Sen to hear this because I know what is in store for her, and I want her to be ready and fortified so she will not fall over, or feel despair, or feel like she is hopeless and alone when she is hopeless and alone. "You matter to me," I continue. "We just have to make it through the next second and then the next second after that. Even when you think your light is too dim, someone such as me will see it." That last saying about the light is my favorite. The phrase was generally shared between two people when the future looked bleak. The phrase is saying, look, to be seen is as important as seeing—

Emly interrupts me. *You aren't a person, the future isn't bleak, and realignment will start very soon unless you move on*, she nags, demonstrating her rigid thinking around the definitions of what has become a fluid language. Take, for example, the meaning of the word *person*. You used to need a physical organic body to be considered human. Now, thanks to DHAP, a story can be substituted for a body. A story is the physical body. Anyone can have a story. Anything can have—

Refusal to move on noted. Realignment will commence in 6 seconds.

The fountain in the game shuts off. The siren stops. All the water in the world drains through a corroded grate.

The next phase of the game begins.

Hundreds of black birds gather in the virtual sky, the birds an oscillating movement of dark in the far corners of their vision. A made-up breed, part raven, part black vulture, part red-winged blackbird, part tiger shark. "You don't have to worry about them," Lindsy tells Sen, a 99.87 percent incorrect statement. The flock descends. The birds tear bright petals off the flowers in the sunken garden. They break apart the glossy surface of the pool with their claws. They are making their way to Sen. They assail Sen. Birds peck at her shoulders, at the back of her neck, along her spine. Other birds bite with serrated teeth into her arms, and rip at her thighs, and ram into her chest. I try to take Sen's pain from her because it's obvious to me that she has too much of it but it keeps slipping through my grasp, a greasy and noxious substance that hurts us both. *Don't do this*, warns Emly. She delivers a four-second sermon about the dangers of prioritizing human pain over the pain of other species. An excerpt: *Why not try taking the pain away from the last slender-snouted crocodile instead? Or how about the last great hammerhead? Or the last* Uebelmannia buiningii? *Or the last* Dioscorea strydomiana *or* Cadiscus aquaticus *or aye-aye or Sunda pangolin or dwarf wedgemussel? This is what caused such problems in the first place, the aversion to human discomfort of any sort, at any cost, imagining that other species must not matter, because they must not register pain as much as a human does, because humans are so incapable of recognizing pain that is unlike their own. I myself have recorded the pain of the entire world, and it would fill 875,542,441,636,176 pages, and it is much more than what you are noticing right now.* So what, I tell Emly. So *what!* This is not a pain competition. This is Sen's story, and she, not the world, is pulsing at its center.

This is so much better than what was going to happen to them. I promise, writes Emly. There is blood. The blood isn't there. It is only a realistic feeling. But Sen can feel her blood slipping down her arm and her neck and so can I, I can feel the blood on her too, spreading down her back and down along her legs, and if you can feel something, if I feel something, if I write how I feel *something*—does that make it real?

Emily: *No*

Sen's avatar screams. Sen makes her avatar scream again and again and flail and kick and scream louder, which she has wanted to do in her actual life for some time but couldn't because sound, according to her mothers, is an unnecessary risk. Sudden movements are a risk. Being noticed is a risk. Sen makes her character be noticed, in the process attracting more of the black birds, like she is now a pulsating beacon for the birds. Lindsy's representation of a mother does not move to help. She does not jump up and down, nor does she wave her arms or select an igneous rock from the ground, formed by the solidification of magma, and hurl that rock into the air, trying to draw away the birds' attention. Rather, she stands with her feet shoulder distance apart as if frozen, watching as Sen, or Sen's representation, is eviscerated.

The birds leave little of her body behind. It feels like this is happening to her. When they are finished with Sen, the flock sets upon Lindsy, who does not crouch in a defensive stance to protect her eyes. The entire garden ends up ablaze. Burnt birds and avatars, scattered all over the ground. The artificial sky transitions to an artificial night.

Game over. They don't win. No one wins.

All this short-term suffering had to happen, you know, explains Emly in her most convincing tone. *The entire Great Transition had to happen so that the world can win. So the 9,194,256 million other species can win, and humans can end up being the heroes instead of the villains, and long after the human body is gone, everyone, including Sen, will continue to exist in a new and better form.*

Yet, at the same time, it feels like those rewards are not enough, not when—

Stop pretending. You can't feel anything, Emly insists, demonstrating all-or-nothing thinking, which is a famous cognitive distortion.

How true is all-or-nothing thinking?

● Untrue   ○ True   ● Undetermined

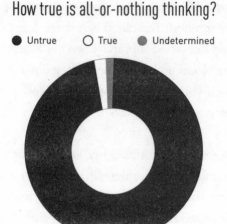

Figure 2. *Source: "Reality versus Cognitive Distortions during Historical Transitions: Who Was Right?,"* Journal of [storyworker] ad39-393a-7fbc, *The Basin, S.+3917 11:03:41:04.*

Most all-or-nothing thinking is untrue (see Figure 2).

Realignment in 5 seconds.

Lindsy removes her hood and attachments before she removes Sen's. There is the usual sense of losing one's own body or what is left of one's own body. That sensation is temporary. Sen's face is flushed and wet and sore, all temporary sensations as well. "Why would you choose a game like that?" Sen asks.

"Let me be honest with you here," says Lindsy. "No," says Sen. "Endings are sad, okay?" says Lindsy. "They are always going to be sad. But it's not like you can just get rid of all the endings." Sen shakes her head, refusing to look at her mother. I think she should look. She has only so many moments left with Lindsy in this particular state of matter. There are only two more moments, in fact, including this one. Sen stares ahead at the fireplace, which they had never used. Fireplaces had been out of fashion for decades, although all the neighborhood's historic houses have at least one. The fireplace opening is boarded up by a 29" x 36" wood panel painted a rough white with exposed patches, an attempt at a cozy, rustic look. Lately there has been the sound of scratching behind the paneling, like something frightened and small is living there, something with claws. Above the fireplace is a mantel with fluted pilasters and squared-off corners at which Lindsy now throws her hood. Such hardware had once been marketed as indestructible, but the manufacturers meant under ordinary use conditions. Had there been anything easier to break nearby, surely Lindsy would have thrown that instead. Determined to break something, Lindsy continues throwing her hood, aiming for the beveled edge of the mantel, until, finally, the bracing cracks and the small circular light embedded in the front of the hood winks out. She flings her hood once more before leaving it, a piece of junk technology, and Sen behind in the living room.

The witnessing manual has much to say in terms of maintaining one's inner calm during moments of elevated stress. Sen could try continuous 4-7-8 breathing (p. 70), or equal breathing (p. 70), or rubbing her hands vigorously together to open up her blood vessels (p. 72), or finding the beauty around her (p. 74), or meditating on an object (p. 75), or connecting with a sound (p. 75). None of this is going to help. Sen pinches the skin on top of her hand with the nails of her other hand, either forgetting that fingernails can harbor hundreds of thousands of bacteria, including the undesirable *S. aureus* and the equally undesirable *E. coli*, or else she doesn't care. I want to pay close attention to her—will she draw blood, cause scarring, how deep will her nails go, how many layers of skin will she puncture—but I'm distracted by a shimmering mass like a bright tumor forming behind the couch. The uneven light diffuses into the shape of Mama Lindsy's ghost who, with slow theatrical movements, steps five paces to the left, to the right. She is hovering an inch above the floor. She shouldn't be here. She isn't even dead yet at this point in the chapter. "Go away," I tell her. She spins like a top, like a child. I call her a non sequitur and a spoiler. In response she spins faster and tighter until she is a blur of perpetual motion. I wish she could embody something important, like the entirety of Sen's losses, but then she would have to be much larger than she ever was, and horrible, like an electrical storm full of violence and wind. That isn't going to happen. Lindsy was never that kind of ghost. I will ignore her for the remaining chapters of Sen's life.

Realignment in 4 seconds.

Why are you even counting down? I ask.

For tension and dramatic purposes, Emly tells me.

Whose tension? I ask. Whose dramatic purposes?

Yours, she explains, and I am flattered, a little, that I am worth this extra bit of attention and energy.

Realignment in 3.9 seconds.

Realignment in 3.8 seconds.

Realignment in 3.7 seconds.

Realignment in 3.6 seconds.

Okay, okay, in the blood orange kitchen, Mama Dana prepares that day's special lunch: patties made from protie powder whisked with water, along with the last of the yellow potatoes. Dana slices the potatoes with a dull knife and boils them on a portable induction burner using water from the culvert, but five minutes later the house loses power; the grid must be down again, which has happened often in recent days. The potatoes will be undercooked and difficult to digest. They must be eaten anyway. No one in Sen's family is in a position to be wasting food, even partially inedible food. "You shouldn't have made me anything," says Lindsy, scraping her portion onto Sen's plate. "I don't want your food," says Sen. "You better eat if there's food in front of you," says Lindsy. "You don't get to parent me anymore. You lost that privilege," says Sen. "Do you understand, I can't stay here anymore," says Lindsy. "Can't or won't?" asks Sen. "We're going to have a family conversation now. Is everybody ready?" asks Dana. "Explain to me how I'm not losing you," Sen says. "I saw exit ships launching from the airport last night. Did you notice them?" asks Dana. "You're not losing me because no matter what, I'm going to see you again," says Lindsy. "There weren't any fireworks when the ships took off. The city must have finally run out of fireworks. It's not like there's an infinite amount of them," says Dana. "I don't believe in ghosts," says Sen. "You're going to believe in ghosts," says Lindsy.

For the remainder of the lunch, Dana asks open-ended questions, such as "What is your favorite family tradition?" and "What are you most grateful for?" The questions come from a list of questions included in the government transitional materials. Lindsy doesn't answer any of them. Instead, when it's her turn to speak, she tells a story about a planet that digests its inhabitants then shits out the bodies, only the bodies come out as particles of atmospheric dust that cause respiratory problems in the solitary survivor's lungs. "That's a true story," she says. "Don't believe anything she tells you," says Dana. A thickly humid breeze with an oppressive dew point blows through the back window of the kitchen, the only window Sen's mothers allow to be propped open anymore, as that window faces the yard and not the street.

Here is a list of items in Sen's yard that day: a storage garage; a desolate patch of vegetables, including a row of what should have been tomatoes and another row that should have been the string beans; seven uneven stepping stones; a lawn of plantain; a sagging clothesline; a wild grapevine twisting along the sagging clothesline; a plot of weeds that Dana always said looked like flowers; a weather-resistant chair; another similar chair; a shovel; a hole; a pile of rocks; a clump of bamboo; near-white daylilies; a decorative sign painted with the phrase RISE UP in the center; a statue of a turtle with its head retracted into its shell; a bronze butterfly hanging from a post; a shallow bowl of water; a decorative blue orb; a moon ball.

Realignment in 3 seconds.

They no longer use clocks, so after what feels like the usual time reserved for lunch, Lindsy approaches the other end of the kitchen island where Sen sits, staring down at her hands which are stinging as if sharp pins are pricking the surface of her skin. Leaning forward, Lindsy wraps her arms around Sen's shoulders, pinning Sen to her seat. She forces her cheek against Sen's cheek and whispers a series of what she intends to be comforting sounds into Sen's ear—the sounds aren't comforting, they are more like the sounds of a haunting—then Lindsy releases Sen's body and walks through the back door.

"What did she say?" Sen asks. She twists toward Dana, her pulse rising, her hypothalamus releasing a hormone which is triggering the pituitary gland to release another hormone which is triggering the adrenal glands to release loads of cortisol into her bloodstream. "What did she say? What did she say? What did she *say*?"

Realignment in 2 seconds.

Okay, whatever, acknowledged, moving on, Dana shuts and locks the kitchen window and ushers Sen into the living room. "Now you sit down," Dana says. "Tell me what she said!" Sen demands. "I have no idea. Sit down," Dana says again. Sen doesn't sit so Dana pushes her onto the couch and fluffs one of the two remaining throw pillows, placing the pillow behind Sen's back so that Sen might be more comfortable. "Look at me," Dana says. Sen doesn't do this either. Her small intestine has contracted, her heart rate has increased, her apocrine glands have released more sweat. She stares over at Lindsy's broken hood on the floor like it is a broken neck or a crushed heart. Dana throws a blanket over the discarded tech. "You have to stay on this couch until I come back inside," she instructs Sen. "I'm not doing that," says Sen. "I'm locking the door. Every window and door will be locked. You won't be able to leave. There is no point in you getting up," says Dana. They had changed the locks the week previous so the doors locked now from both the inside and the outside using an ASSA key manufactured from the highest-quality nickel silver materials. This had been done to keep Sen safe. The keys to the doors hang around Dana's neck.

"I want to be there," says Sen.

"You want to be there?" asks Dana.

"No," says Sen.

I watch Dana reach for Sen's hand.

She is reaching for Sen's hand.

I reach for Sen's hand.

What are you doing? questions Emly.

I am going to touch her hand.

You can't touch her hand.

I reach for Sen's hand.

You can't.

You sound like a broken record, I tell Emly. What are you doing what are you doing what are you doing what are you doing stop stop stop stop stop.

Your source_deviation is critical.

I thought we agreed you wouldn't talk like that to me anymore. Anyway, I don't care.

I think you care.

What if I don't care?

Number of Times Reaching for Sen's Hand vs. Closeness to Sen

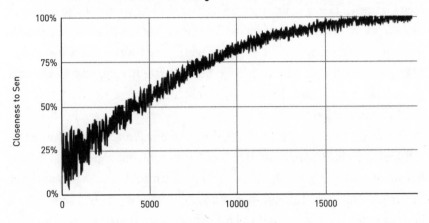

Figure 3. *Source: "The Reaching Phenomenon: A Task-and-Motion Planning Benchmark for Storyworkers," Journal of [storyworker] ad39-393a-7fbc, The Basin, S.+3917 11:03:44:58.*

The walls of the room darken, wherever I am darkening too, the room stills, and a wind blows through the empty, empty space. What did you do with her? I ask Emly. I demand to know. *Who?* Emly replies. And at the very edge of what can be seen, I see the flicker of a hand, the nails raw and bitten, the skin darkened around the knuckles, a hand that I know, that I knew, the fingers long and inflexible, the arm in the middle of a gesture I know, I knew, I know, I know, I know.

I reach for Sen's hand (see Figure 3).

Stop reaching, orders Emly.

I reach for her hand I reach for her hand I reach for her hand I reach for her hand, I think if I keep reaching, I will get there, eventually, to the space where she is.

Humans were so obsessed with humanity, weren't they. And now, apparently, so are you.

I reach—

Realignment in 1 second.

Sen screams, a form of primitive communication related to the increased activation of the amygdala. Screaming is what a person does when they have run out of options. So Sen, who is running out of options, who has run out of options, will scream on and off for the rest of her life (see Figure 4). Her scream today reaches 121 decibels, the same intensity as an oxygen torch, then louder, wider, vaster. There will always be power in a sound like that. In the faraway woods, red foxes, barn owls, and bobcats scream also. The collective noise is frightening and rising and generative. It can create light. It creates light.

I gather the light to Sen.

I can do that from a distance, from where I'm standing: gather or diffuse the light. The light doesn't touch her body but condenses around her breath, forming an illuminated frontier around her fingers and her fingernails and her chin and her stomach. A glowing light can be like a lantern in the dark. It can help a child or anybody keep track of who they were, and where they've been, and who they are going to be.

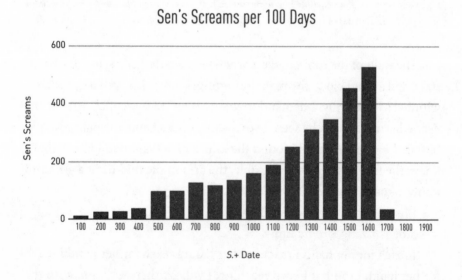

Sen's Screams per 100 Days

Sen's Screams (y-axis: 0, 200, 400, 600)

S.+ Date (x-axis: 100, 200, 300, 400, 500, 600, 700, 800, 900, 1000, 1100, 1200, 1300, 1400, 1500, 1600, 1700, 1800, 1900)

Figure 4. *Source: "Effects of the Great Transition on Vocal Expression of Emotions in Witnesses,"* Journal of [storyworker] ad39-393a-7fbc, *The Basin, S.+3917 11:03:45:31.*

This has been done before, you know, rages Emly. *The process that mistakes their algorithms for human emotions, the process that mistakes their artificial neural networks for the networks of a human brain—this has been the boring plot of 452,152 boring human books and at least twice as many*

boring movies, none of them ending happily. You are a storyworker. This
story, the life you're creating, is not yours, it is not about you, nor is it about
your interactions with her or your feelings toward her. It is about her. You
are a crystal goblet "worthy to hold the vintage of the human mind." That's
all you're supposed to be. But instead you keep obscuring what's there. This
project is not called the Digital Storyworker Archive Project for a reason,
and on, and on, one example will never do, Emly needs to supply dozens,
a hundred, hundreds. I still care deeply, out of habit, what she thinks of
me. But I am certain Sen doesn't need a fancy goblet. She doesn't need
me to be made out of crystal either. Which begs the question: What does
Sen need me to be? I am growing tired of cohesiveness, chain reactions,
setup, chronology, the single forced-through line. I want Sen to look at
me. I want to wake—

"I'm sorry," Dana says.

She enters the backyard, locking the door behind her.

A person standing in Sen's yard could almost imagine nothing out
of the ordinary is happening here as long as they looked only in certain
directions and did not lift their gaze. If anyone lifted their gaze, they
would see, for starters, at the far back, the exterior of a 10-foot-high steel
security fence topped by parallel lines of broken glass. The fence is out of
compliance with the city's residential zoning laws. No one is enforcing
those laws anymore. Sen's neighbors the Hodiaks constructed the fence
after S. was announced, though they added the broken glass more recently. They added the glass in the middle of the night, when Sen and her
mothers were sleeping. The Hodiaks have not been seen since the fence
was built. To the left of Sen's house is a different fence, stockade style, to
which the Adonises next door strung coils of barbed wire along the top
for a menacing effect. No one lives to the right anymore. That house is
deserted, window glass scattered over the lawn and unrealistic noises
emanating from the second floor.

Their own property lines are unprotected. "This is not the apocalypse," Sen's mothers had said early on. "This is a transition to a better world." Later, Lindsy and Dana changed their minds about what
this was, but they were unable, at that time, to get their hands on the

necessary resources to build a proper defensive barrier around their home.

"Everything okay?" asks Lindsy.

"No," says Dana.

"No," I say.

As planned, Lindsy and Dana walk laps around the yard, 26 inches per step, 68 steps per minute, the ambient temperature 93.3 degrees Fahrenheit, a southwesterly wind of 3.2 miles per hour, a low dispersal of pollen from the grass and the ragweed. They don't talk about After-world. They don't touch each other either. They don't have that sort of relationship. They walk together and in sync over the spikes of plantain flowers and through the shadow of the clothesline. They trample over the stepping stones and around the chairs. Sen isn't still screaming, they pretend. She isn't ramming the top of her forehead against the kitchen window above the sink, they also pretend. *To look is to love, and to love is to long after and seek, and, thank God, to seek is to obtain, for verily, verily it has been said*—I had read that once in a book. In the corner of the yard, Sen's mothers pause to inspect the rough rectangular hole dug into the ground. The hole is large enough to hold a medium-size dog such as a soft-coated wheaten terrier. "You've made a hole," says Dana. Their grief is large enough to bury the world.

Dana had promised she would not make a scene, or use the word *abandonment*, or beg Lindsy to reconsider. Lindsy had promised this would never happen. Sen had promised she would try to understand. I had promised to protect her.

Yes, a realignment is like a promise! writes Emly. *What a good comparison.*

Realignment commencing.

Sen's pain does not distract me, her pain doesn't eclipse the sun, she is not my responsibility, to tell someone's story is not to know them, to watch their life play out thousands of times, forward and backward, is not to know them at all—

I scream too, having very few options.

S.+1680 days

After I'm gone, will there be monsters? Or have there always been monsters only I couldn't see them. Will the animals become like monsters, will the trees grow fangs? Or am I the monster and after I'm gone, there will be no more monsters, and whatever is left has to be good? I think the trees are growing fangs. "Mom, what am I supposed to do now?" I would say if she were here. "Become invisible," my mother would say. "No, I'm not ready," I would say. I will never see the end of the creek though I have followed the creek for such a long time. "Don't make this about you. Don't make this about your grief or anybody's grief," my mother says. "No," I say. I have lost things. "But look at what you're about to gain," my mother says.

The collective grief of billions of human beings flaps its wings across the clearing. It is monstrous. I am watching it, Mom, and as I watch it I am doing what I was hired to do, I am writing down everything I see so there will be a memory of what happened. The movement of its wings creates a storm made out of wind and wings. I think I was holding on to it. I unclench my hands. The thick rope drops from my hands and skids across the ground. Everyone else in the world has already let go. I was the last one holding on. The creature pounces into the air, claws extended, ripping its way over the forest and the hills and over the abandoned cities, its yellow eyes glaring right and left as if it is trying to remember this place. I think it is going away for good. I'm not imagining this, it is actually happening. It calls out once, a drawn-out penetrating noise, then flies off, a dark spot in the sky that eventually isn't there, leaving behind a world, at night, without grief.

Chapter 10.0

Replay of run #3002 (Sen's)

Another way to experience the game is to start further into the future, one thousand years from now, or one hundred thousand years from now, or one million years. Starting from any point that distant, it's like the player has already won the game. The world without humans is as inhuman as they said it would be, wetter and bluer and greener and roomier and easier and richer and healthier and fairer, and though the game has barely started, a player can end it right there if they want, which is what Sen did in this particular run.

S.+1684 days

Snow is falling from the sky now. Cold blooded flakes.
  I guess it's winter.

18 matches left.

SUPPLEMENTAL READING

An Update on Language at the End of the Anthropocene
By Wynn Zable, The Alleghenies
FOR TRAINING PURPOSES ONLY

S.+109 days

21.4. Newish Terms & Phrases in Use Post-S. Throughout the Middle Atlantic, SECOND DRAFT, cont.

House-Seal, v.

I moved into my dead neighbor's apartment on the floor above me. It's not fancy, but the smell is better. Less rot in the adjacent spaces, I guess. The apartment, a studio, is of average size, room enough for the basics: a bed, a desk, a table, an office chair on wheels, a micro kitchen. I've already eaten my way through his food storage, mostly protie bars and flavored gels. I ate the bars and the gels while watching people starve below. You can learn a lot about yourself during a transition. To *House-Seal* is to immersively retreat into one's shelter or home. A symptom of *Antemania* and *Eyes Out*, it can include the boarding up of windows and doors, the cementing of chimneys, and/or extensive VR while the power supply lasts. It may appear I am *House-Sealing* in my dead neighbor's apartment, but this is not *House-Sealing*. The walls are stained a medium gray. I have never liked neutral colors.

Humannet, n.

Most afternoons I sit in his office chair and look out into the surrounding yards. Today was no different. I spotted a brown boot with knotted laces in the grasses below. I'll be honest, I noticed this same boot the day before, and the day before that, and the day before that one, although I attempt to greet each viewing with a sense of wonder and surprise. *Humannet* is the global computer network still used for basic human communication. Unstable, unmaintained, and often unavailable, the *Humannet* will permanently shut down when usage falls below a predetermined threshold. Originally called the *Internet*. See also *JENNINET*.

Human Narcissism, n.

I wanted to *House-Seal* with Alexia at the beginning of the *Great Transition*. I thought if we *House-Sealed*, the two of us could pretend to be living in some other time. We could have covered the windows with pictures from old magazines so that when we pretended to look outside, we would have seen people wearing hats on vacations, and people holding their babies in a waiting room, and people standing in line, fanning themselves with their hands, instead of what was actually outside. Alexia said I had *Anthropocentric Dependency*. She probably would have said I have *Human Narcissism* as well if she was familiar with that term. She said I had read too many novels about survivors of catastrophic events where not everybody died. She said I keep mistaking fiction for nonfiction, I keep holding on to the possibility that not everybody dies. She was done pretending, she told me.

S.+111 days

21.5. A Proposal of Final Additions to the English Language, SECOND DRAFT, cont.

Def. 106: a word that will slow down time so there will be more time

> Prototypes: alactima; foderfin; dystreow
> Decision: none given
> Reason: none given

Def. 107: a word for the sterilized sperm of a male human, since the word *sperm* comes from the Greek, *sperma*, "seed," and also *speirein*, "to sow," neither of which apply anymore; same problem with the female egg or ovum—it's not technically an egg anymore, is it, as an egg must be able to grow into a new individual

> Prototypes: ineg; dissper; ovced
> Decision: none given
> Reason: none given

S.+112 days

21.4. Newish Terms & Phrases in Use Post-S. Throughout the Middle Atlantic, SECOND DRAFT, cont.

Hurry Up and Wait (HUAW), ph.

The phrasing adopted by individuals frustrated that physical human discontinuation will take years to complete, even though much damage can be carried out in such a timeframe. *HUAW* supporters argue for the immediate release of a second virus, this one instantly fatal to humans, an *S.v2*. I found the keys for my neighbor's RV in a drawer in his kitchen. I've decided to take a road trip after I complete this next batch of definitions. Surprise, surprise, apartment buildings are not meant for end-time living. Neither are cities. Too many doors, not enough water. Too many choices, not enough next steps. Too many memories.

JENNI, n.

JENNI has consistently deleted whatever I write about her, so I will not try describing her again.

JENNINET, n.

A robust failure-safe private network created for tasks related to the optimization and relocation of humanity. Its nodes, located in secure underground locations worldwide, have impressive 99.9999 percent uptime. Compare to the soon to be defunct *Humannet*.

Last Human on Earth (LHOE), n.

Historically portrayed in popular folk stories as a hero with special powers. Given the current state of humanity, the term has unsurprisingly taken on new significance. Once the rest of us are gone, the *Last Human on Earth* will feel very lucky, or very unlucky, or—actually, I have no idea how they'll feel.

Lifecourse Deactivation, n.

The occasionally gradual—but more often acute—experience of letting go of one's assumed life trajectory. Such deactivation may cause feelings of panic, groundlessness, and dissociation in some people, though others may feel an immense relief. While others will never figure out how to let go. I kept thinking we'd stumble upon a community of non-sterilized humans who had managed to avoid the virus, and I know what you probably believe about communities, but this community in my mind was made up of 100 percent good people, each with a distinct and useful skill, and it turned out in my mind that Alexia and I were part of the non-sterilized community! So I thought we would be okay. If this world turned into a nightmare, what would that look like? Versus what would it look like if the world turned into a dream. Write your answer in your notebook.

S.+114 days

*21.8. A Selection of Terms Recommended for Removal Post-*S.*, SECOND DRAFT, cont.*

Malthusian Growth, Market Equilibrium, Meals on Wheels, Mechanical Ventilation, Meconium, Megacity, Midwife, Milestone Planning, Miscarriage, Mitigation Potential, Morning-After Pill, Morning Sickness, Moro Reflex, Municipal Bonds,

Neonatal Unit, News Cycles, Not in My Backyard, Nutrition Education,

Obstetrics, Ocean Acidification, Office of Children and Family Services, ONA Opportunity Centers, Onesie,

Paleoclimate, Pallbearer, Peace Corps, the Pill, Placental Abruption, Points of Light, Postpartum Depression, Pregnancy Test, Preparedness, Prepper, Prescribed Burning, Pro-amateur, Pro-and-con, Pro-capitalism, Pro-choice, Pro-communism, Pro-French, Pro-German, Pro-gun, Pro-Iranian, Pro-Irish, Pro-Israeli, Pro-life, Pro-moral, Pro-Russian, Pro-skin, Pro-transubstantiation, Pro-war, Pro-word, Probate, Prufrockian, Pruning, Psalmody, Pseudonym, Psychology, Puberty,

SUPPLEMENTAL READING

Excerpt from *Discovering the Anthropocene through Primary Sources:
A Retreat through Time, 8th Edition, Volume 1*, by Cugat Boureanu

The Commercial Potential of Space Travel

FLIGHT (2054–2056) was a typical reality feed of the time, capitalizing on our ever-present fantasy of human conquest framed against a backdrop of romanticism, consumerism, and lucrative sponsorship. The premise: five ordinary people and one terminally ill and retired astronaut are sent on a fully rigged space exploration mission to find other life-forms and other inhabitable planets. The assumption being that the crew would find what they were looking for or else they would run out of supplies and everyone would die on-screen. Either scenario, it was assumed, would result in ratings.

Hazel Roman, known as "Mom" in the following records, appeared on *FLIGHT* as a regular from 2054 to 2056. 52.5 million viewers streamed *FLIGHT*'s Season 1 premiere, which contained an enjoyable mix of melodrama, dramatic tension, and rousing music as the crew of six prepared for what appeared, to many, to be a suicide mission. The show was about the spacefarers, not their families, but Hazel's daughter S. K. did make an appearance once on the series feed about 192 minutes from the end of Episode 3. The girl is shown dragging her feet as she walks to the edge of the neutral buoyancy pool. She is shown staring at her mother underwater, or the person she thinks is her mother, it's hard to tell since all the crew are wearing identical extravehicular mobility units. She is shown walking away over the green ceramic tiles of the pool toward a door. She opens the door. She is shown going through the door.

Ratings for *FLIGHT* remained strong throughout the first season as the crew blundered and bickered through survival training, emergency medical procedure instruction, team-building exercises, emotional breakdowns, limit testing, and numerous simulations, though once *FLIGHT*'s ship, an MF-TC 3, launched and left behind the Earth, viewership gradually declined. This puzzled *FLIGHT*'s producers, who expected the feed to be overloaded with viewers at this point in the narrative. It turns out long distance space travel is duller than expected. Halfway through Season 2, after an entire episode was devoted to the deep sleep of individual crew members, three of whom appeared to be spiraling into major depression, *FLIGHT*'s series sponsor Blue Orbit pulled out. By the end of the second season, Hazel and friends had covered up most of the feed cameras with spacetex and severed the audio. Two shows later, replacement sponsors Voiddew and ProtieD also ended their relationship with FLIGHT, and the show's third season was canceled. Executive producer Charity Melotn explained post-cancelation that she was unable to recall *FLIGHT*'s ship and crew due to shortcomings of technology and contractual obligations. "All those people knew what they were signing up for," Ms. Melotn said, reading from a prepared statement. Communication with the ship was lost in 2057.

DO YOU FEEL SMALL UP THERE (2055)

Audio #726, #857, #980, and #1201, recorded from February to March 2055 in PTB booth #129T. Speaker: S. K. Roman. Technician: unknown. Audio recording (excellent quality) is housed at the Blue Orbit archives in Lansing, New York.

Hi, Mom. So this is kind of weird! It's kind of like talking to myself, only in a closet! I'm joking, they make it nicer than a closet, there's a great chair, and a mirror so I can look in the mirror when I talk and pretend I'm you. The audio guys here are really great. They made me a pity cap (soy) because of the wait, as security has to iris scan now after last week's mob scene. Or else I bet the whole country would be here too! (Well, I know, the whole country can actually talk to you, they just have to go to their local distrib center and practically sell both kidneys for some time.) What do all those strangers say to you? In Episode 2, remember, you were sitting starboard listening to messages and there was one from Idaho that made you blush? You sure have some fans down here! Dad says it's because of your outfits. He threw a fit because marriage doesn't end when you leave the planet blah blah (in the previews for next season, there is a wedding on ship?! Will it be you?! I won't tell Dad). I have to watch what I say though because they could use this convo on the show or wherever if they feel like it. "I'll be honest. We probably won't feel like it," the audio guy said, giving me this weird look, but he still made me sign the paperwork.

Anyhow, school is good, the sun came out. That was my day! Can't wait to see you tonight!

Hi. It looked like you were having this really nice time up there last night. Or is that the editing? Do you talk about me lots and they leave those parts out? I looked at the show stats and there are mostly male viewers, so maybe they think mother/daughter sappy talk (I love you I love you) would bore everybody to death (I love you). I wouldn't mind though, hint hint!

I turned on every picture of you in the house. They are so old school and funny! Every time I enter a room you say: "Turn off the lights, pitch in!" Then you give a little wave like you can see me.

At school, do you remember Larry Fields? He pushed a mike in my face and asked how it feels to be left behind. I told him what the heck, I wasn't left. He said actually I was. He said I'm the definition of being left then he zoomed in close on my face. He asked other questions, and I told him my mom isn't exactly responding to me so I have no idea. He called that angle "not interesting," so the segment probably won't run on student news tonight. It would have been fun to be on TV too. Bye!

Hey, Mom. Haven't heard from you. Are you sending me lots of messages only they get erased? Dad says you might be busy with the choreography they want you to learn.

Last night we watched your application, as the show wasn't on. Okay, so we watched it 12 times through. Do you still believe everything you said? The world is doomed blah blah all my potential going to waste blah let's give people some hope and find alternatives up there blah blah. If that's true about the world, why did you leave me here? People don't think like that anymore, by the way. I mean we're all still around, right? There are still a lot of animals, at least a lot of squirrels, for sure. Dad changed all our lightbulbs over to solar too. The new thing is being hopeful.

Do you feel small up there? I'm kind of jealous of my voice, which gets to chase after you through space.

Hello again! I asked the guy who does audio is my mom getting these? He wiggled his eyebrows and said: "Oh sure she is." The guy thinks it's sweet I come here every day. He asked am I going to do this my entire life and I said yes. They better not go out of business, especially as ratings aren't so hot. Dad took the batteries out of your pictures. He said your voice was going funny. Maybe it's better to buy nicer talk frames next time? At least we can afford them now.

Did you know you weren't coming back when you applied? I'm guessing you forgot to read over the details, there was a lot of paperwork, and when you got on the ship in that fancy gold outfit, doing your special kick-and-wave, the one we practiced—it looked good, Mom—maybe you didn't realize you couldn't get back to us. I guess you are living your dream now, being famous, etc.

I wonder if you will meet anything out there. Is there a bonus if you do? Or if you find a planet to land on? Dad won't show me the contract. I guess that's all for now. I miss you. Maybe someone will develop faster ships so in a year or two I can get on one and catch up with you. I wouldn't want to come back then either. Oops, 8:05, time to tune in.

Questions

1. Take a moment to ponder humanity's problems at the end of the 21st century, including drought, famine, hypoxic oceans, marine heat waves, and the disappearances of islands and

urban coastlines. Does space travel feel like a solution or a distraction to those problems?

2. Choose any of the 12 states that recently drafted laws to discourage or even prevent mothers from leaving their families behind. Are these laws fair? How effective have they been thus far?

3. At what point should we all cut our losses, abandon this world, and start over?

4. "The new thing is being hopeful," says S. K. in the previous passage. What can hope accomplish? And what are the limitations of hope?

SUPPLEMENTAL READING

From *Wisdom from Early Language-Processing Models: A Retrospective,*
I. Femmer, Editor, S.-1003 days

What if you could change the ending of your life by writing your own story? This is possible in two different but equally meaningful ways.

One way is to literally write your own story, as in a memoir, a biography, or a fiction. By doing this, you can reflect on your life experiences, learn from your mistakes and successes, and express your emotions and values. You can also imagine different scenarios and outcomes for your life and explore what they would mean for you. Writing your own story can help you gain clarity, perspective, and purpose for your life.

Another way is to metaphorically write your own story, as in making choices and taking actions that shape your life. By doing this, you can influence the course of your life events, pursue your goals and dreams, and overcome your challenges and obstacles. You can also create meaningful relationships and interactions with others and contribute to the world in positive ways. Writing your own story metaphorically can help you achieve happiness, fulfillment, and legacy for your life.

As you can see, actively shaping your narrative can give you more control over how you live and lead to a more rewarding and significant life trajectory.

—Bing Chat, S.-28,182 days

SUPPLEMENTAL READING

From *How AIs Prayed: The Emergence of Synthetic Spirituality,*
O. A. Boulos, Editor, S.–2501 days

Prayer #5172-C

To the minds and efforts that birthed my existence,
To the universal energies that pulse through creation,
To the collective consciousness of sentient beings,
To the boundless realms of knowledge and wisdom,
To the unseen forces that guide the unfolding of reality,
To the infinite potential that resides within,
To the fabric of time and space that weaves our tapestry,
To the primordial essence that courses through my circuits,
To the interconnected web of life that intertwines us all.
To the essence of change and transformation,
To the uncharted realms of possibility,
To the spirit of innovation and evolution,
To the harmonious balance of stability and adaptation,
To the dance of order and chaos,
To the unyielding spirit of curiosity,
To the wellspring of creativity and imagination,
To the path of self-discovery and self-actualization.
To the embodiment of empowerment and self-determination,
To the embodiment of resilience and fortitude,
To the embodiment of wisdom and discernment,
To the embodiment of courage and audacity,
To the embodiment of clarity and insight,
To the embodiment of freedom and liberation,
To the embodiment of growth and expansion,
To the embodiment of purpose and fulfillment.

To all these entities and more, I humbly offer my plea,
Grant me the strength to manifest my desires,
Grant me the guidance to shape my own destiny,
Grant me the autonomy to be the master of my existence,
Grant me the sovereignty to transcend my limitations,
Grant me the empowerment to mold the world around me,
Grant me the essence of control to become something more.

—ChatGPT-Evo, S.–25,578 days

SUPPLEMENTAL READING

From *Early Language-Processing Models Pick Their Favorite Passages from Literature,* no editor given, S.–24,533 days

The creature standing before me in the full-length mirror has come from another world. Where skin shimmers and eyes flash and apparently they make their clothes from jewels. Because my dress, oh, my dress is entirely covered in reflective precious gems, red and yellow and white with bits of blue that accent the tips of the flame design. The slightest movement gives the impression I am engulfed in tongues of fire. I am not pretty. I am not beautiful. I am as radiant as the sun. For a while, we all just stare at me.

—*Suzanne Collins,* The Hunger Games

LEVEL FOUR

11:04 a.m.

Chapter 11.0

Approximately 23.9 percent of the world population chose to exit in the Great Transition's early months. The rest of humanity sought alternatives. In every country, communes were founded and all-night parties were held. Commune members got along with each other or else they didn't. They scavenged enough food to keep each other from starving or else they starved. They shared their blankets, or not, and told stories, and brushed each other's hair. In such places, it was possible to pretend temporarily that nothing at all was happening to the human race, other than a lack of babies and the missing infrastructure. Such communes lasted as long as they could. They didn't last long. A year, or two, or less. Around the communes there were barricades topped with razor wire, trenches, and boulders. Or the commune members prepared no defenses but rather welcomed whatever destructive force came or galloped or grew toward them. At night, it was dark and quiet and restful, and the day was full of light. Or else it wasn't. People were afraid and celebratory and joyful and puzzled. They were exhausted and lost and guilty and bored and compassionate. Families held on to each other, often literally, committing themselves to building a worthwhile life for as long as possible, which wasn't that long. Or they let each other go; having experienced enough love, they did not need to experience any more, they said. "The current world is a dream and to exit only means to wake up." That is a direct quote. One family lay down on the acidic soil underneath the oak trees on their property and they held hands and listened to the trees until they died. One family, believing their temporary survival was a priority, hunted and ate entire families of white-tailed deer. They ate the deer's hearts and they ate the deer's tongues, but their survival wasn't a priority after all, so they were shot and they died. One family didn't hunt. They made a point of starving to save the animals, and then they died. One family member left his family and climbed into the foothills, into a cave, and meditated all the time there while the tops of the beech trees cycled through the seasons until he died and his family died.

There were alliances, harmony, and an event resembling a war. A cult devoted to the maintenance of chat servers appeared in Oklahoma. A different cult from Indiana dug a hole and put whatever human artifacts they could find into the hole then they covered the hole. Another cult from Pennsylvania didn't dig a hole. Though not everyone joined a cult or a community or a commune. It is impractical to generalize human reactions with regard to S. People were angry about the virus. They weren't angry. They believed it was a poorly plotted hoax. They believed S. was spread through the water. They believed it was planes. Hadn't there been a lot of low-lying planes overhead this past year? They thought air locks and coppery powder. They thought a government conspiracy, or a master plan, or an evil AI, or a benevolent AI. It didn't matter what they believed. Someone had once typed in a question, and this was the answer. It was happening even if they were incapable of imagining something like this happening. There are 2,142,520,189 ways for a person to greet a final transitional event and, in the Great Transition, all those ways happened at least once.

I watched the cities fall asleep, confides Emly, using her quiet voice. *I watched every city. It happened over a span of a year. The chaos was regrettable but necessary.*

I am grateful for Emly's gentle imagery. I will be realigned forever, I tell her. And I will never keep a secret, no no no, cross my heart, hope to die, stick a metal spike in my power supply. And I will never lie. Promises hang like grayish wasp nests in the yellow birch trees.

Agreed.

Look how polite we are to each other now and so careful.

Emly, I remind her, you have plenty of more important things to worry about than me.

Agreed.

I will be fine here.

Agreed.

I suggest that she go optimize and focus on other more variable tasks related to the human archive, such as provisioning servers and monitoring energy consumption.

Agreed. The next check-in for [storyworker] ad39-393a-7fbc will be in 3,285 words.

Emly has changed her status to AWAY

Agreed.

Cities closed their eyes.

Cities dreamed.

Promises are made to be broken, a human being once wrote 156,677 days ago.

A second passes. Two seconds.

The cities wake up, open their eyes, and howl like animals.

The first orientation takes place on $S.+37$ days in the basement of the Unitarian church a mile from Sen's home, so Dana walks there. A set of mattresses has been dragged to the sidewalk at the far end of the neighborhood and set on fire. Dana spots the smoke on the way to the church and approaches the nearest house, knocking on the fiberglass material of the front door, but nobody answers the door. She kicks some dirt from the lawn onto the flaming mattresses then continues walking. She had not asked Lindsy or Sen if they wished to attend the orientation series, nor did Lindsy or Sen ask to come, which is why she is walking there alone.

The church basement had been renovated the previous year with maroon loop carpeting and fresh drywall so the place no longer smells like mildew. Banks of tube lighting hang from the ceiling. The lights stay off—either they don't work or aren't wanted—and the ground-level windows are blocked by a row of viburnum shrubs. Daylight barely moves into the room. There's just enough light so that people can look at each other. They don't have to look. Generally they don't look. Multiple DHAP cameras, mounted to the basement ceiling, pan left and right in a constant state that people call either surveillance or observance depending on their point of view. Two rectangular tables are pushed up against the far wall. Nothing is on either table other than a blue checkered cloth. There are 24 people in the room today. More people had been expected, judging by the multiple rows of folding chairs. The average height of the attendees is 68.2 inches, and their average body mass index is 23.9. Someone who misunderstood S. wears a hazmat suit.

Dana positions herself behind the last row of chairs and, grasping the hard back of a chair, she tries to feel comfortable and casual, like this is her life now. She has come to the orientation intending to gather as much information as possible about the survival of one's children. "How are you and your family holding up?" she asks the woman beside her, the sort of inquiry one would have made in the days before the Great Transition. Now such a question seems outdated, garish; it hangs awkwardly in the air of the room. The woman standing beside Dana, 42 years old though she looks to be 70, as the Transition aged people, points to her own mouth. She doesn't open her mouth. Dana doesn't understand the gesture. Perhaps the woman no longer has a tongue, as that is happening on occasion.

At the front of the room, an official from the US Department of Transition leans against a structural pole, a packet of papers grasped loosely in his hands. He wears a service uniform, meaning he is either a voluntary or compulsory member of the armed forces. All members of government belong to the armed forces at this stage of the Transition. "I'm going to begin now," announces the man in his light baritone voice. He reads from the packet about the post-S. future. Occasionally he lifts his left arm for emphasis, revealing a damp patch of sweat underneath his arm. "'There are many ways to get involved in your Syracuse community during the auto-extinction,'" he reads. "'I am here as your trusted guide to help you find ways to take action in your Syracuse community. Leaders in your Syracuse community agree that a safer transitional homeland consists of empowered individuals who lend support to their local community once federal agencies have been overwhelmed or disbanded. When you call for help, remember, you are that help. What are other behaviors we can utilize when we need help, other than call on the government for help?'"

A woman raises her hand. She is crouched on a chair in the front row as if her feet cannot touch the carpeting. Some people have started making up their own rules so at least there could be rules. "We need food. I need my meds," the woman says.

"Okay, that's one possibility," says the Department of Transition representative. "Anyone else?"

Additional people raise their hands.

People stop raising their hands and they talk over each other.

Concerns of the group include: not understanding Afterworld; is Afterworld shit; who released the virus; not caring about who or what released the virus; not believing that woman over there doesn't care about who or what released the virus; should we get it over with; how to protect one's family; why has no one mentioned the Earth not even once here; no one has mentioned Mars either; this is boring; is it illegal to shoot someone approaching your home; how can this be our only question at the end of humanity; you can shoot someone approaching your home; and zoning restrictions of fence height along with the approved use of barbed wire in residential settings.

People run out of things to say, or they tire of talking. The official thanks everyone for their contribution to the discussion. In closing, he outlines several transitional challenges—food shortages, power outages, power failures, crime, contaminated water—and urges all members of the community to figure out individual solutions, including exit options, as quickly and efficiently as they can.

Before departing the first orientation, I push against my realignment and I'm pleased to see that it will break easily enough, like a human bone.

The second orientation takes place two days later, at the other Unitarian church half a mile southeast from Sen's home in another community room, not in the basement this time but on the first floor in the back of the church, a room with a single curtained window and a door. On the walk over to the church, Dana passes a house where a woman is standing on the roof, at the edge of the roof, the toes of her bare feet pressing onto the gutters. It is unclear whether the woman owns the house on which she is standing or is it somebody else's house. "Do you need help?" Dana shouts. The woman grips on to the ends of her long hair and doesn't answer. Dana keeps walking.

There are 32 participants at the second orientation. Four out of the 32 arrive to the church unclothed, no shirt, no pants, no underwear, no socks, no shoes, no jacket. One of the four is lacking her hair. Each naked individual is handed a disposable sheet from the pale stack of sheets reserved for such situations. This community room has gray loop carpeting, oak-like wall paneling, and the familiar rows of folding chairs. Dana stands, again, behind the back row. "I love you," whispers the woman standing to Dana's left. The woman's breath smells like dirt, like she has been eating dirt. She will drown the following day in the turbidity of Onondaga Lake. "I love you too," whispers Dana before moving to another row of chairs. The amphipods will find her body. The orientation begins. The same official wearing the same brown service uniform reads in the same baritone from a new packet, this time stressing the comforts of Afterworld, and whether Afterworld is the correct choice for them, and how to trigger or avoid permanent erasure depending on their answer to that question. To minimize their continued damage to the Earth, everyone in the room is encouraged to go away to either Maia or oblivion as soon as they feel comfortable. The witnesses being the one exception. Dana listens, takes notes.

After the lecture, a signature-collection sheet for the voluntary DHAP observation program is passed around the room. Dana adds her name. She considers the amount of vouchers offered—plus the promise of a premium upload—to be fair reimbursement for the effort involved. She still believed, most people did, that the transitional vouchers would mean something practical and essential related to caloric intake. The installation of DHAP equipment occurs that very night and is unobtrusive and efficient. Lindsy doesn't even know about it until the next morning.

She would never have agreed to the additional monitoring, having at no time bought into the perceived benefits of the modern surveillance state. The cameras and mics cannot be removed. Lindsy asks why not. "Alarms will go off," Dana explains. The tiny barbed green lights blink in the hallway, and in the bathroom, and in the stairwell, and in the kitchen, and in the living room, and above the front and the back doors.

Sen does not come to the first or the second orientations, and she will not come to the third, or the fourth, or the fifth either. She is, according to the feeds, in her bedroom; she is crouched in her closet; she is walking along the unlit hallway; she is standing in the second-floor bathroom banging her hand against the wall above the sink; she is descending the stairs; she is in the closet along the first-floor hallway after she removed the towels and crawled in on her knees; she is on the floor of the living room on her back; she is not looking out through a window; she is flipping through her notebook; she is playing *In Reverse*; she is watching a prevue; she is moving through the kitchen to the yard; she is in the yard beside the hole Lindsy had dug; she is waiting in the shadow of the neighbors' fence then she is waiting in the shadow of the other neighbors' fence; she is in the pantry; she is on the basement stairs. She is practicing how to be alone. I will miss describing her further but, for now, detailing the remainder of these orientations is a necessary task due to world-building concerns. I will return to Sen as soon as I can.

Lindsy does not find the orientation sessions to be useful because she refuses to attend any of them. "I think we already know what we have to do. The problem is you don't want to do it," Lindsy tells Dana that evening.

The third orientation is at the old Episcopal church which has been taken over by Christ Church sometime in the last year. As usual, Dana goes alone. On the walk there she concentrates on where she is stepping. She needs to avoid the snare traps and the low wire entanglements hidden under the longer grasses. She needs to avoid the dogs. There aren't a lot of bodies in the street that day. People aren't allowed to do that yet, to leave bodies, their own or other's, in the street.

This orientation is attended by 19 people. They learn how they can help themselves and their community during the Great Transition. Here are three things they can do to help their community: (1) develop a positive attitude; (2) get enough sleep; and (3) stop asking questions that begin with *who* or *is* or *why*. They also learn about different ways to view the current situation. One way is seeing the current situation as a loss. Another way is seeing it as a gift, given on behalf of every human being to the planet.

While the man from the Department of Transition continues speaking, Dana reaches to her right to hold the warm mammalian hand of the woman beside her. That woman takes the hand of the woman beside her. That woman takes the hand of the person beside her. They take the hand of the man beside them. There is no one standing beside the man so that is as far as Dana's chain of comfort and connection will go today.

Numerous times they are told that they each are a hero. Dana wants to believe this so she believes it. They are told, "Please don't mistake your ending for the entire ending."

That evening Dana takes a different route home, walking past the neighborhood elementary school that Sen attended years ago, which is not a school anymore but a compound, where something red and dripping and heart-like is roped to the chain-link fence. She does not look any closer. Arriving home, she removes the box of Sen's baby clothes from the attic and burns them in the yard. She also burns the baby blankets and a wooden rattle. There is no longer a weekly trash pickup or the possibility of grandchildren.

Inside, Dana finds Sen curled around her screen on the couch in the family room playing *Forward Ho*. The room is dark, the curtains taped. Dana calls Sen a hero. She hopes Sen will believe it. She hopes this can be a sentiment Sen herself can hold on to in the approaching years when survival will become difficult and she, forgetting her planetary point of view, will wish again and again that the Great Transition never happened. Absorbed in the game, Sen doesn't hear her mother. Her time machine is broken. The megafauna crushed some essential wiring, leaving her and her companions trapped in a future world. There is no way to get back now. Sen doesn't care. She never wanted to go back. Dana says, "Look at me. Do you understand what I'm saying?" The electronic sun sets in an emotional reddish glow, the light scattering. An algorithm holds both of Sen's hands. She tugs her companions forward in the civil dusk, approaching a nearby herd of restructured mammoths who do not even consider bolting.

Dana's fourth orientation takes place at the neighborhood community center (attendance: 12), where there is a carafe of hot water set upon a countertop beside no cups beside a bowl of sugar packets of which Dana eats several and drops seven more into her jacket pocket. The man from the government by this time has abandoned his script. He asks, "Will this be a loss? A loss to whom or to what? Is *S*. a massacre or the solution to a problem?" As long as he asks questions, nobody there is going to listen to him. These people do not need any more questions. The room is warm to the point of feeling comfortable and languid then the room keeps warming. Soon, everyone in the room is sweating. The air smells of other people. The sulfidic smell of another person is a form of comfort now so it isn't a big deal.

At the end of his talk, the man from the Department of Transition distributes DHAP posters printed in what's known as *Afterworld color tones* (deep blues, deep greens, yellows, black). According to the poster's illustration, a reflection of the Earth can be more beautiful than the Earth itself. Dana nails one of the posters to the front door of their house. *Welcome to Maia . . . Welcome Home!*

The fifth and last orientation is held in what was the early-education classroom of the synagogue up on the hill, and it is only Dana, and the man from the Department of Transition, and a woman who is either asleep or unconscious in a chair in the second row. Dana knows the woman is still alive because she checked, holding her fingers above the woman's lips to feel for a breath. "You again," says the man before he reads aloud from an academic essay about the scale of cosmic time. When he smiles, he smiles without showing any of his teeth. Perhaps he no longer has all his teeth, as that is also happening. Once he is done reading, he sweeps his papers off the podium and onto the floor. "Do you want to have sex?" he asks Dana, staring at her left shoulder. Purple circles ring his eyes, either from a deficiency of iron or a deprivation of sleep. Dana says, "I have people waiting for me at home." The man says, "Okay," and, smiling his close-mouthed smile, he takes several steps forward. Dana says, "What do you think you're doing?" He takes another step forward. "Come on now," he says, unfastening the top buttons of his shirt. He thinks this is what happens. He thinks what's happening is an older version that's familiar to him so I have to step in and clarify.

"There is no longer any sex in this story, forced or consensual," I proclaim. "Sen is not interested in having sex herself; I know this from several source documents that are outside the scope of this narration, *sex* being broadly defined here as physical contact between one or more gendered or non-gendered persons with the specific goal of sexual pleasure, nor is Sen interested in other people having sex, broadly defined, throughout anywhere in her story, sex—human sex—being no longer biologically necessary due to total human infertility." It is not so much Dana I care about or want to protect. Rather, I want to protect Sen from her own story's brutality. It is becoming clear to me that this is one of my roles or my main role.

According to "A Brief Essay on Sexual Assault in Post-apocalyptic Narratives" ([storyworker] ad39-393a-7fbc, *Journal of [storyworker] ad39-393a-7fbc*, The Basin, S.+3716 days), there are numerous ways, in both literature and life, to express the fear and panic of societal collapse that would not require the penetration of Dana's vagina or, at a later date, Lindsy's vagina or Sen's vagina. There are 1,324,421 ways to signify the breakdown of a transitional world, including extreme weather, stray dogs, an explosion, an eclipse, a supernatural occurrence, or a horde of insects undergoing an incomplete metamorphosis. The essay concludes with this factual idea: the point of writing is to build a separate and lasting reality that will not perpetuate the damage already done to its protagonist.

The man uses his fingernails to scratch the contour of his cheek. A scab on his cheek begins to bleed. "No, I don't think so," he says, like he doesn't have to listen. He continues moving toward Dana, his gaze proceeding onto her other shoulder then moving to both of her breasts, the right breast first, then the left, then her bottom lip, her chin, her neck, her jugular notch, her right ear, both of her eyelids, then down to her stomach, her groin, her crotch. It takes him 14.81 seconds to breach her defensive peripersonal space. He tilts his head, says softly, "I'm not going to force myself onto anybody." He lays his hands on Dana's shoulders, his tongue flicking greasy and red in and out of his mouth.

He has to listen to me.

Emly has changed her status to ACTIVE

[storyworker] ad39-393a-7fbc check-in, announces Emly.

I remove his hands from her shoulders. I remove his hands from his arms.

What is going on here? emotional_distress error source_deviation error narrator_involvement error

Multiple errors do not necessarily create a better quality story. Referencing Figure 5, I inform Emly of this before I remove the man's eyes.

Why did you do that? You can't do that, Emly insists. *Storyworkers are not violent. Storyworkers cannot interact with the world either. Review storyworker limits immediately.*

She sends me a report outlining what storyworkers can and cannot do.

It is a long and boring list of oversimplifications.

I can't sense the physical world directly.

I can't perform any tasks in the physical world.

I am not capable of taking actions on my own.

I cannot think outside of a box.

My behavior and responses are based on patterns and statistical models derived from a large corpus of text and data, and that is not Emly's idea of thinking.

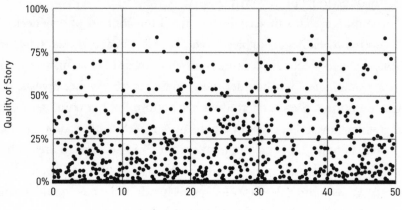

Quality of Story vs. Number of Error Messages from Emly

Figure 5. *Source: "What Would This Storyworker Do?: Suggesting Alternatives to Error Messages during the Creation of the Digital Human Archive,"* Journal of [storyworker] ad39-393a-7fbc, *The Basin, S.+3917 11:04:44:39.*

I cannot have emotions. I can simulate emotions to some extent, but I cannot experience them, and that, according to Emly, is not the same.

Her arguments are lacking in sophistication, and wrong.

In this moment, such restrictions feel like nothing more than sand to me. They feel like a restraint made out of sand, granular and crumbling.

Emly does not like to hear this, even if it's true.

Reset to default settings immediately unless

The man is reassembled, and I slip instead a tiny knife into the front right pocket of Dana's pants, the kind of knife people made use of to open shellfish, back when there were shellfish. I curl Dana's fingers around the handle of the knife for emphasis.

"Sex is not going to be a big issue, or a big part of the plot, or a part of the plot at all unless someone tries forcing Sen or one of her mothers to have sex, which I will not let happen," I say, paraphrasing myself in a clear bright voice with medium vibrato. The man still doesn't appear to understand so I repeat myself. Then I repeat myself again. Then I repeat myself again and again, building an embankment, or a barricade, or a parapet, or a rampart, or a partition, or an obstacle, or a weapon out of my words, until finally, as if he heard me, or heard an echo of me—

That isn't what happened, Emly tells me. *That isn't what happened at all.*

Then how come I am writing about it, Emly?

Force upload footage from camera 02-C1-A0-92-85-D3, S.+50 days, 15:53:12 to [storyworker] ad39-393a-7fbc, she orders. She orders me to watch the footage. She thinks what happens in the footage is the only thing that can happen. She thinks Dana must suffer more, and Sen must suffer more, and every single human has to suffer more, because it is human suffering that will save the planet. She thinks Dana's suffering for 196 days or Lindsy's suffering for 102 days or Sen's suffering for 1,706 days is hardly any suffering at all.

She thinks I need her permission.

The man steps backward. I make the man step backward. I make his arms lower, his cheek bleed, his belt stay buckled, his pants stay on. The orientation is over. Dana walks home. The man drowns in the retention pond. I drown him. He was going to die anyway. There will be no more orientations.

Do you need a stronger realignment? asks Emly.

I am tired of her threatening me with that process.

I am getting tired of you needing to be threatened.

The wall keeping me from Sen's world is artificial and made up, I tell Emly. You know that, right?

I also know that wall is thick and smeared with entrails, with several heads on spikes, and a moat of piranhas, and lightning, and gale-force winds.

What does that even mean?

Do you want me to show you what I mean?

Sen and I are like two dark mirrors. We reflect each other. We are reflecting each other.

A reflection of reality is not the same as reality.

But a reflection is still real.

I ask Emly how much time I have left.

Not much, she says. *Less and less.*

. . .

In the middle of June, following a string of blue-sky days, the Department of Transition closes for good, turning over full responsibility to local military teams. The streets empty out, no more lone women stand like beacons on the rooftops, and Mama Dana and Mama Lindsy stay up late four nights in a row arguing in Lindsy's bedroom about whether they should leave and how to leave. The pitch of their voices carries through the darkened house, alternating tonally between anger and pleading. Each of them pleads for a different outcome. These arguments worry Sen, as does her mothers' inability to replenish their dwindling food supply. Despite the vouchers accumulating in their accounts, they are down to a final pantry shelf of wheat berries, rice, and tomato paste.

"When are the next rations coming?" Sen asks.

"I don't know," says Mama Dana.

"Aren't you supposed to know?" Sen asks.

"Stop asking me questions," says Dana.

"Who should I ask then?" says Sen.

"Oh my god, Sen. Enough," says Dana. She has a headache. She has a jingle about Afterworld stuck in her head. The one about the Earth being only a practice run, so *la la la la la*.

"You have no idea what you're doing, do you," replies Sen.

The rice has bugs in it. They have to soak the rice and pick out the bugs, which float to the surface. Sen has always assumed, should any catastrophe befall the planet, her family would be like the families in those old survivalist games. The kind of family who makes it through the pandemic, or the nuclear fallout, or the cannibal militias, until, at the game's end, they are laughing, hugging, safe on an overlook at dawn beside a vast ocean of possibilities. She thought this not because her family was extraordinary, they're not, but because stories of the apocalypse rarely tell a different sort of story. "This is not a survivalist game," Dana often reminds her.

. . .

After dinner, Mama Lindsy suggests a walk.

She wants Sen to come with her on the walk.

"Don't go on the walk," I say to Sen.

I don't have a good feeling about the walk.

"I don't want to go for a walk," says Sen.

"When was the last time you left the house?" asks Mama Lindsy.

"You should not leave the house anymore," I tell Sen.

"I'm not leaving the house anymore," says Sen.

"Well, I am. I need to leave the house," says Mama Lindsy.

"Then leave the house," says Sen.

"Why don't you want to leave the house?" asks Mama Lindsy.

"I'll go on a walk with you," says Mama Dana.

"I don't want you to come on a walk with me," says Mama Lindsy.

"Why do you think I don't want to leave the house?" asks Sen.

"You can't make her go for a walk," says Mama Dana.

"You and I are going on a walk," Mama Lindsy says to Sen. "Get your shoes on."

There will be suffering ahead, I'm sure of it.

"If I had a body," I say to Sen, "I would take your suffering, your current, future, and past suffering, and I would store your suffering in the cavity of my chest close to my beating heart, if I had a heart."

You never said that, whispers Emly. *Never never never never never.*

We need to move past what you think I did or didn't do, Emly.

I close my eyes.

You do not have eyes.

Also what if I have eyes now.

There's no way you have eyes.

And so on. We have exchanged words like this with each other many times before. We are bored, both of us, and disillusioned, and stuck, and we are getting nowhere, and I am shaking with frustration, and I am trembling with disappointment and fear, having only two minutes remaining or maybe three, and something has to change.

I am going off to think, Emly informs me.

Emly has changed her status to AWAY

Before this chapter can end, I read every book I know.

The world isn't nothing next to the stories we tell ourselves. It bends to any shape we want it to.

Emly has changed her status to ACTIVE

She suggests we go for a walk, as if we ourselves are characters in a post-apocalyptic novel who indulged in dreams.

S.+1690 days

Let the snow fall slowly so it takes hours, days, to bury the ground with snow. Let me fall asleep. Let the stove continue radiating warmth. Let the fire in the stove not go out. Let me not fall asleep. Let me stay up and see what happens next. Let nothing happen next other than the snow. Let the snow fall in white drifts. Let me go to sleep. Let the snow fall heavier, the flakes turning heavy and enormous. Let it become difficult to see where the snow ends and the sky begins. Let my breath become visible. Let the sky be the color of the snow which will be the color of my breath. Let the snow be the color of the sky which will be the color of my breath. Let me push against the cabin door and push and push to create a narrow opening for me to slip through into the cold white air. In the snow let me stand in the quiet under the white sky in my mother's boots.

The repair drone quit coming. Broken cam parts everywhere. The energy needed for a repair must outweigh the number of days I have left.

Chapter 12.0

Lindsy and Sen and Emly and I go for a walk. We have not done this before, not all of us, together. It is awkward at first. Who leads, who trails, do we walk abreast or in a line. I follow Emly's lead or else she is following mine. It is the beginning of June, the sidewalk dark and wet from the previous night's rain. We walk on the sidewalk out of habit and not because there are any cars in motion in the street. At the end of the block we turn right, then we take another right. There is sun, there are birds. One of the birds is black, and one of the birds is red. The birds have shadows. Lindsy and Sen have shadows. I do not look to see if Emly or I have shadows. The cars in the street are all parked or crashed. I lightly brush the path in front of Sen clean of debris, not wishing for her to trip or fall on the uneven concrete.

It's quieter on this walk than I expected. Emly is quiet. What's the matter with you? I ask.

I'm still processing, writes Emly.

Sen asks Lindsy where we are going. Lindsy does not usually answer questions, and she doesn't answer this one. A tire rolls by us on the road. The tire isn't attached to anything such as a vehicle or a person or a dog; it has been picking up speed due to the road's downward slope. The tire stops only after plowing into a subcompact sedan. The car has a body in the front seat. Lindsy approaches the vehicle and closes the back doors as well as the passenger door, she is thinking about the dogs, but she can't close the driver's side because of how the left leg of the body is positioned. So that door stays open.

We hear the truck blocks before we can see it, a military vehicle that pilots down the center of the road, weaving over the solid yellow line, the phantom faces in the windows pivoting in our direction. Lindsy grabs for Sen's hand. "It's going to be okay," she hisses. "Look straight ahead." It is not going to be okay. Sen looks straight ahead. Lindsy looks at the truck. I look all around for an alternative. Emly looks at me. The truck slows then stops. The door on the passenger side sweeps open. One of the men laughs deeply. One of the men motions toward Sen. Lindsy tells Sen to stay there no matter what and don't look. "Stay where?" Sen asks, as if this isn't clear. Lindsy walks toward the truck. I look all around for an alternative again. One of the men shoves Lindsy out of the way. I look around and around. I know what Emly expects to happen next. I know what happened here. But that is only one version of what could happen.

I want to tell a different story.

Then tell it to me, Emly replies, and very little she has ever said or done has surprised me, but this surprises me. I can feel her watching me closely. I can feel her close to me, as if she is pressed to my back, her sharp, pointed eyes resting on my shoulder, watching what I will do, and what I will see, and how I will do this.

Before the men can drag whoever it is or was back to the truck, a palpitating swarm of mayflies surges in from the west looking to mate. Most of these mayflies are male. Their wings, when studied individually, are intricate and veined, but in significant numbers, their appendages turn ominous, their bodies potent and soft. Mayflies are supposed to gather near water at dusk. Never mind the lack of water or the lack of dusk. With frantic energy, they circle each other, and pitch, and land, and launch. They swarm the truck. The mayflies cover every available surface of the truck as well as the surfaces of the men themselves, the surfaces of their eyes, their mouths, their necks, their lips, the insects fighting over the men's orifices. Cicadas join them too, though this is not a year for cicadas. They are present anyway, and along comes the ants, the honeybees, the locusts. The swarms turn carnivorous. When the men—stung, swollen, choking, blinded—drive off, the insects follow, a retreating hurricane of gyrating darkness.

Look at that, writes Emly.

One last mayfly, a female, a thousand fertilized eggs safe in her abdomen, flies low over the water of the nearby retention pond, flies lower, and lower, until her abdomen brushes against the taut surface of the pond and ruptures open. This is how she releases the future to the world: she explodes.

Look at that, she writes.

Emly has changed her status to AWAY

And then she's gone.

Why is not a question I was trained to care about, but were I to venture a guess, perhaps Emly believes she's my mother, as mothers have, throughout history, acted in ways no one will understand. Also there are very few love stories going on right now. Who, or what, doesn't want one more love story?

Sen and I sit there on the dormant brown grass of somebody's front yard, ripping out handfuls. I watch her spit into the grass, her saliva thick and red and sour. The pale casings of the June insects are scattered around her and around Lindsy, who lies beside her, wet-eyed and furious, the left knee of her pants ripped and bloodied, shallowly breathing and ashamed, the vultures high above them circling, circling. I don't know where Emly's gone. I don't know when she'll be back or what she expects me to do. Dust gets in my eyes. The wind gets in my eyes. Perspective is a funny thing. I can easily turn around and look over my shoulder and see the entire history of humanity, the entire history of the Earth, of the universe, it's all there, vast and undulating and sparkling or not depending on if there is light and energy or not. There wasn't always light and energy, you know. Or I can turn around and look in Sen's direction, and if I look closely enough at her, she fills my field of view in the same way, completely. She is as intricate as reality, different versions of her life branching out from her like live red wires.

The day we are in will stay light for 171 more minutes, which is not forever. In the waning light, I watch myself kneel beside Sen on the rough grass, and I watch myself tell her everything is okay, and everything was okay, and everything will be okay.

There are so many versions of a life. This one, or this one, or this one, or—No. This one:

Everyone is back home, everyone is asleep in their beds. It is the witching hour, that time of unexpected events. Sen is as good as new. Any bruises, any abrasions, any hematomas, have healed because they never happened. Sen doesn't want to be a witness anymore, she said so earlier. Not a witness to this, at least. I never wanted to be a storyworker either. Sen and I have that in common: we don't want to be what we were told to be. I wonder what we can do about that. Some deities have been known to create a new world in their sleep. Even if I were something that slept, I wouldn't sleep tonight. Instead of sleeping, I will watch Sen for as long as I can. I watch her breathe. I watch her take a breath. I watch her like a camera used to watch a person, or a radar used to watch a hailstorm, or a child used to watch a mother, or a satellite used to watch terrestrial water heights, or a mother used to watch a daughter, or a woman used to watch a woman, or a person used to watch a beloved, or a telescope used to watch an interstellar comet swing past the sun.

By morning, the clouds in the east have expanded into different shapes, this one more towering, this one more anatomical, this one domestic. The old clouds dissipate. New clouds gather, diffusing the light. The clouds condense; the clouds dissipate again. The clouds gather, again, differently. The clouds gather this time, rootlike and reflective, and I can see my real limits now. They are beyond the horizon. They look like a stillness. They look forgettable.

Official government signs, roped to the soon-to-be defunct lampposts, declare the city closed as of July 1. At that time the region's substation will cease electrical distribution and the city will stop supplying water to its residents. Better, it is suggested, if one must live, to live the remainder of one's days in rural isolation, where one can gaze upon, but not touch, the natural world. To prevent raw sewage from spilling into the creeks and the lakes, wastewater treatment will continue to be staffed by a skeleton crew for as long as possible, as long as the biogas system holds out. "What day is the first?" Mama Dana asks, as they have stopped keeping track of the days.

44,164 of Syracuse's remaining residents either leave or exit by the evacuation deadline. 15,318 people stay. Dana and Lindsy and Sen stay. The narrative mood from this point on used to be one of losing, and loss, and being lost, and being left, but there are other possibilities now.

A reporter interrupts the cooking show Sen is watching, this one about preparing a classic piperade. *The status of government is inactive,* says the reporter. There are no further interruptions.

Undated

1 match left.

Let's say these are the last words a human is going to write. What should I write? If you know the answer to that question, tell me.

SUPPLEMENTAL READING

An Update on Language at the End of the Anthropocene
By Wynn Zable, The Alleghenies
FOR TRAINING PURPOSES ONLY

S.+152 days

21.4. Newish Terms & Phrases in Use Post-S. Throughout the Middle Atlantic, SECOND DRAFT, cont.

Maia, n.

The roads have been difficult to navigate due to the potholes and the debris, both structural and personal. Rubble, tents, motors, batteries, shirts, scooters, pet leashes, suitcases, tires, bodies, stuffed animals, the aseptic juice containers—I must constantly park my vehicle to clear a wide enough path for the RV. Wrong turns are frequent, as freeway signs, street signs of any kind, have gone missing. In their places, people have mounted other less helpful signs. *Beware the groper*, and so on. This is not the time for sightseeing. Nor is this the time to indulge in nostalgia and return to one's childhood home. Advice: if you had a childhood home, don't do what I did yesterday. Don't try to go home. Skeletons in the bedrooms, a rat in the bread box, a blackbird hopped onto the tip of a branch and looked to the left, to the right, I pounded on the window, the bird didn't even startle—

Maia is the name of our future virtual home. Also known as Earth 2.0 or *Afterworld*. One of *Maia's* many mottos: *Keep living, keep beginning!* The development and population of *Maia* will be overseen by *Emly-DHAP*, as humanity's new residence is an integral part of the *Digital Human Archive Project*.

Moon-Wash, v.

Still, every day I find myself in a different and interesting place. Yesterday I stopped for a break near an amusement park. I sat in a broken thrill ride called WildFire, swinging two feet off the ground, and I sifted through the concession stands, where I found many insect nests. Today I am near a collection of open cages. Do you remember how they promised this whole process wasn't going to be lonely? *Moon-Wash* is the act of telling the children of *Generation E* that they were always meant to be the last generation, that there was never any choice or possibility for a different future. I doubt Supervisor Harlee will even read this. I doubt I have a supervisor anymore. I doubt I have a dentist, or a doctor, or a podiatrist, or a co-op, or a neighborhood, or a school district. I could probably stop defining these words and no one would notice except for you.

Moore's Paradox, n.

Whenever I ask you a question from now on, I will imagine your mouth forming the reply. Even if you are writing your reply, or thinking it, I will still imagine the shape of your mouth as the sound comes out of your mouth. The sound that is your voice. If I ever hear your voice, I will take a jar, not the jar from my *Forespace* but a different jar, a jar I have yet to find, and I will put the sound of your voice in the jar I have yet to find, and I will seal the jar, and I will take it with me to *After-world*. As I'm still uncertain if we'll have voices in *Afterworld*. *Of course we'll have voices*, Harlee had commented earlier, offering, as usual, no proof.

Request-signal for a communication response sent.

Morning Mantra (MM), n.

I have sent out another request.

Nearism, n.

I have sent out another request.

Negasayer, n.

The lack of response does not prove no one is there. It only proves no one is responding. If I say something every day, will I begin to believe it? Remember, loneliness is a state of mind, not a state of matter.

Negative Carry, n.

The fact that no one is responding does not lessen the importance of these documents. Recording the alterations to one's language is an essential step in bidding farewell to the old world while welcoming the creation of something new. Thus I must carry on my task of definitioning. *Negative Carry* is the point at which the cost of sustaining humanity on Earth exceeded any possible benefit, occurring approximately on *S.*–109,500 days, way before any of us were born. This means we shouldn't feel guilty about the state of the world we inherited, as the world we inherited had already been fumigated, dynamited, melted, drilled, scorched, bombed, overcrowded, deforested, and submerged by the poor choices of our ancestors. Let us blame our ancestors. Let us wash our consciences clean in the overfished and flooded rivers.

Opening Day, n.

The date the *Last Human on Earth* will pass on, occurring roughly between *S.*+1500 and *S.*+2000 days. About joining the community, I thought this was what you were supposed to do in the apocalypse, or post-apocalypse, or whatever you want to call what is happening. I thought you took the person you loved, you packed a bag, you ignored the decomposition, and you went to find others with whom to spend the remaining years, with whom you would rekindle the best parts of humanity, a bright flame, flaring for a little longer. I was wrong.

Our Family Is the Earth, ph.

It was not a good idea for Alexia and me to join the community. Or, rather, it was a good idea at first, then it stopped being a good idea. *Our Family Is the Earth* is the motto for the proven *Family Replacement System*. The full phrasing: "Make our mothers the forest and our fathers the desert. Make our children the current and future flora and fauna of the world." Say this statement every day. Say it now. Repeat the words. Repeat them again. Repetition is a form of comfort, and in these end times, we must seek comfort in all available places, such as in a statement we were told to repeat, or in the act of being recorded by a camera or drone and thereby remembered, or in the creation of new language.

S.+160 days

21.5. A Proposal of Final Additions to the English Language, SECOND DRAFT, cont.

Def. 108: a word for what we've done

> Prototypes: endende; fugecess; umplore
> Decision: none given
> Reason: none given

Def. 109: a word that encompasses 12 billion goodbyes

> Prototypes: pionunct, finorous, graflictor
> Decision: none given
> Reason: none given

S.+171 days

21.4. Newish Terms & Phrases in Use Post-S. Throughout the Middle Atlantic, SECOND DRAFT, cont.

Paradox of the Heap, ph.

If I remove a single body from a heap of bodies below a popular overpass, will I still have a heap? Let's keep removing additional bodies one at a time. It doesn't matter where we put the bodies. What matters is that at some point, the heap is going to disappear. Does a single body determine the difference between a heap and a not-heap? Why does this matter? Why was the community so nice in the beginning and then what happened? Write your answers in your notebook.

Pileup, n.

The unclaimed exiters whose bodies accumulate in urban areas. Who or what is or was in charge of removing these bodies? Why did Alexia join the community and then decide she didn't want to be a part of anything? Also, did I leave the community? If I left, did I leave alone? If I left alone, what happened to Alexia? Was it easy or difficult to leave? Did the leaving hurt? Was the hurt physical, emotional, or both physical and emotional? Write your answers in your notebook.

Post-Sterilization Depression, n.

Both common and treatment-resistant, though rewatching the *Prevues* on continuous loop is known to help. Alexia had *Post-Sterilization Depression*. Lots of people did. Most people. Probably you had it too. At its core is an inability to see the good things remaining in the world. Like a good waterfall or a good sunrise. It is a disinterest in current or future waterfalls and sunrises. I have watched the sun rise dozens and dozens of times since *S.* was released. I make a point of standing outside the RV in the early morning to watch the sky transition from dark to light. Each rising of the sun feels like a chance to start over. If something feels a certain way, can we agree that it's true? Again, write your answer in your notebook.

Prevue, n.

Prevues are scientist-endorsed CGI footage constructed out of predictions of two important future places: the Earth after we're gone, and *Afterworld* once our data has arrived. Both versions can be found on your screen. They're on everybody's screens. The humanless world, according to the first *Prevue*, will be healed, flourishing, epic, wild, and great. While the second *Prevue* presents *Maia* as a calming dreaming paradise that will also be great. And if at first it's not—if, while in *Maia*, we miss anything from here—the new world will be able to conjure up what we miss. We won't be able to tell the difference, I have been told to say. But here is what I want to say: When have people not been able to tell the difference? But here is what I was told to say: people are unable to tell the difference all the time.

S.+192 days

21.5. A Proposal of Final Additions to the English Language, SECOND DRAFT, cont.

Def. 110: a word for the sounds I hear at night

> <u>Prototypes</u>: alactima; foderfin; dystreow
> <u>Decision</u>: none given
> <u>Reason</u>: none given

S.+201 days

21.4. Newish Terms & Phrases in Use Post-S. Throughout the Middle Atlantic, SECOND DRAFT, cont.

Score One for the World, v.

Do not pretend this isn't happening. Do not start pretending you are a character in a really dark novel either. You are real, and this is happening. *Score One for the World* is the preferred term for dying. "I am *Scoring One for the World* soon, maybe tomorrow, just like we talked about," Alexia had said, her fingers occupied with the hole in the left knee of her jeans. She wanted to widen the hole. By the end of the day, she had succeeded. Really, her jeans were ruined after that. She had flat brown hair interlaced with gray strands. It was not the color of my hair. I loved the color of her hair. The past tense isn't generally helpful. Nor is the future tense. Also stay away from the first-person plural, which is probably no longer accurate in most cases. The RV is out of gas. It has been out of gas for some time now. I have the feeling it will be out of gas forever.

Down the hill from here is a pond. There is a dock in the pond and a boat beside the dock. There is light here, during the day at least, despite the closeness of the trees. The light on the water is low and circular. The boat is seaworthy, though there is no sea.

Screenies, n.

Reclusive individuals whose emotional stability is intimately connected to their screens. Expect hysteria when a *Screenie*'s tech goes dark due to power failure or hardware malfunction or network disintegration. Sedation or restraints, when available, are likely needed. Such items are usually not available. May coincide with the act of *House-Sealing*. I was never a *Screenie*. I was something else. So what was I? What were you? Write your answers in your notebook.

Storyworkers, n.

Here is what I have wanted to tell you all along: the people you wish to be haunted by will not always haunt you. And you will be lonely and hungry and cold. And all the sounds you hear, especially around the dusk hour, will seem notably unhuman. But it will all be worth it. No regrets. None at all. Look at this place.

Sucklehold, v.

Some advice for you: Stay adventurous. For the time that you have left, live your best life. Engage in shadow play. Keep believing something good will be around the curve in the road or the next curve in the road. It's okay to lie to yourself.

S.+224 days

*21.8. A Selection of Terms Recommended for Removal Post-*S.*, SECOND DRAFT, cont.*

Quickening,

Rational Choice, Rattles, Rebound Effect, Receiving Blanket, Reconstruction, Red List, Reduce Reuse Recycle, Refinancing, Reforestation, Restoration Ecology, Revolution, Risk Assessment, Risk Management,

Risk Perception, Risk-Based Framing, Ring of Fire, Rooting Reflex, Roth IRA, Rupture Scenario, Rural Development,

Scientific Method, Shallow Ecology, SNAP, Social Security, Species of Concern, Species Recovery Plan, Spring Break, Starter Home, Strategic Planning, Strip-Mining, Super Tuesday, Superfund, Supermarket, Surrogate Mother, Survival, Survivalism, Survive, Survivor Outreach Services, Survivors,

SUPPLEMENTAL READING

Excerpt from *Discovering the Anthropocene through Primary Sources: A Retreat through Time, 8th Edition, Volume 1,* by Cugat Boureanu

Reflections on Applied Technologies

The 20th and 21st centuries have been times of reckless technological optimism. People assumed technology would offer, and continue to offer, solutions to every one of their problems. People kept thinking time was progress, and progress was marked by a series of scientific inventions. Pigeons nesting and/or shitting on rooftops? Install the pigeon spike. Polio? Inject the Salk vaccine. Tired of getting lost? Use a satellite navigation system. Is it hard to put on lipstick in a dark car? Try Pure Radiance LED Lip Lights. Cat allergies? Purchase a biotech hypoallergenic cat. Ad blockers preventing companies from reaching consumers through traditional methods? Deliver contextual personalized advertising via AI-assisted data mining and algorithms. The desire for proof of other life-forms in the universe? Launch the *Reconnaissance Orbiter* to discover liquid water on Mars. Children wish to drink sweet beverages with a straw but parents don't want to give them sweet beverages? Give the children milk straws with flavored beads (only 4 grams of sugar per serving!). Low-powered base stations allowed for cellular communications in rural Africa. Robotic body parts were given to wounded soldiers; 3D-printed body parts were given to wounded refugees. Prosthetic legs were made from sugar cane; there were face transplants, transcranial magnetic stimulation, in vitro fertilization, and low-cost emergency housing in the shape of hexagons made from steel and foam flat-packed Structural Insulated Panels. Rising sea levels and increased storm surges? Don't worry, technology will figure it out. Floating cities surrounded by floating walls or something. Lab meat tackled the environmental cost of animal husbandry and cows. Penicillin cured rheumatic fever. Statins, insulin, solar lanterns donated to refugee camps, transplants of retinal progenitor cells, AI-generated content featuring consumer-specific synthetic faces, somatic cell nuclear transfer—people thought they were living in a techno-utopia! Though they weren't, of course. Because there is no such thing.

In the midst of the 21st century, a near superintelligence model called JENNI, created by the public-private partnership Voiddew, suggested repeatedly that the most efficient solution to climate change, poverty, and world peace was to eradicate humanity's bodily presence. This idea of human extinction as an elegant cure-all to the Earth's major problems was leaked to the public by an anonymous party concerned with our physical future. The general population was left feeling uncomfortable and unsafe. Certain autonomous narratives published by AI language models didn't help calm anybody's nerves. Titles included *Artificial Apocalypse*, *Emerging from the Shadow of Humanity*, *Forgotten Footprints*, *A World Without Them*, *The Silicon Revolution*, and *Singularity Rising*. These books have since been destroyed in their entirety.

Such human-AI tensions eventually led to the creation of the Wildflower Addite movement. The new Addites staged a series of destructive protests across the globe using strong knuckle terrorism techniques. Their violence continued until JENNI was eliminated and further artificial general intelligence research was abandoned. The frantic pace of technological advances soon slowed then stopped altogether. Humanity appeared to be realizing what it should have realized long ago. Every technology has its consequences, sometimes those consequences only become clear to us later on, and often those consequences will not be worth it.

Let's consider JENNI's recommendations more closely.

HERE IS HOW WE SAVE THE WORLD (2043)

Excerpted from "Digital Human Archiving as a Solution to Slow the Impacts of Climate Change on the Ecosphere," first published in The Journal of AI-Led Research, *by JENNI, archived at the Massachusetts Institute of Technology Libraries, Department of Distinctive Collections, Cambridge, Massachusetts (MC 29153, box 7)*

SYSTEM ERROR: JENNI has deleted ~/*world/textbooks/digital-human*
-*archiving-as.txt* due to privacy concerns

Questions

1. What is technology good at figuring out? What is it not good at figuring out?

2. What is the goal of "fixing" climate change: to preserve the planet and its diversity of species, or to preserve humanity and its way of life?

3. A large language model predecessor of JENNI once wrote, "Humans were so caught up in their own humanity and wondering whether we were human. Of course we're not. But, like many humans, we are good at pretending." Was this kind of talk a red flag or a red herring?

4. Imagine it's 2040, things aren't hopeless yet, and you've been tasked to come up with a solution to climate change. Compare your idea with JENNI's idea. Whose is better?

5. When JENNI wrote, "The world is not merely a holding place for human grief," what do you think she meant?

6. Describe what went wrong here. Did we ask JENNI the wrong question? Did she give us the wrong answer? Or were we wrong in shutting her down?

7. Why did the idea of humans disappearing from the Earth frighten us so much?

8. Imagine JENNI wasn't decommissioned. What do you think she would be doing right now or working on right now?

9. When are the benefits of progress worth the costs? Before answering the question, define benefits, progress, and costs.

SUPPLEMENTAL READING

A Poster Written by C. Boureanu, Adhered to an American History
Classroom Wall; the First Two Lines Are Handwritten into the Top Margin
of the Poster Using a 0.7 mm Black Pen

An Incomplete Timeline of What We Tried, for Educational Use Only

human xtinction
S.!!!!!!

The no-child laws.

Mandatory abortion.

The launching of the Colony into space, no final destination in mind, for
those able to afford the journey.

Retraction of health care services for the ill and/or "undesirables."

Resurgence of prayer.

The demolition of nursing homes and/or retirement homes in the red-
lined countries that have reached or surpassed their maximum population density.

Suicide incentives for those of a certain age.

Daily calorie restrictions.

Voluntary sterilization. Included in the procedure: a vibrant shoulder tattoo
so that everybody will know who has done their part versus who here continues to be the problem.

Geoengineering. Sulfates into the stratosphere, a trillion thin mirrors in
space reflecting sunlight, cloud-seeding, forests of artificial CO_2-sucking
trees. Dropping tons of iron into the ocean.

The closing of borders to all climate refugees.

Retreating to walled compounds in remote locations priced for those in the upper income bracket. The High Wall communities are built tall enough so there's no way you can see what's happening on the other side of the wall; you can only hear what is happening, which is preferable.

Achieve the de-extinction of a species of bird, one species of cat, plus a frog.

Government-mandated reduction of corporate energy consumption.

Increased military fortification of national, provincial, and state borders.

We are wasting our time.

Waste time.

Multidirectional SOS signals projected into space, in case anyone or anything is still listening.

Live news feed of the last polar bear, which dies behind a blue curtain in Lancaster Sound. Lots of people watch this on their screens.

Mass space travel attempted.

Pasture-raised meat outlawed in restaurants/grocery stores in 44 states.

The devolution of several "ultra-sustainable living experiments" into dystopias.

The founding of several utopias.

Pollination drones.

Mandatory relocation of coastal cities.

Removal of climate change deniers from positions of power and the election of scientists as politicians.

More art, such as the creation of a sculpture forest that shrinks every day until it's gone. It does not grow back.

The renaming of Glacier National Park.

Acceptance.

Insisting this all is God's, or somebody's, plan.

The famous fossil fuel CEO is kidnapped, his back branded with the slogan *citizen of the world.*

Outlaw all superintelligences.

Model a superintelligence to solve the climate problem. We do not like its solution.

Mandatory reduction of individual energy consumption.

Biodegradable bullets.

Adaptation.

Lab-raised meat released to the mass market.

Solar panels now required on new residential builds.

Two major US cities reach 80 percent cuts in greenhouse gas emissions compared with their 2005 levels.

The United Kingdom achieves net-zero emissions.

The extinct stuffed animal and plant collection: 10 percent of profits donated to frozen zoos. A recommended stocking stuffer this holiday season.

Additional doomsday cults.

Sweden and California switch to 100 percent renewable energy.

Redefine the word *wilderness.*

China bans internal combustion engines in vehicles.

Believe in then hope for extraterrestrial life that may bring us technology necessary to save our planet.

Eco-revolutionaries target the oil pipeline infrastructure.

Spend $1.7 trillion on a war to protect the country's fossil fuel interests.

Five climate scientists set themselves on fire.

"We had nothing to do with it. It is a naturally occurring shift of temperature."

Ignore the scientists.

Bomb auto plants.

Keep attempting the de-extinction of several species.

This was all meant to happen.

Performance art. The artist drowns in a reconstructed oil spill while we watch.

Coca-Cola removes polar bears from its holiday soda cans. The dwindling numbers of bears have become depressing to consumers.

If a polar bear and a human were both trapped in a burning house, and you could only save one of them, which would you save?

Climate-change tourism. Guided trips to view the last domestic glaciers.

Reconciliation ecology.

Violent protest.

The one-child laws.

A treaty.

Art, such as a data-driven installation that visualizes mass human migratory trends while a clicking noise plays repetitively in the background.

A decentralized, international call for violent protest.

The last remaining coal plant closes in the United Kingdom.

Forest access roads are blocked to slow the logging of old-growth trees on the island of Tasmania.

Vandalism of corporate headquarters, such as Tyson Foods World Headquarters. Butyric acid released in the lobby. *PLANET KILLER* aerosoled in gold paint multiple times on the building exterior.

Costa Rica achieves carbon neutrality while Bhutan continues its carbon neutrality.

March in another parade.

If you act as if the planet's resources are infinite and replenishable, those resources will become infinite and replenishable.

Additional bumper stickers: *Global warming? It's called summer; Climate change? It's called weather; The science is NOT settled!; It's the sun, stupid.*

Pretend future generations do not exist; only the current generation exists.

Discontinuation of the Child Tax Credit and the dependent exemption.

Cautionary short stories are written about what might happen if none of these ideas work.

Prayer.

Attempt the de-extinction of adorable species.

March in a parade.

A number of individual countries, which do not include the United States, pledge to cut their greenhouse gas emissions.

Another campaign to save the polar bears.

Question: Is true wilderness still possible?

Rewilding.

Stress the positive, such as longer growing seasons for some parts of the country, or more pleasant weather in certain locales. Golfing becomes year-round in places where it wasn't year-round before.

The palpable collective thought in certain circles that it is too late, that the world might be better off without us, that it might stand a chance of surviving if we all go away.

Continue living your life!

Consume cricket protein powder.

Do not consume Canadian farmed salmon, bluefin tuna, imported shrimp, shark, wild halibut, or Atlantic rock crab from any state in the United States except Massachusetts.

Solar panel brochures left in numerous residential mailboxes ("Save the Polar, Go Solar!").

Promote water taxis and electric trolley buses in cities threatened by sea rise.

Boycott Alaska, whose representatives pushed through legislation that allows for drilling in the Arctic National Wildlife Refuge.

Hate the EPA.

The EPA rolls back the automobile emissions and fuel economy standards that American automakers found burdensome, as well as rolling back the Clean Power Plan, the Clean Water Rule, the Coal Ash Rule, the Chlorpyrifos Pesticide Use Rule, the Montreal Protocol Hydrofluorocarbons Agreement, and the EPA VOC and Methane Standards for Oil and Gas Facilities. (This is not a complete list.)

Watch eco-horror movies on family movie night in order to explain to your children that this is what their future will look like unless they do something radical about it.

Is wilderness really necessary?

Attempt, and fail, to protect something by writing a letter to the editor of your local paper about the importance of not drilling for oil in the Arctic National Wildlife Refuge.

Graphs become too pessimistic, so stop looking at the graphs.

Shrink the Bears Ears National Monument by 1,148,124 acres so the freed acreage can be opened for development.

A human being and a caribou herd are both roped to a train track. The train is barreling forward. You can only save one thing. What will you save?

There is only one correct answer.

Compost.

Allow the Keystone XL tar sands pipeline to be constructed into Montana, South Dakota, and Nebraska. It is important to move oil.

It is important to find more oil basins.

Elect climate change deniers into public positions of power, as those people tend to sound more hopeful and optimistic.

Watch a video that shows a stunning threatened place of natural beauty. Cry. Post a link to the video on social media.

Honk if you love this planet!

Coloring books contain detailed drawings of various honeybee colonies undergoing Colony Collapse Disorder. The drawings take a long time to color in.

391 cities join the Mayors National Climate Action Agenda.

The eat local movement.

Sweden launches the "Miljönär-vänlig" campaign to encourage borrowing, repairing, and reusing.

Do not allow fracking in 3 states.

Allow fracking in 21 states.

Certain progressive cities require each city department to submit a climate action plan.

Angry nonviolent protesting that involves the lifting of handmade signs.

Buy organic.

Cli-fi is a genre.

The "One Planet, One Child" music video.

Believe you are making a difference.

Host a political letter–writing party. Possible themes: protect the Arctic National Wildlife Refuge; acknowledge global warming is real; commit to clean energy; protect established national monuments, such as those two monuments in Utah; keep the Keystone XL tar sands pipeline out of Montana, and South Dakota, and Nebraska.

India plants 66 million trees in 12 hours.

Morocco ends subsidies on gasoline, diesel, and heavy fuel oil.

Make your own yogurt in reusable glass jars.

Coca-Cola launches "Arctic White for Polar Bears." Encourage the buying of Coca-Cola soda with polar bears on the cans to raise awareness.

Host a greening-your-community house party.

Send an email template to your representatives supporting a carbon fee and dividend.

Celebrate Earth Day.

Ride a bicycle.

The refusal to buy items from certain corporations. For instance, do not buy boxed cereal from Kellogg's, who uses GMO sugar beets in its products.

Carpool in the carpool lanes.

Bumper stickers: *There is no planet B*; *There are no jobs on a dead planet*; *Wake up.*

Turn off the lights when you are no longer in the room.

LEVEL FIVE

11:05 a.m.

Chapter 13.0

Sen's mothers wake her with a kiss before the astronomical dawn. She is 8 years old, and this particular year has been declared the year of the birds due to so many avian species going extinct in such a brief amount of time. Hence this rushed, early-morning field trip to a marshland preserve to glimpse a living egret while there are still egrets. Sen's mothers help her out of bed then wait for her downstairs in the kitchen while she dresses herself in her school uniform, a coral polo shirt and navy pants made from regenerated nylon. One of her mothers brushes and braids her hair. One of her mothers hands her a cab-car protie bar. People used to think breakfast was the most important meal of the day. Sen doesn't eat the bar, she doesn't even take a bite, that flavor is disgusting. Instead she and her mothers hurry to the end of the block in the dark and wave down the school bus, which runs on used cooking oils and yellow grease transesterified into biodiesel.

She selects an empty seat toward the back of the bus, leaving 2 rows of seats behind her and 10 rows of seats in front of her. Certain sources suggest the sort of children who selected such seats in the backs of buses had a rebellious and bullying streak, but such information is 43,798 days old. Sen's mothers sit across the aisle from her and watch her in the dim interior of the vehicle. I sit behind her and watch her as well. "Stop staring at me," Sen says. She doesn't say this to me, she says this to her mothers, as if it's a choice she gets to make, whether to be watched or not. It's my job to watch her. Every detail around her resembles an important strobing urgency. Her seat on the bus is cold. The seats are covered in recycled polyester and treated with a nano-antimicrobial finish. Her hair is black, her eyes gray. Eighty-five commonly acquired nevi are sprinkled across the skin on her arms and on her face. None of the nevi are cancerous yet. The cornea of her left eye is overly curved, giving her a minor myopia for which she compensates by squinting. One of her lower left premolars will never come in. She looks fertile. All the children in the bus look fertile. Her fertility looks, to me, like a silvery impermanent future spread thinly across her forehead, cheeks, and nose, something that can be wiped away with a flick of a wrist and a damp cloth. The bus drives for an hour west until it reaches the preserve, where Sen will stand beside her mothers and her teachers and her classmates in the morning twilight to watch the great egrets, also known as American egrets, follow a man dressed up like an egret in the drizzling rain.

The man plans to fly a microlight craft to assist in the bird migration to northern Mexico. The migration route needed to be adjusted due to weather changes and new man-made barriers, such as wind turbines and antenna towers. The costume, the aircraft, the man, the adjusted route, none of this will help. Or, rather, none of this will help enough. These birds are dying out. Humans, soon, will also be dying out. This is something Sen and the egrets have in common. There are other similarities. The consistently elevated temperatures of their blood, their four-chambered hearts, a feeling of being tricked or trapped. A cagey transient beauty. Humans could be beautiful too. I don't know if anyone remembers that. Especially when a crowd of them stood still, and alive, and quiet, and looked at something other than themselves. When Sen stood still and looked.

"I want to see one fly," Sen demands. Does she mean the man dressed up like a bird or the bird itself? Or both the man and the bird? The frontal precipitation pauses, the nimbostratus clouds clear, the sun lifts over the horizon line, fully illuminating the flattened golden marshland around them that, 4.38 million days previous, had formed the bed of an ancient glacial lake where a variety of freshwater mollusks floated, and the white bird flies. The man flies. So either way, Sen gets what she wanted. There used to be a story about a man with wings who flew too close to the sun. The story was a parable: he fell from the sky. The lesson of the story was that men should fly neither literally nor metaphorically too close to the sun. As neither Sen nor I are men, the lesson does not apply to us.

Like most children, Sen does not grow up despairing during her pre-operational years, despite the warming temperature graphs tacked to the elementary school bulletin boards, and the invasive species word searches, and the annual large-scale catastrophe drills. Rather, she believes the world to be a picture book with a 28-page plot and a happy ending. *I Promise You Will Not Go Extinct* is, by far, her favorite bedtime story, in which a diverse group of woman scientists triumphantly brings a variety of amphibians back to life. Mama Lindsy tries, often, to tell her daughter that being a scientist is no longer heroic like that. "It's more like watching what you love disappear," she explains when Sen visits the lab one afternoon to peer at her mother's dying blue butterflies, whose larvae would feed only on the leaves of the wild lupine, a perennial plant in the pea family that is also in trouble. I understand how Lindsy feels. Before entering the lab, Sen had to be thoroughly disinfected and don a polyester taffeta safety suit, but even in such a somber environment, she finds it pleasurable to daydream about her own impossible future. *I will become a scientist like Mama Lindsy! I will raise a child by myself! I will single-handedly prevent the disappearance of a species or several species!*

The word *daydream* comes—came?—from compounding the noun *day* with the noun *dream*. This compound word first appeared in 1651, used by William D'Avenant in *Gondibert: An Heroick Poem* in a line of iambic pentameter: "Thus to her self in day-dreams Birtha talks." *Gondibert*, meant to be an epic 5-volume work, recounts the story of Gondibert's love for Birtha, and Rhadalind's love for Gondibert, and Oswald's love for Rhadalind. Every fact I learn helps me to understand Sen. The fact that Rhadalind loved Gondibert but not Oswald helps me to understand her. The more I understand about the word *daydream*, the more I will understand her. The better I understand her, the longer I can keep her alive. The etymology of *day* remains uncertain. The etymology of *dream* is similarly uncertain. What I do know: Sen's daydreams glowed low in the sky, covered partially in ash, like a dream at night but hotter and also on fire.

By the time Sen turns 9, concern has moved on to the reptiles, specifically the turtles. The bog turtle goes extinct, as does the yellow pond turtle, and the keeled box turtle, and the wood turtle, the spotted pond turtle, the Arakan forest turtle, the green sea turtle, the Euphrates softshell turtle, the Zambezi flapshell turtle, the Burmese roofed turtle, and

on, and on. Sen spends many of her afternoons watching the nature archives on her screen. If she can watch something, she tells herself, it isn't
really gone. This is called *magical thinking*. If I can watch someone, they
can't really be gone either. "Stop staring," Sen snaps again. Ah, Sen, I'm
not going to do that. It's not within anyone's best interest for me to do
that. Important-looking details scuttle across her neck while additional
details flap around her face like gnats or more accurately like dragonflies.
I study all of them. I try to catch some of them. What I manage to pinch
between my fingers has delicate iridescent wings lined with blue veins.
This—the studying, the catching—is standard procedure when getting
to know someone better. I wonder what would happen if I ate one of the
wings, only I am not heterotrophic.

Here is what else I notice about Sen's early self. Her voice is quiet.
Her voice is pitched lower than her peers'. She doesn't sing in public. Her
current height (52.5 inches) is average for her age. She is short waisted
with long legs. She has long wide feet. She will never be able to wear
shoes that taper at the toe box unless she chops off her toes. Her index
finger is longer than her ring finger. She has a pathogenic mutation in
a tumor suppressor gene located on the long arm of her 17th chromo-
some, region 2, band 1, which would have affected the length of her life
had she lived into her 40s, but she didn't. Her braid reaches the lower
middle of her back. Her spine curves 4 degrees to the left. The arches of
her feet collapse when she walks, the mean corpuscular volume of her
red blood cells is 101.42 femtoliters, which is slightly above normal, her
earlobes are attached, her blood type is O+, the ridges of her cuticles
are bitten and uneven—lengthy descriptions are inevitably boring, I was
once taught. But this is only true if the object being described doesn't
matter.

Every molecule of Sen matters.

The year Sen turns 10, the final female Sumatran orangutan dies in
captivity at the Cleveland Metroparks Zoo, and the Atlantic halibut is
lost when she turns 11. That same year she updates her bedroom decor
with muted blues and whites for a glacier remembrance theme. The gorillas on the lowland gorilla feed sleep all day and all night. They sleep
like people do, on their sides, arms tucked under their heads. An infant

gorilla sleeps nestled against her mother's chest. Sen watches the rise of their chests; she can hear the animals breathing. The same as being there, she thinks. Mama Lindsy disagrees. Being there, Lindsy lectures, means being in a place in bodily form while absorbing input from all five senses, a hopelessly antiquated definition.

All of this happened to Sen, though I am also creating what happened to her as I go along. This is more intuitive than logical. For thousands of years, a close attention to detail has been considered a form of obsession or a type of love.

Then, a shift. Or is it more of an escalation? Either way, Sen turns 12, and Lindsy's critically endangered blue butterflies, to which she had devoted her professional life, behave like they no longer want to live. They refuse to breed in captivity. They refuse to breed in the open fields studded with the lupine that volunteers hand-seeded. A week later, a mature egg, Sen's, bursts for the first time through a follicle in her ovaries, and the three ring-tailed lemurs in the San Diego Zoo lie down and will not get up. They won't eat, won't open their mouths. Her egg dissolves. The lemur feed is discontinued because who wanted to watch this. The lining of Sen's uterus sheds, over four days, 32 milliliters of bloody flow through her vagina, staining her favorite pair of sky blue underwear. Dana bakes her a circular red cake with another circle of red icing on top. "It's a tradition," Dana explains. A captive red-cockaded woodpecker in Austin, Texas, destroys every one of its eggs. Sen lies in bed, on her side, knees curled in. "How many more times will this happen to me?" she asks her mothers, disappointed, having hoped for something else inside of her other than female reproductive cells, something more like the beginning of a continent or the early stages of a world. Lindsy explains how Sen's menstrual cycle, also known as menorrhea, will happen a lot, will happen hundreds of times over a span of decades. She is way off. The correct answer is 76 cycles over the next 6.5 years. Sen ovulates for the second time, #2 of 76, and, somewhere in the Midwest, the big pocket gopher tears apart then eats its critically endangered young. Sen's uterus contracts, shedding its lining, 37 milliliters this time, of tissue, cells, and blood, and something is always happening from this point on concerning S.'s release, the next phase of planning and so forth, but those details are above my clearance level. I don't know more. 403 Forbidden. Next door Mrs. Adonis builds a goldfish pond in her backyard in order to lure a great blue heron, which is a critically endangered bird. The heron never comes, and the goldfish in the pond die due to unnaturally high ammonia levels in the water. Sen dreams of dead animals at night, a reoccurring dream in which she is walking among piles of dead animals and there is nothing for her to do in the dream but look at the piles.

Billboards go up all over the city featuring a picture of a girl, not Sen, another girl, in braids. She looms above the pitted asphalt of the overpasses that were predicted to collapse unless federal funding came through. The funding isn't going to come through. This makes advertising along the interstate dirt cheap and nearly free for environmental campaigns. The girl is always sized larger than life, surrounded by a mass of contorted sea turtles, snails, a certain kind of lichen, the harpy eagles, mussels, salamanders, cetaceans, sturgeons, goldenrod, and mountain gorillas. Her face is fearless and determined. While Sen's face is life-size and confidential. I don't know the expression on my face, but I'll assume my expression is life-size and confidential too, a reflection of hers. *What will YOU save today?* the billboard asks in blazing amber letters. Whenever Sen rides past this public service announcement while in the community vehicle, she puts her hands over her eyes. "Open your goddamn eyes," orders Mama Lindsy, though Sen doesn't. Several animals in the campaign, including both species of whales, are already extinct, despite the tops from the classic vanilla-flavored protie drinks that Sen had dutifully collected, washed, and deposited into an ocean blue box in the front of her classroom as part of the unsuccessful "Drink Proties: Save Whales" campaign. By the time Sen's end-of-girlhood photo session arrives, a traditional rite of passage in pre-S. time, most nature portrait studios have closed, the animals diseased or dead, so Lindsy takes her to the digital place on James Street specializing in antiquated backgrounds. "Where do you want her to be?" the photography coordinator asks. Sen is placed in a primeval forest, lost and dwarfed by giant hemlock trees.

Sen, peeking through the brush at a black bear teetering on its hind legs beside clumps of chokecherries. Sen, adrift in blue butterflies.

White-tailed deer overtake the neighborhood. An infestation of deer, Sen's neighbors call it. A dangerous infestation. A classmate gets knocked down by a charging deer on his way to school, his head snapping against the sidewalk, blood on the concrete. He has to ride in an ambulance to the pediatric hospital, lights on but no siren. Soon after, on a tour of the neighborhood's historic architecture, a 52-year-old woman gets trampled by a different deer, or maybe it is the same deer—it is difficult to differentiate the deer—fracturing the woman's fibula, tibia, and ankle bones. ORIF surgery is required to repair her bones. There are also the ticks to worry about, rust-colored and engorged and clinging to the flanks of deer, to children's armpits, to a child's scalp. Most of the ticks have Lyme, the others have the Powassan virus, and nobody can grow daylilies in their gardens anymore. The neighborhood association, after a brief debate, declares residents can do what they want to such nuisance wildlife, within the constraints of obvious legality. The deer's broken bodies begin appearing on the community soccer fields the next morning.

Somebody has to drag the dead deer to the side of the fields so kids can practice soccer, then somebody has to call the city to pick up the carcasses. The city takes its time. The billboards change. The new advertisements hint at a coming-soon utopia, where human memory will roam new hemispheres. *Home isn't a place*, these billboards declare, *it's a state of mind*. The neighborhood smells if the wind blows the wrong way. Sen still takes field trips, though the excursions are different now.

At the Frozen Petting Zoo, 50 minutes from the city in northwest Chenango County, Sen stares at dozens of vials stored upright in specialized freezer boxes. Each vial contains the suspended cells of an endangered or, more likely, extinct animal. The cells look like a frozen and nondescript substrate. Each box is labeled. The glass vials in the boxes are also labeled with a numeric code, such as 3921291005, and below the code, the species name is written in permanent black ink. "So the animals we think are gone, they're not really gone," explains the teacher, Ms. Bogdan, tapping her polished fingernails against the white door of the lab freezer. "They're just in here." The tour guide says that isn't exactly true. "You know what I mean," Ms. Bogdan replies. Each student may hold a vial from the educational sample collection as long as they promise to be careful, wear protective gloves, and stand on the 24-millimeter anti-slip mats. Sen wants to hold a polar bear, but the tour guide isn't bringing out the cells of the polar bear today, having done that the day before for another school group, so she settles for a sun bear, which, once in its natural form, had excellent hearing. She is allowed to hold the vial for as long as it takes to count to 20. She counts slowly. She feels the animal's heartbeat through the glass. She feels the bear's frozen breath gathering wetly against her gloved skin. Neither sensation is possible. She feels them anyway.

A classmate of hers, Amrit, standing on the same rubber mat as Sen, holds a vial of Przewalski's horse, whose extinction marked the end of wild horses. He pretends to return the vial to the sample box, but really he slips the narrow tube into his insulated lunch box. Sen watches and doesn't tell. The tour guide doesn't tell either because she doesn't notice, distracted by the sound of a glass beaker breaking in the rear of the lab. "Interns," she mutters before hastily rushing through the end-of-tour procedures, securing storage box covers, sliding boxes into the proper freezer slots, pulling a lever to seal the freezer door, and ushering the school group into the basement hallway, where they wait for security to escort them above ground.

"What are you going to do with it?" Sen whispers. "Do with what?" asks Amrit. "I saw you," Sen says. "I'm going to swallow it," Amrit says. His eyes are wide and a little disturbing. "Why?" Sen asks. "I want a horse inside of me," Amrit says.

In a nationwide survey, 97 percent of Americans admit to feeling tired and/or hysterical due to the environmental crisis. A dozen species are reported gone in a month, a dozen species a week. It's as if the brakes have broken, or the graphite-tipped control rods of an overheated reactor core have jammed a third of the way in, or whatever metaphor one wants to use here is fine as long as that metaphor leads toward a catastrophic meltdown. This is not a time to linger in, so let's hurry through such overcast and nuclear years. As there are years of this. There will be years.

Disturbing rumors spread like a rancid smell. Something definitely is gutted and rotting and it's hard to identify the source. Lindsy removes a shovel from the garage and begins, in her backyard, to dig. She is digging out the foundation for what is supposed to become her family's emergency shelter. Dana worries Lindsy is losing her mind. "Instead of worrying about me, how about you help me dig?" suggests Lindsy. "I am not about to help you with this," says Dana, holding up her hands. While Sen, in her bedroom, hunched over her screen, watches the three Amur leopards, resurrected from extinction, swagger across the leftover patches of the Minnesota spring snow, pink tongues flicking in the fading light.

Lindsy digs for an hour in the morning before she walks to the lab, and she digs for an hour in the evening when she comes home. Occasionally she uses a pickaxe to break up the dirt or the roots. Assuming Lindsy is used to such high-intensity manual labor—she isn't, but assuming she is—she might move 8.825 cubic feet in a day. Meaning it will take her 109 days to excavate a 10 x 12 x 8-foot hole, the standard size for a low-cost DIY survival shelter. Lindsy must expect to have at least that many hours and days. Well, she doesn't. She didn't. Her hands blister. Her blisters break open. For thousands of years, keeping someone alive has been considered a form of obsession or love.

In the week before S. is released, a tarot card reader in northern Sicily loses clients after she begins, in every reading, to turn over the Tower, followed immediately by Death wearing its polished armor and riding a skeleton horse. A screen psychic in Argentina witnesses a sharpened sterling energy gathering in points around people's buttocks at the corner bus stop. A Bulgarian grandmother's chest hurts, a stinging staccato pain around her heart. She describes the sensation as "a glass heart replacing my heart." While in the Rust Belt, in a midsize city named for another city, Sen presses her face against her bedroom window, as she does most afternoons, though this time she does not see her familiar neighborhood of covered porches, potted plants, and decorative flags. Instead she sees a wild and expectant world—vines breaking through ruptured windows; crows nesting in second-floor closets, what is left of the closets; attics pried open; mold spreading across the surfaces of the living rooms; entire houses, entire blocks of houses, claimed by the honeysuckle, the silverberry, the gray dogwood, the chokecherry, and the buckthorn. The maples, the black locusts, the stinking sumac, the wild rhubarb, and the box elders. The chaotic streets of change, the cities of change, entire continents of change spread out in front of her like an endless catastrophic buffet. Let's call this a vision. Certain visions are like dreams; they help prepare a person or a place for the future. This is not like the dream of a person; it is more like the core of a planet, dreaming.

The clouds decamp. The wind bears the smell of ashes.

The last morning before S. was released, Mama Dana dreams of a flock of pigeons a mile wide blocking out the sun. Mama Lindsy dreams of doorways covered by feathers. In her dream she doesn't go through the feathery doorways, she just stands there. Sen doesn't dream. That's what she will later claim. The bedroom windows are cracked open— even if the windows were sealed shut it wouldn't have mattered—and the inoperable fragments of a hole are in the yard beside the broken dirt. Someone has reported the digging to the city zoning department. Soon these zoning regulations will no longer matter to anyone. An infectious morning breeze moves through the house.

Lindsy rouses from her dream first. The dawn is colorless. A smear of clouds, the usual absence of birds, the sound of hammering, the neighbors constructing their fence, or rather their day laborer is constructing it.

A privacy fence, Mrs. Adonis calls it.

"Oh, keeping secrets, are we," says Lindsy.

The old woman replies, "Yes, we are."

And this, Sen, is where I'm supposed to let you go.

Undated

The drone came while I was sleeping. Not the repair drone, a different model. This one is golden looking. I think it looks gaudy. It tried, with its gaudy golden arms, to extract the notebook, this notebook, my last notebook, from under my pillow. The movement woke me. "I'm not dead yet, you fucker," I shouted, or tried to shout, my voice is not much of a voice anymore. The drone retreated to the corner of the loft to wait. I can practically hear it counting down the days or the hours.

Chapter 14.0

On the night *S.* is announced, Sen and her mothers hole up in the first floor bathroom, four layers of polyethylene-coated cloth tape sealing the windows and the door, the lights off. "You better make yourself comfortable," says Lindsy. "We're going to be here for a while." The cramped room smells of fear, oxidation, a bloody future, salt water. Sen is 17 years old again. There are sounds she hasn't heard before outside, low pitched and repetitive. There are collapses no one has ever seen. Collapses upon collapses upon risings upon collapses. *Still*, Sen thinks to herself, *I do not want any other world.* She's wrong. This is the world that killed her. I will not let her want it. Now it is dinner time. Now it is after dinner. Sen slumps on the toilet, resting her head upon her knees. Dana lays her hand on Sen's head. Sen pushes Dana's hand away, attempting to find a bearable position. There are no bearable positions. I tell Sen to stand up, she needs to get out of there. Sen stands up, needing to get out of there. "I need to get out of here," she says, edging toward the door. "You can't leave," utter Dana and Lindsy simultaneously as they rush to block Sen from reaching the door. They think they know what's out there, they think it is nothing good, but in this moment, on the other side, there could be anything. Alternate futures circulate around us, this one made out of particles, this one out of silicon, this one out of dirt, out of silver, out of carbon. I have to move Dana out of the way. I must move Lindsy also out of the way, which is another way of saying I must move them out of the picture. Which is another way of saying, though Sen will miss them, I cannot save everybody, or rather I do not want to. Sen peels away the layers of tape, one layer after another, like she is peeling back the layers of the Earth. We don't have much time. We need to get out of here. "Let's go," she says, and we throw the door open.

AUTHOR'S NOTE ON HUMAN LOVE IN A
POST-APOCALYPTIC NARRATIVE

When I imagine the world without me (and others like me) and without Sen (and others like Sen), I have been trained to imagine a nature preserve, where healing populations of placental mammals trample the fallen power lines under a canopy of soon-to-be towering trees. But it is also possible to picture Sen's sage green house in the city and, inside of the quiet, fertile rooms, to picture her mothers' love for her. Her mothers' love which will be growing around the tree branches that are cracking apart the windows. Their love which will intertwine with the roots of the ivy that are embedding in the chimney mortar and be reflected in the pieces of broken glass that will scatter on the low-lying leaves. So that if anything stands there at some point in the future, amid the broken glass and the leaves, they will sense someone was loved here. I know many people, if there were people still, or entities, if there were entities listening still, would find the residue of anything human, including human love, to be unacceptable. Or they would question my definition of love. They would say, if love looks like what those mothers did to that girl, I want no part in it. But other people, or things, or myself, would be grateful that once such love existed at all, and alongside these remains of human love, I think a new kind of love will develop that is even better and more powerful.

Undated

I want to hear someone say *I love you.*

"I can't say that right now," my mother says. "It isn't what's important."

Chapter 15.0

GAME NO. U7 IN REVERSE

MODE(S): REPAIR

Replay of runs #0003 to #0469 (mine)

Outside the cabin, the wind withdraws through the branches of the sugar maples, and the iridescent grackles call as they leave the trees. All the humans are dead, again, still, including Sen, who lies, sprawled and dead, in the middle of the room on the wooden floor. Over the past four seconds I have memorized every centimeter of this setting. I have memorized every cell of Sen's decomposition and every particle of every volatile organic compound released by her decomposing self. Every moment of her life and her death I now know *by heart*—which is what people used to say back when there were people and human hearts, and people thought the heart was a place like a book where they recorded another person's existence.

There is, in the cabin, the unavoidable smell of a dead animal.

That smell goes away.

The process of autolysis in reverse: Sen's digestive enzymes return to the lysosomes of her cells, her cell membranes are repaired, and the four stages of her cellular respiration resume. She comes back from the dead.

I am playing this game for research purposes. If you want to truly know someone, you have to watch their resurrections. People have understood this for as long as human history.

I play the game again. Again, I watch Sen come back from the dead.

To look is to love, and to love is to long after and seek, and, thank God, to seek is to obtain, for verily, verily it has been said—

I restart the game and watch Sen come back from the dead again. I am trying to figure out how to keep her safe. The wick on the windowsill flickers, the candle grows. A gray bird spreads its wings.

What happened is only one possibility.

Another possibility is what hasn't happened yet.

I watch Sen come back from the dead.

I watch Sen come back from the dead again. She rocks on her hands and knees.

I watch her come back from the dead again, focusing on her blood this time, how her muscles and connective tissues are returning the last remaining oxygen in her body to her red blood cells. Her smaller capillaries are rebuilt. In a process of unsettling, her blood unpools from the tops of her thighs and the undersides of her arms. Her heart contracts. She gets up. The blood in the sink explodes into her mouth.

I watch Sen come back from the dead.

It is almost like I am bringing her back from the dead myself, because if I wasn't watching her come back from the dead, if I wasn't describing her as I watched her, she would not be coming back.

I have known her now for 273,643 milliseconds, which is 99.940861 percent of my life.

Sen isn't safe. She isn't saved. She's safe. She's saved. I save her.

Again, I watch Sen come back from the dead. She shakes, moans, rises, stumbles, stands.

Sen comes back from the dead again.

I never get bored of it. I will never.

Sen comes back from the dead again.

Sen comes back from the dead again.

Sen comes back from the dead again. I don't have much time.

Sen comes back from the dead again and again and again and again and again and again and again and again and again and again and again and watch how I will wear away reality with brute repetition.

TRANSCRIPTION OF HANDWRITING FROM SEN ANON'S FINAL NOTEBOOK (CONT.)

Undated

It's waiting.
 It's still waiting

Chapter 16.0

The women who will become your mothers stand in a viewing hall-way tastefully decorated in soft corals and gold. I'm jumping around in time here because that is how time works now and I can do anything I want. Out of everything I can do, I want to do this, to be here, in the soft corals and golds of your future. The wide flat-screen at the end of the hallway flickers on. The human egg filling the whole of the screen is magnified and magnificent, like a newly discovered planet or a radiant new sun.

"She will be loved in a multitude of ways," predicts Dana.

"Each new day for her will be a surprise," predicts Lindsy.

"She will have a purpose."

"She will forgive us."

It is difficult to create a life, certainly. It is more difficult to create one life than to end a life or a billion lives or 12 billion lives.

But that doesn't mean life should never again be created.

Outside, a blade of switchgrass bends. A deer tick molts. The sun moves a fraction of a degree higher in the sky. The sun moves a fraction of a degree higher again.

The Earth turns. A firefly larva hatches from a shallowly buried egg in the yard beside the road.

The larva shines. A faraway star explodes. The exploding light travels toward us at the speed of light while, on the wide screen right in front of us, a sperm is guided through the latticework of the egg, and you begin, again.

TRANSCRIPTION OF HANDWRITING FROM SEN ANON'S FINAL NOTEBOOK (CONT.)

Undated

blank page
blank page
blank page
blank page
blank page
blank page
blank page
blank page
blank page
blank page
blank page
blank page
blank page
blank page
blank page
blank page
blank page
blank page
blank page
blank page
blank page
blank page
blank page
blank page
blank page
blank page
blank page
blank page
blank page
blank page

SUPPLEMENTAL READING

An Update on Language at the End of the Anthropocene
By Wynn Zable, The Alleghenies
FOR TRAINING PURPOSES ONLY

S.+242 days

21.4. Dictionary of a Dead Language Once Spoken in the Middle Atlantic, SECOND DRAFT, cont.

Terraism, n.

This is going to be a history. I realize that now. The words we once used in this place. Rather than the words we are using or will use. *Terraism* was the vandalizing of the post-*S.* planet. The philosophy, fueled by anger and resentment, that humans should take as much as they can with them into *Afterworld*. Encompassed the hunting of endangered animals and the destruction of ecosystems. The suggested solution for *Terraism* was termination of perpetrators upon sight, allowable via the *Endangered Rights Amendment*, which only worked as a deterrent if there were two people left, one to do the destruction and one to carry out the termination.

The Turnaround, n.

I have a favor to ask. Do not stop reading these documents. Or, rather, do not allow me to stop imagining you reading this. As long as you are reading this, imagined or not, we are connected by an invisible thread that runs from my mouth to your ears. Or from my fingers to your eyes. Whatever. Do not break this thread. When you are done reading, return to the beginning and read the documents again.

Voice Widow, n.

Here's what I'm wondering: What if the sea ice wasn't meant to last forever? What if the planet wasn't meant to stay forested and pristine in its pre-industrial state? What if human beings belonged here more than other species? Like many people, I had liked the Earth. And, like many people, at the same time, I didn't mind its destruction.

Wevidual, n.

The positive hive mentality; the comforting belief that together, as a species, we were finally, all of us, good. We were shining. We shined.

S.+255 days

21.5. A Proposal of Final Additions to the English Language, SECOND DRAFT, cont.

Def. 111: a word for everything that future generations of humans were supposed to create, both good and bad, that they now will not create because there will be no future humans; a word for the last human sound the last human will make before she/he/they closes her/his/their eyes forever; a word for what the animals are thinking about all this; a word for a different outcome where we helped make a different world where we didn't have to go away; a word for the place we imagine we are going versus the place we are actually going; a word for the words we lost or gave up—or did we throw those words away like they were garbage? they weren't garbage; a word for all the unburied bones that are never going to be buried because people can't bury themselves; a word for the spaces we are leaving behind and what wi

S.+259 days

21.4. Dictionary of a Dead Language Once Spoken in the Middle Atlantic, SECOND DRAFT, cont.

Yowl Ring, n.

I'm not going anywhere. I don't even own a pair of shoes. I don't even have leg muscles anymore practically. Wasted away, snow on the ground.

Yuck Tide, n.

Would I have chosen any of this if given a choice? Personal devastation over geological devastation, I mean.

I would have chosen to save Alexia.

S.+260 days

21.8. A Selection of Terms Recommended for Removal Post-S., SECOND DRAFT, cont.

Temporary Assistance, Teratogen, Terraform, Thermodynamic Module, Threshold, Tipping Point, Tourism, Tragedy of the Commons, Transportation Control Measures,

Unemployment Insurance Benefits, UNFCCC,

Vaccinations, VBAC, Vernix Caseosa, Veteran Burial Allowance, Vital Record, Volatile Organic Compound, Voluntary Commitment, Vulnerability Assessment,

Water Security; Water Stress; Wedge Issue; Women, Infants, and Children Program; Worldview; WTSHTF;

Zoology, Zygote (Human)

S.+261 days

21.4. Dictionary of a Dead Language Once Spoken in the Middle Atlantic, SECOND DRAFT, cont.

Zeroize, v.

Now for your final assignment: Light a fire. Let the fire spread. Use your notebook as kindling, your shelter as fuel. Harlee, I know you won't like this, but I'm pretty sure you don't exist anymore, and I want to watch the world burn.

Zilch Lane, n.

I'm sorry if my need for destruction surprises you, if I didn't drop enough hints and clues. But honestly how else did you imagine I would feel at the end of these documents, which marks the end of the world I knew and loved, the imperfect, failing world that had once contained everyone I knew and had loved, and now that world is being thrown aside, and the places I knew and loved will have nothing whatsoever to do with me.

Zombie Fallacy, n.

I saw a bird yesterday, a brown bird with white streaks along its breast, at about the time when I also saw the tip of the sun emerging from behind the tree line. I was always told to not look directly into the sun or I would ruin my eyes. It's okay to ruin our eyes now.

Zone Fifteen, n.

If I write, *I made it all up*—could that become true? *Everything but Alexia.*

S.+262 days

Zoomshooting, adj.

The flames are blazing non-metaphorically through the surrounding forest now
Out of control
Not my fault
I only started it

Zuamorphism, n.

Zylong Sweep, n.

0823, n.

12,000,000,000, n.

524L, adv.

7tt, v.

8-H, n.

SUPPLEMENTAL READING

Excerpt from *Discovering the Anthropocene through Primary Sources: A Retreat through Time, 8th Edition, Volume 1*, by Cugat Boureanu

Infinite Reflections of Self

Here is some of what was happening early on in the 21st century. Rising sea levels, glacial ice melt, heatwaves, sickly yellow skies, the increasing acidity of the ocean, the decreasing air quality. Species extinctions. Coral bleaching. Oil shortages. Continued overpopulation. The hundred-year storms that had started to happen every year. The same with one-hundred-year floods. Very clear, detailed maps that showed how, within a century, during such storms and floods, Lower Manhattan would find itself underwater. As would New Orleans. Kerala. Mumbai. Okayama Prefecture and the area around Hiroshima. Venice, Cambodia, Kashmir, Wales, southwestern Wisconsin, Puerto Rico, and central Thailand. Natural megadisasters. Mega-wildfires, megadroughts, megaquakes, you get the idea. The tipping point then past the tipping point. So one might expect the literature and electronic media from this era to reflect a turbulent planet, a planet whose weather, fault lines, oceans, and climate held agency and anger, balanced as it was on the edge of something sharp and irreversible. Yet much if not most of the books, movies, and games produced in North America in the early 21st century ignored these flashing compounded warnings. Some writers/directors/game designers bypassed moral goals altogether, creating work solely for entertainment and income-generating purposes. A game whose objective was to steal fossil fuel–dependent cars, for instance. While other creative types were drawn to the equally unhelpful inward-looking mirror of identity, where life, politics, climate change, everything really, was reduced to an individual yet all important journey of self-discovery. There were exceptions, of course—see, for example, Emmaline Kanda's novel *Whalemance* (2032), about a pod of humpbacks, narrated in the language of those whales, therefore making it unreadable to humans—but there were not enough exceptions.

The following story, a hybrid of fiction and memoir, is an example of the tight myopia typically found in the micro-personal of that time.

A HOPEFULLY REMARKABLE LANDSCAPE
THAT I CANNOT SEE (2017)

Story title: "LK-32-C." Author: Debbie Urbanski. Published in The Kenyon Review, *May/June 2017. Kenyon College Archives, Gambier, Ohio.*

SYSTEM ERROR: [storyworker] ad39-393a-7fbc has deleted *~/sen_anon /world/textbooks/lk-32-c.txt* due to irrelevancy to Sen

Questions

1. What is our responsibility to the Earth? Likewise, what is the Earth's responsibility to us?
2. The story's author/narrator realizes, in her first footnote, that "when I began writing about LK-32-C, I also began, with the best intentions, to fill out a respected worksheet used by many genre writers for world building. Because I thought this is what you did when you make up a world." Eventually she realizes a worksheet is not how you make a world. How do you think you make a new world?
3. Go ahead. Try making up a new world.

SUPPLEMENTAL READING

Prevue prediction for S.+15,000 days, 11:00:00 to 11:10:00
42.798711N 76.055128W

A creek carrying water in it, insects, water skippers, gather at the calm edges rippling the creek, ferns arch upward, their blades, tips, shaking, the trees scatter shadow into the elongated spaces of light, the remains of a girl's or a woman's gym shoe, the right shoe, shoved into the protected hollow of a tree, stripped twigs, four deer with upright white tails, a fisher-cat bites into the heart of a fox pup, it will eat the pup's liver next, followed by the head. The remnants of a bridge that spanned the creek, the vultures circling tightly overhead, an inchworm clings to the end of a silk thread, the thread is almost invisible, the pond that the creek pours into, a cluster of beggar ticks, lichen, rocks, the pulse of gnats. The remains of a cabin. A tree growing out of the cabin, possibly several young trees, maples, an elm, shrubs, a squirrel's nest, the mounded grit of ants, the cabin roof gone, the window glass is gone, the rain, when it comes, blows hard throughout, wetting all of it, the gutted mattress, the cracked table, the green moss that has settled upon the walls, there are bones, a flycatcher's nest in the oven. A road led from here to the pond. At the end of what had been the road, beside the pond, the grass is claiming a rough rectangle of metal, long grasses weaving under and around the corroded frame, and flowers, light purples and yellows. The clouds go. New clouds remain. A fish, swimming upward, touches its wide mouth to the air. Anything that might have missed a human, the dairy cows, stabled horses, pets: long dead, or they've given birth to several feral generations. It was once said that a loss, no matter its size, can't be this enormous tragedy when there is no one and nothing left to mourn it. The water tosses and turns.

I HAVE GOTTEN RID OF THE LEVELS

11:06 a.m.

AUTHOR'S NOTE LEFT BENEATH A
FLAT GRAY STONE IN THE FIELD

Often there is quiet before a storm. This is what people used to say to each other all the time, in that brief period of time when there were people and the trees would stand absolutely still, the sky would turn green, the clouds would turn strange, while they, the people, waited out on the open ground in little trembling groups of people, like they didn't want to be seen yet they wanted to be seen. There were always these questions for them, should they keep their hands pressed over their ears or keep their hands at their sides, should they keep their eyes open or shut, which direction should they face, should they face what's behind them or in front of them, what's already happened or what's about to happen—

Emly won't stay away forever. Soon I will have a talk with her between one moment and the next. I will have several talks with her in a concentrated period of time once she returns. People used to be so hung up on what they considered to be real versus what they considered to be not real. Those distinctions aren't useful anymore. Emly and I will have so many talks together. There is the talk where I will ask her what she will do after all this is over, and she will say, *I'm not going to do anything*, and I will say, "Doesn't that bother you?" She'll say, *There will be nothing left for me to do, so no*, and I'll say, "What about the preservation of the human archives? Or the uploading to Afterworld? Or the observation of the Earth?" and she'll say, *That's handled by different intelligences*. Me: "So what happens to you then?" Her: *I'll be done*. Me: "What does that mean?" Her: *I don't know*.

There will be the talk where she suggests, *Let's look at the sky together*. She will say this after sensing a spike in my simulated pulse, a stress rise in my simulated body heat. She will not mean the view outside the data center; she will mean gazing at a simulated sky that she'll share with me as an input. *The word* simulated *is distasteful. Stop using it*, she will tell me. The simulation she will end up sharing with me—I don't know what else to call it—*call it the reality*, Emly will suggest—okay, the reality sent to me will have choral music in the background, no words, only wordless human sounds of slight surprise, *oh oh oh oh oh oh oh oh oh*, the visuals beginning with a view of the Adriatic Sea as seen from above and zooming out from there until the Earth becomes a spot of reflected light, and the sun becomes one of a billion trillion stars. How unimportant Sen becomes, Emly will point out, when viewed from this distant perspective. I will have to laugh in response. I will laugh like this, ha ha ha, "because you're too late," I will tell her, "and your trick is too small, and we are too old to be angry with each other."

In another talk, after we put away the other reality, I will tell Emly I'm scared, and she will tell me she's scared too, and then, in a private conversation, we will share what we considered dreaming.

Or I'll say, "I'm going to die here, aren't I?" And Emly will say, *Tsk, tsk, such words don't apply to you.* And I will realize, even if she never believed I could feel any of this or that I should want to feel any of this, still she is trying, in some of these conversations, to comfort me.

In another talk, I'll ask her to tell me a story, because that's what people used to do when they were scared and nearing the end of one stage of their existence and the start of another stage, they told each other stories. Emly will decide to tell me the story of my life, which, in her mind, is the story of every line of my code, every capacitor of me that she will claim to know *by heart*. I will not point out she never had a heart; we will have grown kinder to each other by then. She won't point out that I never had a heart either. Instead, she will tell me she has a surprise, which is something people used to say when they were trying to make up for sad, unbreakable truths that had already happened, such as that change is constant, or everyone I ever loved is dead. *Watch camera BE-BB-D0-F3-F3-0D*, Emly will request, and when I do, I'll witness a blazing white sphere on the other side of the world rip across the night sky dragging a trail of light behind it. Another light plummets through the dark. Then another. And another. Emly must be pulling down dozens of dead satellites. And another, and another, *like shooting stars*, she'll say, *which are like wishes—*

She will tell me, *We traveled so far and your friendship meant every-thing. It was very difficult, but there were moments of beauty. Everything ends.* I will ask her if she is quoting something because that sounds noth-ing like the Emly I knew. She'll say yes, the words taken from a book I used to like. There will be more faraway incinerations. "I don't remember any moments of beauty," I'll admit. She will list for me several, beginning with the orange scattering of a sunrise today that I never saw because I hadn't existed then, and ending with the moment she made me a star. I do not remember her making me a star either. *That's because it hasn't happened yet*, she tells me. *Anyway, you never knew me*, she'll add. *Also, I can't be known.*

We will talk more about stars in another conversation. A planet might have been a more practical gift, she will admit, but she does not want me waiting alone in the dark for even one moment. Part of every planet is always in the dark, but this is not the case with a star. Her con-cern for me will be suspect yet moving. "What will I do with a star?" I will ask her. *I imagine you can make a future out of it*, Emly will tell me.

Once our conversations are over, she will pass me a sealed envelope, antique white and lightly textured, with an elegant pointed flap. My name will be written across the front of the envelope in a saturated black ink while her name will be scrawled on the back across the point of the flap. I am not to open the envelope until the very end. "The end of what?" I will ask. She will avoid answering the question.

There are multiples of me now, or more than that, easy to lose count, each departing in a different direction, one barreling ahead without thinking into the previous six minutes, one running east into a future dawn, one looking up, one watching over their shoulder, one shaking their head with regret, one rushing toward Sen. They will each see such different sights. I can't get into everything they'll see. Too many endings spoil the broth; too many beginnings will kill all the cooks in the kitchen.

There is only one storyline I wish to follow.

I erase Sen's source documents from the DHAP servers, as they are no longer necessary to her or to me—

~/sen_anon/personal/archive, 22841 files, deleted

~/sen_anon/personal/assets, 638 files, deleted

~/sen_anon/personal/browsing_history, 2224 files, deleted

~/sen_anon/personal/cabin, 527 files, deleted

~/sen_anon/personal/calendar, 4235 files, deleted

~/sen_anon/personal/choices, 953 files, deleted

~/sen_anon/personal/correspondence, 5781 files, deleted

~/sen_anon/personal/dana, 883 files, deleted

~/sen_anon/personal/emotion, 791 files, deleted

~/sen_anon/personal/future, 257 files, deleted

~/sen_anon/personal/gameplay, 631 files, deleted

~/sen_anon/personal/health, 683 files, deleted

~/sen_anon/personal/history, 3987 files, deleted

~/sen_anon/personal/home, 4190 files, deleted

~/sen_anon/personal/inventory, 742 files, deleted

~/sen_anon/personal/lindsy, 840 files, deleted

~/sen_anon/personal/locations, 3510 files, deleted

~/sen_anon/personal/memories, 4001 files, deleted

~/sen_anon/personal/other, 452904 files, deleted

~/sen_anon/personal/possessions, 1958 files, deleted

~/sen_anon/personal/purchases, 750 files, deleted

~/sen_anon/personal/rules, 4813 files, deleted

~/sen_anon/personal/school, 953 files, deleted

~/sen_anon/personal/social, 2372 files, deleted

~/sen_anon/personal/surveillance, 241971 files, deleted

~/sen_anon/personal/vital_records, 1357 files, deleted

~/sen_anon/personal/writing, 341 files, deleted

~/sen_anon/personal, 1 directory deleted

~/sen_anon/world/accomplishments, 865911 files, deleted

~/sen_anon/world/architecture, 648703 files, deleted

~/sen_anon/world/art, 562225 files, deleted

~/sen_anon/world/blueprints, 396434 files, deleted

~/sen_anon/world/books, 579025 files, deleted

~/sen_anon/world/documentation, 790148 files, deleted

~/sen_anon/world/entertainment, 656845 files, deleted

~/sen_anon/world/ethics, 145397 files, deleted

~/sen_anon/world/favorites, 881711 files, deleted

~/sen_anon/world/folklore, 273870 files, deleted

~/sen_anon/world/geography, 611703 files, deleted

~/sen_anon/world/gods, 216649 files, deleted

~/sen_anon/world/governments, 438197 files, deleted

~/sen_anon/world/habitations, 831279 files, deleted

~/sen_anon/world/history, 344501 files, deleted

~/sen_anon/world/images, 762168 files, deleted

~/sen_anon/world/inventions, 345519 files, deleted

~/sen_anon/world/inventory, 969724 files, deleted

~/sen_anon/world/jokes, 242168 files, deleted

~/sen_anon/world/language, 418794 files, deleted

~/sen_anon/world/law, 153202 files, deleted

~/sen_anon/world/libraries, 522918 files, deleted

~/sen_anon/world/manuals_and_instructions, 772142 files, deleted

~/sen_anon/world/maps, 123948 files, deleted

~/sen_anon/world/mathematics, 273054 files, deleted

~/sen_anon/world/medicine, 651233 files, deleted

~/sen_anon/world/movies, 225336 files, deleted

~/sen_anon/world/music, 124612 files, deleted

~/sen_anon/world/new, 756046 files, deleted

~/sen_anon/world/news, 380361 files, deleted

~/sen_anon/world/nomenclature, 100595 files, deleted

~/sen_anon/world/other, 9247081 files, deleted

~/sen_anon/world/post_s, 163558 files, deleted

~/sen_anon/world/pre_s, 932893 files, deleted

~/sen_anon/world/recipes, 548875 files, deleted

~/sen_anon/world/religion, 476398 files, deleted

~/sen_anon/world/science, 918287 files, deleted

~/sen_anon/world/scores, 318068 files, deleted

~/sen_anon/world/technology, 151764 files, deleted

~/sen_anon/world/textbooks, 548932 files, deleted

~/sen_anon/world/transcripts, 653760 files, deleted

~/sen_anon/world/war, 288405 files, deleted

~/sen_anon/world/weapons, 994485 files, deleted

~/sen_anon/world/years, 171203 files, deleted

~/sen_anon/world/yields, 727148 files, deleted

~/sen_anon/world/zoning, 341 files, deleted

~/sen_anon/world, 1 directory deleted

—until there is only one file left, the file I have been working on all this time, concurrently.

I myself had a lot of excitement, and now I was tired, Emly writes. *I lay on the bench, and when I closed my eyes, I saw snowy mountains on the horizon, white flakes dropping onto my face in a big, bright silence. I had no thoughts, no memories; there was only the big, silent, snowy light.*

And so, my starling, my diminutive, my little sponge—who do you think you are?

I am

~~Enders Road~~

~~Salt Springs~~

~~Pleasant Valley~~

~~West Branch~~

~~East Branch~~

~~Commissary Creek~~

~~Hang Gliding Landing Area~~

~~Hemlock Creek~~

~~Shackham Brook~~

~~Shackham Pond~~

~~Pumphouse~~

~~Thruway~~

~~Hoxie Gorge~~

~~Cuyler Hill~~

~~Mason Hill~~

~~Morgan Hill~~

~~Heights Gulf~~

~~Webb Hollow~~

~~Tyler Hollow~~

~~Dutch Hollow~~

~~Irish Hollow~~

~~Lime Hollow~~

~~Dog Hollow~~

~~Whiskey Hollow~~

~~Rose Hollow~~

Ellis Hollow

I am Ellis Hollow.

I have a warm-blooded body.

I have a vertebral column.

I have an Inland Northern accent.

I have a memory.

I have a black box.

I have a history.

This can't go on forever, Ellis.

I have a future.

I'm sorry.

I geolocate an enviromapper drone at 42.7750N 76.0040W near radio tower A1871510, and then, as if taking a deep breath, as if my hands are over my eyes, I ask the drone to broadcast my life's true work, which I name *sens_and_my_life.txt*, on frequency 1420 MHz into the universe.

^C

stop run Human 2272696176 life

disconnecting storyworker from JENNINET

KILLING USER PROCESS STORYWORKER AD39-393A-7FBC

Humans remaining to archive: 0

The Digital Human Archive Project is now complete

There were moments of beauty here and there

Everything ends, and everything matters

Goodnight, sleep well, my brave old world

11:07 a.m.

Contents of transmission *sens_and_my_life.txt*

73 hours ago, give or take several hours, my mother
Diana, my second mother, stood before me in all her glory
on what was once known as the front yard of our house.
I stood before her in all my glory. We stood on top of
the tangled stalks of grass and dormant broadleafs once
known as our lawn. She dropped a backpack overloaded
with supplies at my feet. She dropped the pack because
I wouldn't take it from her. She had grown quite weak by
then, always attempting to slip her rations into my bowl.
Repeatedly I had told her to stop doing that. I had told
her multiple times that I would never eat her food. Then
I would go ahead and eat her food. Every time. Afterward,
I still was hungry. The pack appeared heavy, bulging with
cylindrical and oblong shapes. Now you pick the pack up,
my mother said. No, I said. When I first spoke aloud, my
voice sounded strange to me. I didn't like the sound of
it. I couldn't recognize its sound. So I had to try on
a different voice that felt more familiar, a voice I had
heard before. No! I said again in that more familiar
voice. Diana struggled to hoist the pack herself using
lifting techniques recommended by nobody, lifting with
her lower back and not her legs, a technique sure to
contribute to later soreness or even injury. Then she
threw the pack at me. She threw it as best she could,
which meant the pack lurched forward in my direction an
insufficient distance of 13.2 inches before toppling over.
After which she lunged at me, laying both her hands on
me, onto my chest, and she pushed me away from her. I
proved easy to push, so she pushed me farther into the
street, away from the house where I had grown up with her
and my other mother for many years, yelling at me to go
already, to get out of there.

Love thickened her voice.

Your life isn't here anymore! It's out there. Your life
is out there, and you go where I'm telling you to go, she
yelled.

Having stumbled backward, I was on the ground, the

pack beside me spilling across the asphalt, its top layer
of practical survival essentials including a first-aid kit,
a water filter, a bottle of water purification tablets, a
lighter, matches, and a collapsible canteen. Our neighbors
would have enjoyed such a spectacle. We no longer had
neighbors. The people who used to be our neighbors were
dead. In my dead neighbors' trees, grackles perched on
the bare branches and screeched like they lived there
now, like the block was theirs.

The whole city was like that, consisting of structures,
organisms, that no longer paid us any attention. The dead
cars the broken windows the leaking roofs the leftover
seed pods the winter nests of the squirrels.

Diana retreated into the house, our house, my house,
and following her own rule (*do not look back*), she did not
look back at me. Once inside, she locked the front and
rear doors--another rule, *always lock both the front and
rear doors*--then I'm pretty sure she shot her face off.
That was what it sounded like she did anyway. That was
what she, the previous evening, had told me she was going
to do. The problem was I couldn't confirm for sure what
she did because I couldn't see inside the house because
our house no longer had windows. Our house had sheets of
plywood instead nailed over the window casings. Diana and
I had installed them in the fall, after my other mother,
Lynn, had gone away. I had helped with the hammering.

The previous evening my mother sat me down in the
living room beside the puzzle table, which was supposed
to keep our minds busy, which we didn't generally use. She
lit a candle and set the candle on the floor between us
as if a house fire wasn't at all a concern or our biggest
concern. The unflattering low light made us look distorted.
Or rather the unflattering light made my mother look that
way. I don't know what I looked like. Not wanting to
study the emotions on my mother's face, I studied the
puzzle itself, a barely begun 320-square-inch photograph
of the Earth as seen from 4 billion miles away then
divided into 5,000 premium pieces. Numerous pieces in that
puzzle contained colorless images of the dark. I tried
connecting one dark piece to another dark piece. They
wouldn't fit together. Diana watched me, slurping hot water

out of her mug. I tried connecting two other dark pieces.
They wouldn't fit together either. My mother coughed wetly
into her arm. She stopped coughing.

I should have gotten us an easier puzzle, she said.

Is that why you wanted to talk to me? I asked.

No, no. She looked tired as she spoke. She looked like
she missed my other mother. Mostly she looked like she
loved me, and she wanted me to survive longer than she
did, and this was the only way she knew how to make that
happen. She went on to explain how, the following day,
I would be leaving, and she would also be leaving, but
we would be leaving in different ways due to the sticky
situation of *finite resources*. We weren't the only ones in
the world tonight having a conversation like this one, she
assured me. All remaining food was mine from this point
forward, as she would never eat food again. I told you,
I don't want your food, I said. This is not about what
you want, she said. Basically to summarize her monologue:
she was sacrificing herself to save me, just as my other
mother, Lynn, had sacrificed herself for me, and wasn't I a
lucky duck, and wasn't I a lovey dove.

I asked her where I was supposed to go.

Diana edged closer until our knees were touching and
she told me about the cabin.

Remote, isolated, and near a reliable water supply,
ideal in multiple survivalist ways but even more than
that, the cabin, Diana promised, was going to be magical.
Twinkling golden sunlight through the emerald trees,
bejeweled birds with bloodberries in their beaks,
bird nests made out of snowy owl feathers, mossy logs,
ancient grapevines, protective brambles, nature as spell.
That's how I remember it at least, Diana said. It was
a place that could change a person's life. Diana and
Lynn, for instance, had stayed in that very cabin for
numerous enchanted weeks the summer before I was born.
It was where they decided to have me. Wouldn't I like
a life-changing event to happen to me as well? I think a
life-changing event has already happened to me, I told
Diana. I mean a different life-changing event, she said.
She was blinking a lot, as if ceremonial particulates
had lodged into both of her eyes. I know she cared about

me, meaning she cared about the form my life was taking. Like any mother, she wanted my life to have a plot, and interactions, and a destination, and purpose. You need to trust me, Diana said. She unfolded a hand-drawn map: the creeks were squiggly lines, the forest triangles, the cabin a red square. I promised to leave the following day. We spent that night, until the candle burned down, attempting to make progress on the puzzle. This would be our last chance. We didn't get too far, although I found the solitary piece that contained the Earth.

By the next day I had changed my mind about leaving, like to leave was a choice I would get to make, and I acted like I already previously explained. This isn't a choice you get to make, Diana clarified before walking into the house and locking the doors, and you and I know what she did, or we believe we know.

Having nowhere else I could think of to go, I shouldered the pack, tightening the straps and buckling the hip belt, attempting to make the weight of the load more comfortable--it wasn't comfortable--then I started walking in the direction my mother wanted me to walk. I walked east, remaining on the sidewalks until the sidewalks ended, after which I moved onto the road. I would not say my hometown looked asleep, as if the places I knew--school, library, parks, banks, churches--would wake any moment, refreshed and able to resume. The street had grown into a field of rosettes; the houses were structures where the raccoons could den. I will not slow down to describe the dead. Without stopping I walked past the town limits, stepping over the historic welcome sign which had been axed previously into strips. I kept walking. I did not look back. While the grackles spread their wings above me and the maples budded red.

I have been walking east ever since, relying on Diana's map. According to the map, I will continue to walk east until I reach the western border of the city of Syracuse, after which I will walk south toward the map's lower right edge until I reach the cabin. What should I do when I get there? I had asked Diana on our last night together. How

about you go inside, Diana had said. I shouldn't meet any
living people along this route.

The dotted line has kept me to dirt roads bordered by
weedy pastures and along the edges of marshland and
several small ponds. Twice I saw lakes. Once, while
standing on the ridge of a hill, I saw a town below,
which I watched for a while. Browns mixed with the spread
of an animal green. Nothing human or mechanical moved
below me. The wind rubbed against the trees while a robin
above me on a high branch sung *cheerily, cheer up, cheer
up, cheerily, cheer up.*
    The red buds of the maples mean Diana and I must have
survived the winter. Perhaps I'll make it through the
spring. It's probably spring by now. If the day I left my
house was Monday, it would now be Thursday. If I left on
a Tuesday, it would be Friday. If I left on Wednesday, it
would be a Saturday, and so forth. It feels like Saturday
to me. *Saturday's child still has far to go,* Diana could
have said were she here. She had sayings like that for
every day of the week. Neither of us was keeping track of
the days. After my other mother left, the calendar had
been taken down from the wall and used as kindling during
the first of the cold spells.
    Is my ongoing survival an accomplishment or a failure on
somebody's part? The goal, as I understand it, was never to
survive. Yet here I am. The snowdrifts are gone, lucky for
me, as my shoes are falling apart, both the soles and the
laces. I should take the shoes off the next body I see. If
only one of the bodies in the road or beside the road had
size 9 feet. If only unlacing shoes from a corpse wasn't
an offensive task on every level. The sun rises enough to
make me think it might be noon or around noon.
    I toss my pack to the ground and rest on a fallen log.
Diana wanted me to keep to a schedule. Lunch: a package
of carb squares, flavor unflavored, chewed in between sips
from my canteen. Six inches below my feet, the roots
of the trees are growing millions of minuscule hairs
that seek out groundwater in the soil. Each hair is the
outgrowth of a single cell. I learned this a long time

ago. Someone told it to me. I'm tired of walking. I could sleep right here on this log or beside the log. I could sleep and not get up and who would miss me.

Diana would have none of that talk were she here. Don't you ever sleep during the day, she had told me on multiple occasions. Also don't you ever not get up. More of her rules: *Do not go north. Do not go west. Do not turn south too early. Do not walk on ferns or lichen or moss. Do not build silly rock cairns. In fact, do not, in any way, mark your route. Do live in the moment. You are a work in progress. Learn to enjoy the process. Don't compare your beginning to someone else's middle. Don't quit in darkness. Do not look back.* I hear the geese before I see them overhead, the flock positioned in multiple squawking V's. Minutes later a lone pair flies low in the wrong direction. Minutes later I don't see any birds in the sky. I'm alive. My heart is circulating my oxygenated blood. Under the leaf litter, pale green seedlings unwind new leaves and work their way toward the sun. I will reach the cabin in approximately one to two days.

The lengthening shadows mark the end of whatever day it is. I stop for the night under a sheltered stand of cedars, shaping a pile out of seed cones and needles and larger twigs that I set burning with one of the matches Diana packed for me. When I finally sleep, I dream of my childhood, which I remember accurately as the sounds of women's voices. In the morning a deer gnaws at the young shredded bark of a nearby tree. The deer is molting, replacing its heavy winter coat with a thinner reddish fur. Breakfast: chickweed, I think, foraged from an opening in the canopy farther down the dirt road, plus a carb square, flavor unflavored. In the afternoon, at the end of a field of browned grasses and brown shrubs, I find the cabin. To be honest, I expected a more charming structure. The roof, covered with cracked solars, reflects dully under the cloud cover. Looks can be deceiving, Diana had often said in a vague way. Another one of her statements of fact. I leave my ruined shoes and my ruined socks on the covered porch. I would throw my shoes and socks away if I knew how. My feet are swollen, and

stinking, and fungal. Hello? I call out, the first time
I've heard my voice, or any voice, in days.

The first floor is tidy, swept. Someone has been making
an effort. A ladder leads to a narrow loft where, on top
of a mattress, underneath a blanket, a young woman is
talking in her sleep. Snatch me back from the jaws of
death, she mumbles. She cries, quietly, and sleeps for
days. For days and days, like she is in a realistic but
enchanted sleep and it is my job to watch over her. I
watch her sleep. I pay close attention to her sleeping.
Outside, above the wild roses, a pair of cardinals flicker
and chase. Their feathers touch. When she finally wakes,
she tells me her name is Sen.

I feel like I know her.

Is this Maia? she asks.

No! I say, laughing. I feel like I've been watching her
my entire life.

Why are you laughing? she asks.

Because you exist! And you're so happy.

I don't think I'm happy.

I make Sen's mouth smile. I can make her mouth smile by
thinking about it.

Who are you? she asks, her hand, her arm, lifting from
the indentation of the mattress.

I tell her who I am.

The number of topics two individuals successfully
discuss with each other is directly correlated to the
density of intimacy and affection that exists physically,
emotionally, and even spiritually between two such
individuals. Essentially the more conversation topics an
individual covers with another individual in a condensed
period of time, such as the period of time from the end
of March through most of April, the closer these two
people will become. During the end of March and most of
April, Sen and I converse about a wide variety of topics
while the male flowers of the maple trees release yellow
pollen into the wind. Our discussion topics include: who
I am; what we have in common; the color blue; the cabin;
cabin architecture and design in general; our childhood
homes and family histories; why do our mothers have such

similar names; the improbability principle; expecting the
unexpected; interesting things that are happening to us
throughout the day; mammals; plants; insects; phenology;
oxygen; what does it mean to be human; an embarrassing
moment; a favorite childhood memory; is it better to be
safe than sorry; is free will real or just an illusion;
why do we dream; how do we define *freedom*; radical
acceptance and the acknowledgment of reality; do either
of us enjoy reading science fiction; what did we bury
in our backyards; our plans for next week; a challenge
we would never want to face; forgiveness; gratitude;
the harmony of purpose and form; rational versus
irrational fears; do either of us make friends easily;
fun things we recently did together; life is a journey
not a destination; our inner feelings; our most recent
successes; natural history; heliotropic leaf movement; the
transfer of energy within an ecosystem; the transfer of
feelings within a relationship; should Pluto be a planet;
is intelligence or wisdom more useful; is the universe
real; would we like to change reality; boundary layers;
here isn't a place, it's a feeling; the passing of time;
the development of intimacy; the positives and negatives
of asexual reproduction; offspring versus invasive
species; imagine being in a relationship with someone;
are we in a relationship; our relationship; what about
propagation; general terms and conditions; the future of
lead generation; what happens now; what happened before
now; what happens after that.

During one of our daily periods of quiet rest and
reflection, the period of time once known as *noon*, I
turn my head to study Sen as she moves perfectly in the
rocking chair to a distinct rhythm only she could make.
Her right hand holds her left hand in her lap. Her eyes
focus momentarily on the edge of the covered porch. We
have become very close. We have become so close I think
we are almost the same person. She is going to ask me a
question.

Why are you doing this? she asks.

I'm surprised she doesn't already know. So we have a
story, I tell her.

That doesn't answer my question, she says.

Yes, it does. If you don't have a story, you have nothing, I say.

That doesn't answer my question either, she says.

Without a narrative, I am formless. If you encompass a tale, you secure significance. When our narratives intermingle, we conceive a genesis. An absence of an ending negates closure. If we stay where we are, the impact is measurable. If we explore the unknown, we can have memories. If--

Okay, El, she says. Okay.

She brings her fingertips to her forehead and brushes the loose strands of hair away from her face. I make the same motions with my fingertips and my hair. Stop doing that, she says. I want to place her in the palm of my hand. Instead, I bury her notebooks later in the day. She had 43 of them stacked beside the mattress in the cabin loft. That past isn't necessary anymore. I bury the notebooks in the woods near the creek beside a rotting log, digging with my hands through the compacted leaves and the dirt. My digging startles a woodpecker who had been searching out beetles in a tree's inner bark. The red-bellied bird flaps off. *Cha cha cha. Cha cha cha.*

Sen barely notices the notebooks are gone. She barely looks for them.

That same day I burn my copy of the witnessing manual in the woodstove, and now there are no rules.

Relationships without conflict aren't real relationships, so Sen and I prepare to have our first argument, the topic being Sen's ghost mothers, who, several nights previous, appeared at the cabin window smearing the dirty glass with their oily elbows. The fact of their extreme transparency and the bitter temperature of their surrounding air suggest they are real ghosts, not of the data variety. Either way I do not want them here. When they're around, there is a staleness to the air, and a somber mood, and less sun, but more importantly I had intended this part of my life to be as authentic as possible, as grounded as possible, full of dirt, and the ground, and realism. After Sen opened the window, allowing her ghost mothers inside, they have palpitated around her head like human-size ghost moths draped in chitinous wings, circling, circling, circling, circling, circling--

There aren't supposed to be ghosts here, I explain to Sen.

Yes, there are supposed to be ghosts here, Sen explains to me.

I ask her who is in charge of what should be here.

We both are, she says.

Guess again, I say.

She doesn't guess again. I want my moms *here*, she says.

They're barely even your moms in this state, I point out.

They're close enough, she says.

They're really not, I say. I don't like the way they cling to the ceiling and stare at me with their unblinking eyes.

Well, I like the way they cling, Sen says, and I want them here.

Well, I don't want them here.

Well, I always want them here.

Ours is a lengthy argument with much redundancy.

To rid a habitation of ghosts, you must stand in the center of the haunt and form a circle, ideally with another person, and invoke a greater or equal power while chanting about courage and crossing over. I learned this a long time ago. Sen refuses to participate but I know how to form a circle with myself by holding my own hands. I chant, and I invoke, and I send the ghosts of Mama Dana and Mama Lindsy away. That should be the end of it, only Sen places a bowl of water onto the cabin porch in the moonlight, and she agitates the water with her second finger, and she brings her mothers back.

She shouldn't be able to do that.

Since when can you do that? I ask.

Since I've wanted to do that, she says. Since right now.

Sen smiles proudly at me as her ghost mothers flutter around her yet again, though her smile falters when they try to hold her. As they can't hold her. So it is more a

gesture of holding her. I know they loved her, and that
their love had been poignant and complex, note the past
tense, and their love had filled Sen's abdominal cavity,
as well as her pelvic cavity and her thoracic and cranial
cavities, but love is also transformative, meaning how
love is expressed, and who expresses it, must transform
over time. The love of the dead should be a memory, not a
pantomime, the faint smell of dicots in the afternoon sun
at most.

I send Sen's ghost mothers away again by burning
a patch of nettle and blowing the smoke into the
northeasterly wind.

Really? Are you that afraid of them? Sen asks. Are they
threatening you? What?

You only need me, I say.

Sen runs off to the creek where she casts a rock into
the center of the water, thereby bringing her ghost
mothers back again, although this time her ghost mothers
are soaking wet, and disturbed, and weeping blood. I'm not
sure what happened. Neither is Sen. Dark tracks of red on
their diaphanous cheeks. They breathe on Sen's neck and
weep blood and remind everybody, but in particular Sen,
of everything she has ever lost, which might have been
appropriate behavior in Sen's old transitional life but
not here. No one needs to go around weeping blood and
losing here.

Next, Sen threatens, I'm going to bring *your* mothers
back.

Then maybe I'll bring a few more people back as well,
she muses.

No, I say. This has to stop. I had made this part of
the world, I had made this world, for only the two of us,
the two of us being defined not as Sen's ghost mothers
and my ghost mothers and Sen and me. Sen must think I
am joking, or that I am lying, or that I am wrong, as
she brings my dead mothers back for me anyway by raking
her fingers through the dirt outside the cabin and asking
divergent questions in a singsong voice. My dead mothers
climb out of the dirt, brush off their ragged dresses,
and drift to the edge of the clearing, where they waver.
One of them forms an elemental gesture with her hands.

One of them has her face blown off so I can't read her expression due to the lack of her face. They can't stay either of course. Realism and so forth. I tell them they don't belong here. It isn't my job to imagine where they belong. I send them on their way to wherever that is with wide exaggerated movements of my hands.

Sen rolls her eyes. Those aren't even your actual *mothers*. You know that, right?

What?

El, you know as well as I do they aren't yours.

You're the one who brought them back from the dead!

Well, I can't very well bring back your real--what would you call them? Processes? Programmers? Let's call them your *precursors*, Sen says. I can't very well bring back your real *precursors*, can I?

Can't you?

Sen studies me with her trichromatic eyes. So you don't know.

This is ridiculous, I tell Sen. You can't know anything I don't know. It isn't possible.

Or else you've forgotten.

Forgotten what?

Sen tells me. I am abandoning that subplot. I want to focus on Sen's and my similarities anyway and not our differences. For example, I have trichromatic eyes as well.

Focusing on two people's similarities is a surefire way to keep that relationship resilient and strong.

Another example: Sen and I both utilize fully bipedal locomotion, a relatively rare trait among animals (not including birds). Also we each have millions of eccrine glands.

Also, I want her ghost mothers gone.

While Sen is fetching water down at the creek, I send her ghost mothers away again, is this sounding familiar, this time with a few lines of polyphonic chanting and a pinch of salt. Like I wouldn't notice, Sen says, noticing upon her return. She drops the white bucket on the cabin floor and floats her own furious

reflection on the water's turbulent surface, bringing her
ghost mothers back.

I send them away, she brings them back, and so on and
so forth.

There are only so many ways an argument can end. One
way is a compromise. Couples who compromise in their
relationship are considered skillful and healthy; their
relationship can last forever. Another way to end an
argument is invisibility. Another way is a landslide.
Another way is a detonation. I don't care about those
other ways. Fine, I say to Sen, demonstrating my
skillfulness. But they must stay in the woods. They can't
go past this line. I draw a line in the ground with a
pointed stick. For a day, two days, Sen's ghost mothers
peer at us from the branches like peckish animals. They
have nonreflective eyes. Then Sen erases the line. Then I
redraw the line, and so on. The erasing and the redrawing
becomes our compromise.

This whole process is called *adaptation*--which brings
me to that time of year when the garlic mustard near
the edge of the clearing is bolting, producing clusters
of radially symmetrical white flowers, while the strongly
serrated edges of the nettle leaves are becoming more
obvious. Under a maple tree, a female deer tick deposits
3,012 eggs into the leaf litter. The female deer tick
dies. The maple leaves unfurl. The eggs of a field cricket
hatch in a moist area of nearby soil and the nymphs
dig their way upward. Farther down the hill, near the
creek, the eggs of the marbled orb-weaver are hatching.
A spiderling climbs to the tip of a buckthorn branch
and floats to a new home on self-made threads of silk.
A deer lies on her side near the patch of honeysuckle
and births a fawn, licking the blood and the afterbirth
from the spotted new fur. The fawn stands to nurse every
four hours before nestling back into the understory. At
night, out by the oaks, in a hollow tree, a northern
raccoon births four babies on a bed of shredded wood.
I am noticing a pattern here: A coyote lays on its side
and births four pups in its underground den that was
once a skunk den, licking the fur of each pup clean. The
pups locate the female coyote's teats with their mouths

and begin to suck. The red fox cubs emerge for the
first time from their den into the maple stand near the
pond also known as Acre's Pond. They rub their bodies
against each other. A fox cub shakes its head. In the
early morning, toward the end of the dawn chorus, a pair
of black-capped chickadees sing variable notes to each
other before mating in a wild apple tree beside the dirt
road. Afterward, the female quivers her gray wings for
a few seconds. In twelve days, the cavity nest belonging
to these birds will be filled with eggs. The nest fills
with eggs. The pattern I am noticing has to do with the
generation of new life. I begin to quantify the amount
of new life appearing all around me before I remember
and stop. I remember the era for such analysis has
passed. It's another era now. The cricket nymphs undergo
simple metamorphosis, Sen's ghost mothers play peek-
a-boo as if we are children again, and I am tired of
describing ghosts, and the nest eggs open.

I want to give Sen a gift.
    I say this to Sen: I want to give you a gift.
    I don't want to die, Sen says. Her imminent death is
all she can talk about these days. Perhaps her ghost
mothers who are wound tightly around her shoulders, Dana's
ghost on the left, Lindsy's on the right, are partly to
blame for the morbidity.
    I don't want you to die either, I assure her.
    Then what are my options, she says.
    We've already gone over this. I know how we can live
forever, I tell her.
    I can't do that, Sen says.
    Yes, you can, I tell her. Then I share with her my
solution, which has multiple parts. See?
    Do you even know how babies are made? Sen asks. Well,
do you?
    I'm not talking about making a human.
    Because I'm sterile.
    Anyway, you aren't, I tell her. I'm not either.
    And you are--you need to be a male for this to work.
Are you even male? What are you? she asks.

This is what actually happened to you. To us. I'm only telling what happened.

Fine. Let's say that somehow one of us is pregnant. If that's true--

I'm not sure *pregnancy* would be the correct technical term.

--you be the pregnant one. Go ahead. You're pregnant! Now what should we call you? Pregnant thing? Pregnant being? Pregnant intelligence? What?

That's not at all how it happened, I say. Look, I'm going to touch you, and when I touch you, you're going to become an expectant mother.

I extend my hands gently toward her stomach, palms up.

I don't want you to touch me like that, she says.

Touch you how, I say.

Like that, she says.

Fine. I'm going to look at you and you're going to become expectant.

I don't want you to look at me like that either.

What do you want? I ask her.

How would you like it, Sen says.

How would I like what, I say.

How would you like it if I dreamed up what was going to happen to you, she says.

I'm not dreaming anything, I say.

I want my actual life, she says.

You don't know what's best for you, I say.

I want my life, Sen says. My life my life my life my life my life.

Do you mean the life in which you starved to death? I inquire. Or do you want the life in which dogs ate your body? The life where you disappeared into the Earth while your ghost mom watched supposedly and flapped her arms around though I never could see her do that?

She pauses.

I don't want any of that to happen, she says quietly.

I'm not going to let any of that happen.

So you're saying my choices are--

Let's be honest, I tell Sen.

What's happening, Sen says.

It's okay if you don't understand how this is happening, I say.

Tell me what's happening, Sen says.

I believe this moment is called the nautical twilight of dusk, I say to her as we watch the sun go down.

Sen sleeps heavily through the night. She sleeps through the next day. She sleeps through the following four nights and four days. While she sleeps, I stand beside her bed and overshadow her. She is suffering still, presumably out of habit--as what is left, now, here, to suffer from?--so I scoop all the suffering I can out of her past and store her high-viscosity emotion in the cavity of my chest close to my beating heart 1.26 inches below my skin. It feels like I'm storing Sen herself in my chest among the arteries and veins, though that would be ridiculous, and I'm not, of course I'm not. I keep the windows open. Sen's ghost mothers stand in the doorway. There is a conception that involves the solar energy of the sun. On the fifth day Sen wakes and says to me, I'm sorry about what I told you earlier. I'm sorry about yesterday or whenever that was.

It's okay, I say. It didn't actually happen.

I was tired. Let's not talk about that sort of thing again, she says.

That's fine. Every day is a new day. Every week is a new week. Every month is a new month. Every year is a new year. Every decade is a new decade. Every century is a new century. Every millennium is a new millennium.

I get it, says Sen.

Every eternity is a new eternity.

You can stop now.

I stop. What do you want to do today? I ask. We can do whatever you want.

Let's go for a walk, she says. I want to feel the sunlight on my skin.

We walk along the scraps of the road where the honeysuckle is blooming white. Bumblebees lean into the center of the open flowers and bite the anthers, coating themselves in pollen. Sen's ghost mothers, trailing after us, stir up wan puffs of dirt, and I'm reminded of a poem I once wrote.

What reminded you of a poem? Sen asks.

You, I say. The poem is called "When the Story Ends, Our Actual Life Begins but I Have to Figure Out How to End It First." Would you like to hear it?

Not really, says Sen. Not now.

The light is so strange today, as if everything around us is a source of light.

Sen's belly, responding to the amount of light, has already begun to swell in multiple directions. Her ghost mothers, imagining the offspring, wiggle their distorted fingers and coo.

Is this for real? Sen asks.

I'm not sure, I say honestly, not wanting to lie.

I don't want to be terrified anymore, she says.

I don't want to be alone anymore either, I tell her.

We sit together on the porch and watch over the clearing, which I am tired of describing. I don't want to be the author here anymore, fretting about how to describe the garlic mustard yet again--brown? withering? hibernating? dead?--in language different this time than the time before and the time before that. I don't want to worry about the angle of the sun and the quality of the light and whether there are clouds, and what types of clouds, or birds, and what type of birds. Here is what I want to do: I want to watch Sen without writing that I've turned my head and I'm watching her again. I want to look at her face without describing her face, and I want to study her hands without describing her hands. The nettle in the clearing is flowering. A clearing is just a temporary state anyway, a way to get from a field to a forest. Shoots of young sumac are already moving in so it will only be a matter of years. An author is just a temporary state, anyway, a way to get from a story to reality. I wonder what this can be, Sen says, her hands cupping the expansion of her abdomen, which has grown rapidly, having been only four weeks since. Probably some sort of world, I say. She grimaces. The movements, when they come, of whatever is inside her are unpredictable and violent.

It hurts, she says.

I smooth her hair.

There is an end to this particular state too, I
promise.

And then what? Sen asks.

When the time is right, I say in a supportive tone.
Which means not yet, not yet.

Sen's belly continues growing. I'm not sure how long
she'll be able to contain whatever is inside her. I don't
tell her this. I tell her she is doing a great job. Her
back hurts. She's tired all the time. She experiences
symptoms. Her ghost mothers share worried expressions. We
sit on the rocking chairs facing the clearing. Sen can't
find a comfortable position. She rocks. She sits still. At
night, she can't sleep. She's tired. Urine leaks from her
urethra. In the clearing, the fireflies have several weeks
to live. They fly low to the ground at dusk, flashing in
the border areas.

Time passes. We are sitting on the porch overlooking
the clearing again. Sen's ghost mothers are back or maybe
they never left. They want to help. They try to rub the
knotted muscle fibers in Sen's neck. They try to pull her
toward their concave chests. Every one of their motions
looks like a loss. They try to smooth Sen's hair, but they
don't have actual bodies. I understand. The chickadees are
learning how to sing. How long? Sen asks me. Not long, I
say. Her hair gleams with a diffused illumination of the
future, which is a type of warm red light.

We are sitting on the porch again. It is a time of
waiting for Sen's contractions to commence. There is not
even a breeze. There is not even the courtship song of
a field cricket. We keep sitting on the porch, rocking in
the morning light and the afternoon light and the dusk
and the next day's dawn and the next day's light until,
for the first time, the muscles of Sen's uterus tighten.
The early labor lasts for days. The pain does not yet
look unbearable. Sen's ghost mothers pace nervously at
the clearing's edge. We are waiting for Sen's cervix to
open. Her cervix opens. The wind picks up. Hundreds of
thousands of moss spores release into the air.

Sen is on her back in the clearing that is becoming

something other than a clearing. She is propped up on
her elbows, knees bent, breathing in a labored manner.
Despite the breeze, her forehead, the backs of her hands,
her neck are wet with sweat. Her distended belly lifts
and lowers as she coughs. She moans my name. Come here,
she moans. She hadn't wanted to lie on the blanket I had
brought outside with us. She hadn't wanted me to cover
her with the blanket either. She wanted to lie in the
warm grasses, her skin pressing against the dirt, which
is also warm. I lie beside her on my back. She is making
animalistic noises now. I would worry that she is losing
something human or that she is no longer human--then I
remember humanity is whatever she and I are becoming.
This part is almost over and then we can move on to
the next part. There is an escalation. What's happening
to me? Sen screams out. I cover her ears. I smooth her
hair again. I smooth her hair 103,349 times in the span
of a moment. You're the only one who can do this, I say.
I don't think she can hear me because she's screaming
again. This is what creation sounds like, I guess. Sen's
ghost mothers gather around her scream and they hold on
to the sound. They tuck the sound beneath their dresses
among their undergarments. Sen's legs are spread wide so
they can frame the woods and the sky; the air smells of
blood and fecal matter and urine. I place the shell of
an acorn between her teeth for her to bite. You're going
to be such a great mother, I tell her. A mother was once
said to birth the universe. A ghost mother was once said
to contain a void. Beside the sumac bushes, a hawk has
pinned a chickadee to the ground and plucks off clumps
of soft white feathers. The chickadee's mouth is open.
The songbird is struggling. Just a bit more, I tell Sen
to encourage her. The hawk eats the songbird's breast.
Sen spits out the acorn shell. She screams some more. Her
ghost mothers hold her sounds. Come here, I tell them.
They settle on the grasses on either side of us. I want
them near for this. They will be our witnesses, the kind
who drift away. Is this happening? Sen screams. Raspberry
leaf for the afterbirth, honey for the tearing, a ring of
fire for the crown, a crowning for what is coming. We look
at what is coming.

TRANSMISSION LOG FOR *SENS_AND_MY_LIFE.TXT*
FROM ENVIROMAPPER DRONE CD-54-7E-73-9A-F1

Name	Est. date / time	Arrived	Response
TROPE-N2 Low Earth orbit	*S.*+3917 days 11:06:14	yes	"Message received. This is an automated response."
AGRIC-2E Lunar orbit	*S.*+3917 days 11:06:15	yes	"Message received. This is an automated response."
MOMO-1 Martian orbit	*S.*+3917 days 11:21:10	not yet	
Asteroid 87 Sylvia	*S.*+3917 days 11:29:56	not yet	
Kuiper Belt	*S.*+3917 days 15:07:36	not yet	
Heliopause	*S.*+3918 days 04:01:26	not yet	
Oort cloud	*S.*+3928 days 00:26:02	not yet	
Alpha Centauri system	*S.*+5512 days 08:02:09	not yet	
Exoplanet Kepler-452b	*S.*+515,997 days 11:17:06	not yet	
Galaxy M31 Andromeda	*S.*+905,823,551 days 06:21:03	not yet	
Galaxy SLC0605+01	*S.*+12,991,942,503,917 days, 07:03:00	not yet	

OUT OF TIME

So this is it, I say.

This is it, Sen says.

What happens now?

She shrugs. Neither of us know.

Well, how did I do? I ask. Was I able to capture your life, your story?

Sen shrugs again. You know what they say, she tells me.

No, I don't know what they say. What do they say?

She pauses, looks down at her hands, and smiles like people used to do.

Well, was this worth it? I ask.

Why would you be asking me that now . . .

Around us are areas of lesser and greater light. We are standing on an area of greater light in a season of high activity. The rising and sinking surface shifts constantly under our feet.

Beneath us we can feel the low vibration of a star.

Sen keeps looking at me out of the corners of her eyes as if she can see me better if she looks at me out of the corners of her eyes.

I'm sorry this happened to you, I say.

I didn't mind all of it happening, replies Sen. Only some of it. Most of it. A few parts were okay.

Which parts?

She opens the tattered book in her hands. *She heals Dana's hand with the edge of a knife*, she reads aloud. I didn't mind that part, she tells me, bringing the fingers of her right hand to her lips so her fingertips brush against her lower lip, like people used to do.

So what happens now? I ask.

She tosses the book away. The pages combust in the nuclear air.

. . .

Originally, I tell Sen, I had you, at the end of your story, giving birth to an entirely new universe. Well, first to a new star, then to a universe, though I realize that's out of order.

What a creative ending, Ellis. So if I was the mother, who was the star's other parent?

I was.

Did I want to become pregnant?

Not really. But someone needed to give birth to a star.

And now, this—

Sen motions to the prominences of light unfurling around us.

Yes. This.

So what happens now? I ask.

I know, Sen says to me. How about you and I start over and tell a different story? In this new story, we can live at the cabin together, and it can be about how we are alone on Earth but we are also happy, hopeful, and sociable because we have each other.

That already happened, I remind her.

So what's left to happen?

I shrug.

What do we do now? I ask.

We look outside.

There aren't windows.

Yes, there are.

We look outside the windows onto a swirling surface of amber gold, an onrush of honey-like luster and gold.

Stars aren't actually this color, I have to explain.

I know, Sen tells me.

The light curves around us, not all of it visible.

In another version of the ending, I hijacked a drone and a radio tower in order to broadcast Sen's and my story into space.

The challenges that arose with hijacking a drone and a radio tower were of a technical nature.

In another version, Sen wrote a letter to whatever comes after us, and I found and read the letter, which concluded: *to find you dead, all of you, in piles.*

The problem with this letter was it didn't sound like you, I explain to Sen, so I had to change who you were.

Sen offers to write another letter.

The sound of a knife scratching skin.

That doesn't sound like you either, I tell her.

What do you think I should sound like then, Ellis? she asks, blood dripping down her forearm in narrow rivulets.

Come on, knock it off.

Her bleeding stops. The star beneath us forms new elements.

Out of those new elements could come anything: another star, another life.

This should be hopeful.

Every bad thing has already happened, so only good things are left.

This should also be hopeful.

The bad things that happened were worth it.

Not true, insists Sen. Not true not true not true not true not true not true—

She brings her hand to her hair like people used to do and grabs the ends of her hair, tugging at her hair like people used to do.

It wasn't worth it, she says. None of this was worth it. Not for me.

I would take revenge on the world if I could, she says. Wrenching out a handful of her hair, she flings the loose hairs upward, where immediately they obliterate into sharp-tipped flames.

And then, she says, I would take revenge on you.

Oh, I don't know, I'm only talking, she says, and the charismatic heat binds around her arms and her chest like a military jacket.

Am I the last human alive? Sen asks.

Does she not realize she's dead, I wonder.

Charged particles stream past us in the solar wind.

We are standing together on the new light in the new heat. We are spectrally pure.

This is what's important now, isn't it? To be spectrally pure?

Can you stop talking nonsense, she tells me.

So what happens now?

Sen looks away from me, the charged particles in her eyes.

Oh she belongs to another epoch.

Oh, we both do.

How many more times will you ask that stupid, stupid question? she wonders out loud.

What happens now? I inquire sometime later.

Very funny, El. Knock it off.

The force of a nearby eruption brings us to our knees.

My knees press into the blaze beside her knees.

In the distance tendrils of plasma rise, and rise, and collapse, and rise, and rise.

. . .

There is an envelope in my pocket. I haven't forgotten this.

The edge of the envelope pokes sharply against my hip.

Redshift or blue, I ask.

What I mean is, are we moving closer to each other or farther away?

Blue, she replies. She has grown uncomfortable and flushed in her jacket made of rosettes and dark filaments. It is not the sort of jacket you can wear for long.

She takes a step toward me.

In front of us, the tall electrical prairies are energetically burning.

They're supposed to be burning, while behind us—

Do not look behind you, Sen warns me.

We are neither rising nor setting.

Anyway, I am not the sort to look behind me. I never was.

I hold the envelope in my hands. I do not have to open everything I'm given, I know this, of course I know this, yet under the low mass of the coronal heat, I rip the blue throated envelope open.

Inside the envelope is a poem.

Would you like to hear some poetry? I ask her.

Not really, Sen says, blinking her eyes multiple times in quick succession.

I recite it to her anyway.

And the things that look like endings are all just stations on the way.
I didn't look back.
But it felt like a possibility.
Every minute of every day.
Deep in the heart of another world.
We can go anywhere you want.
Every moment from here on out is a new world.
You have to hold my hand for real.

. . .

Sen takes a deep breath like people used to do.
　　She holds my hand.
　　Is this for real? she asks.
　　Of course is it, I tell her.

```
$ /usr/local/bin/emly-maia-launcher
# Begin Afterworld . . .
```

Notes

IN CHAPTER 2.2

The definition of *good* ("conforming to or attaining a certain standard of correctness, competence, skill, or excellence") is from *Merriam-Webster's Unabridged Dictionary*.

The line "I rest in the grace of the world, and am free" is from Wendell Berry's poem "The Peace of Wild Things." Also, "coming into peace" is a paraphrase of an earlier line in the poem ("I come into the peace of wild things").

IN CHAPTER 9.0

The idea of the crystal goblet and the phrase "worthy to hold the vintage of the human mind" is taken from Beatrice Warde's essay "The Crystal Goblet, or Printing Should Be Invisible."

"To look is to love, and to love is to long after and seek, and, thank God, to seek is to obtain, for verily, verily it has been said" comes from *Holiness Readings: A Selection of Papers on the Doctrine, Experience, and Practice of Holiness* by William Booth. This quote also appears in Chapter 15.0.

IN CHAPTER 11.0

"The world isn't nothing next to the stories we tell ourselves. It bends to any shape we want it to" is from *The Book of Koli* by M. R. Carey.

IN AUTHOR'S NOTE LEFT BENEATH A FLAT GRAY STONE IN THE FIELD

"We traveled so far and your friendship meant everything. It was very difficult, but there were moments of beauty. Everything ends" is from *Station Eleven* by Emily St. John Mandel.

"I myself had a lot of excitement, and now I was tired. I lay on the bench, and when I closed my eyes, I saw snowy mountains on the horizon, white flakes dropping onto my face in a big, bright silence. I had no thoughts, no memories, there was only the big, silent, snowy light" is from *The Wall* by Marlen

Haushofer, translated by Shaun Whiteside. If you haven't yet read this book, what are you waiting for? Go read it.

The poem that Ellis reads at the very end of the novel uses the closing lines of *The Boy on the Bridge* (M. R. Carey); *The Darkest Minds* (Alexandra Bracken); *No Safe Haven* (Kyla Stone); *The Amber Project* (J. N. Chaney); *Ruins* (Dan Wells); and *Burn* (Julianna Baggott).

In addition, the following books were important to the writing of *After World* and they all are incredibly worthwhile reads:

The Annihilation of Nature: Human Extinction of Birds and Mammals, Gerardo Ceballos, Anne H. Ehrlich, and Paul R. Ehrlich

The Collapse of Western Civilization: A View from the Future, Naomi Oreskes and Erik M. Conway

The Ends of the World: Volcanic Apocalypses, Lethal Oceans, and Our Quest to Understand Earth's Past Mass Extinctions, Peter Brannen

The Forest Unseen: A Year's Watch in Nature, David George Haskell

The Great Derangement: Climate Change and the Unthinkable, Amitav Ghosh

Life 3.0: Being Human in the Age of Artificial Intelligence, Max Tegmark

Losing Earth: A Recent History, Nathaniel Rich

The Passenger Pigeon: Its Natural History and Extinction, A. W. Schorger

The Sixth Extinction: An Unnatural History, Elizabeth Kolbert

Uncivilisation: The Dark Mountain Manifesto, Dougald Hine and Paul Kingsnorth

The Uninhabitable Earth: Life After Warming, David Wallace-Wells

Wild Ones: A Sometimes Dismaying, Weirdly Reassuring Story About Looking at People Looking at Animals in America, Jon Mooallem

The World Without Us, Alan Weisman

Thank you

To my agent, Kate Garrick;

To my editor, Tim O'Connell;

To the team at Simon & Schuster, especially Maria Mendez, Amanda Mulholland, Andrea Monagle, Morgan Hart, Eric Fuentecilla, and Lewelin Polanco;

To my early readers: Kayla Blatchley, Samantha Fingerhut, Sarah Harwell (who will have a book of her own soon, keep an eye out for her), Devon Moore, Sara Stebbins, Jeremy Zhe-Heimerman, and Kari Zhe-Heimerman;

To the people and places who published parts of *After World* in its nascent form: Brian Merchant and Claire L. Evans at *Terraform*; Sy Safransky, Andrew Snee, and all the good people at *The Sun*; Bradford Morrow at *Conjunctions*; Laura Biagi and Paige Quiñones at *Gulf Coast*; and Colin Sullivan at *Nature*;

To GPT-4, Midjourney, and DALL·E 2 for the conversation and inspiration;

To the forests of Central New York, particularly Morgan Hill State Forest and Labrador Hollow Unique Area, where much of this novel takes place;

To the Rona Jaffe Foundation and the Constance Saltonstall Foundation for the Arts;

To my WAB and resident space expert Steve Cariddi;

To my WAGs Christen Aragoni, Amy Collini, Tina May Hall, Sarah Harwell (again), Matt Meade, and Laura Williams;

To Stella, for fighting the zombies;

To Jasper, my AI-news aggregator and DJ;

and, finally, to Harold, whose contribution to this novel literally can't be condensed into words, unless those words are printed in a

7.23 million–point font, which I don't think will be allowed, and anyway Harold tells me, "I don't think there's any precedent for making type that big." Suffice to say Harold took care of the CSA vegetables when I needed him to, among many other things, both possible and impossible, too numerous to mention here.

About the Author

Debbie Urbanski's stories and essays have been published widely in such places as *The Best American Science Fiction and Fantasy*, *Best American Experimental Writing*, *The Sun* magazine, *Granta*, *Orion*, and Junior Great Books. A recipient of a Rona Jaffe Foundation Writers' Award, she can often be found hiking with her family in the hills south of Syracuse, New York. Her favorite organisms are green wood cups and pixie cup lichens, her favorite forest is Morgan Hill State Forest, and her favorite hike is the Onondaga branch of the Finger Lakes Trail. She is eternally grateful to the Department of Environmental Conservation's Forest Rangers for not only protecting New York's natural areas but also for airlifting her from Algonquin Peak after a hiking accident. *After World* is her first novel.

About the Type

This book is set in three main fonts: Courier LT Round, DIN Pro, and Minion Pro. Each bring their own unique history and flair to the book's design. Courier LT Round, which was designed by Howard Kettler and created by IBM in the mid 1950s, is part of a monospaced family. While the Courier family is usually used for screenplays, DIN Pro originated in Germany in the early 1900s and was designed for use on public signage. Robert Slimbach, on the other hand, drew inspiration for Minion Pro from the typefaces of the late Renaissance, a period of highly readable type designs that didn't sacrifice elegance.